LIES BENEATH THE MYND

A DI GEORGIE FRASER MYSTERY

SASKIA VAN DER ZEE

DOVE COTTAGE PRESS

To Woody and Suki; for life-long, beautiful friendship

"As long as you keep secrets and suppress information, you are fundamentally at war with yourself...The critical issue is allowing yourself to know what you know. That takes an enormous amount of courage."

– Bessel A. van der Kolk, The Body Keeps the Score: Brain, Mind, and Body in the Healing of Trauma

1

Snow drifted on the wind in fine powder. As far as the eye could see, the undulations of hill and valley, carved by meltwater in the last Ice Age, glittered beneath a cobalt sky.

Once, Joe Ingles had thought he'd never love anywhere as much as his childhood home on the North Devon coast. The long beaches and deep dunes of Saunton Sands and Woolacombe where he'd worked as a lifeguard, surfed and sailed. Finding the Long Mynd had opened his eyes.

This wild landscape had captured him as surely as he'd lost his heart to his new life. On seeing it, few thought the Mynd to be one entity. Rather, it resembled a mountain range, perhaps unsurprising given how it had been formed. Vast sheets of rock, crumpled and pushed up by the collision of tectonic plates, as with the formation of the Alps. Over the course of eleven thousand years or so, it had become this network of heather and bracken-strewn hills, interspersed with steep valleys – gutters, batches and hollows as they were known locally – and chattering, rushing streams.

From where he stood on Cow Ridge, the engine of the quad

bike idling behind him, he looked across to the Iron Age ring-fort on Bodbury Hill and let his gaze sweep across towards the Carding Mill Valley, hidden from view by the steep, craggy slopes of Devil's Mouth Hollow. Funny to think that the busiest route up the Mynd, a path any locals avoided on a weekend, was invisible from up here, as was the reservoir, screened by woods and nestled in a hollow just north of the Devil's Mouth. Not that there would be any hikers or day trippers there yet. It was Sunday and the National Trust visitor centre wouldn't open for another couple of hours. Besides a couple of crazy fell-runners, in shorts and T-shirts despite the snow, he'd seen no one. Not even the pair he'd been looking for.

A flash of movement above him caught his eye and he swung his gaze upwards into the dazzling blue, squinting past the early morning sun. Seizing the binoculars which hung on a strap around his neck, he trained them on the dark speck, adjusting the focus until the bird came clearly into view, hovering over a crag on Long Synald's above the Burway. There was no doubt. Pointed wings and facial markings that resembled a black moustache. Was the other one there somewhere too, scanning for prey beneath the light dusting of snow? Often, the pair seemed to hunt together. Niamh had seen them over near the Lightspout Waterfall a couple of days earlier, though he suspected they were nesting somewhere on the crags above Townbrook Hollow. A location that would have to be kept secret.

The bird, so famous for its speed, lazily surfed the air currents, like the gliders from the club on the south end of the Mynd. Joe swapped binoculars for a camera and took several photographs, logging the time and location on his phone. Then, alerted to the fact that he would be late for breakfast, he walked back to the quad bike and clambered on, pulling on his gloves before he put the bike in gear.

As he made for the Burway, the steep, single track road that wound up and over the Mynd from Church Stretton, his phone buzzed against his chest and he stopped to check it, worried that it might be Effie, his landlady, wondering where he'd got to. It was his mother.

-Are you working today? G and I thinking of a walk on the Mynd.

He wasn't officially working. The peregrine spotting was to scratch a private itch. A second text followed the first as he was typing his reply.

-Effie's invited us to lunch. Is that ok?

He smiled. Since he'd taken the job in Shropshire, she had been so careful not to tread on his toes, or cramp his style, as she called it. Missing the point that she was one of the reasons he'd moved there. If he hadn't wanted to be around her, he'd hardly have accepted an offer of living accommodation from her oldest friend. Oldest in all senses of the word. Effie had just celebrated her seventy-third birthday

He resisted the temptation to respond with a *duh* and instead replied that of course it was fine. He'd love to see her, and Georgie was always good company. A bit weird having a detective for a step-mum, if that was what their relationship was, particularly as he had been a suspect in her murder case when they had met, but they got on well and he liked how happy she made his mother. Not his mum. The woman he called Mum was in North Devon and had adopted him as a baby. He hadn't met his birth mother, Marianne, until he was twenty-four, the summer before last, in the shadow of the Devil's Chair. An unlucky place according to legend but it had been lucky for him.

The surface of the Burway glittered with frosted snow, broken only by the imprints that his quad-bike's fat tyres had made on the way up. Going down would require more care, particularly on the bends, with a sheer drop of well over two-hundred feet to his left. At least he was unlikely to meet any traffic coming the other way, removing the need to cram into a passing space against a wall of rock. Marianne hated driving up the Burway.

He put the bike into low gear, and stuck to the inside of the bends, wishing he'd kept his camera handy when he spotted a small herd of ponies on the other side of the Carding Mill Valley. They stood out stark against the white landscape, no doubt enjoying the sun on their fur after a cold night on the hill.

As he glanced down into Devil's Mouth Hollow, something else caught his eye. A flash of sunlight on metal. Something large, reflecting the morning's glory. Something that definitely shouldn't be there. Tucking the bike into a passing space, he switched off the engine and walked to the side of the road, where the hillside fell away beneath his feet. He wasn't surprised Marianne hated it. One foot wrong and he'd be plunging, if not to his death, then to a very serious injury. Holding one of the striped reflective posts that marked the way for vehicles after dark, he leaned over to get a better look.

A silver car lay on its side about a hundred feet below, wedged between two outcrops of rock. Joe's mouth was suddenly dry, a hammering in his chest. Head spinning with possibilities, he tugged his phone from his chest pocket and, after a brief hesitation, while he wondered who best to call, he pressed not Marianne's number, nor 999, but Georgie's. She answered on the second ring.

"Joe? Everything ok?"

2

DI Georgie Fraser had been looking forward to a Sunday off work. A whole day to spend with Marianne. Neither of them working; fine, crisp weather – the first cold snap of winter – and a long walk in the hills, rounded off with good food and a roaring fire.

Joe's phone call had put an end to those plans. Of course, she needn't have responded herself. She could have put a call through to the station in Shrewsbury and got her sergeant, Mike Harley, who was covering the Rural Crime Unit that day, to take it. As it was, he would meet her there, but something about Joe's find had made her nose twitch. After a week-long search for missing teenager Sam Gray, the last thing anyone wanted to find was a silver car, abandoned or worse in a remote valley.

"Do you think it is him?" Marianne asked, from the passenger seat. The dogs were in the back of the police Land Rover, surfing as the vehicle turned off the A49 and into Church Stretton by the police station. Georgie was based at the new building in Shrewsbury but knew all the local officers who formed the Safer Neighbourhood Team. They'd done most of the work so far looking for Sam Gray. Today being Sunday, they'd be enjoying a well-earned morning off.

"It's a bit of a coincidence if it isn't," Georgie said. "The lad went missing with a silver hatchback car and, from the sound of it, that's what Joe's found."

"And he sounded all right? Joe, I mean."

She had already asked at least once and Georgie smiled. Marianne had as much maternal concern for her twenty-five-year-old grown-up son as the average new mother for their first-born. But perhaps that wasn't surprising. She was a new mother. And he was her firstborn. Her only child and unknown to her for twenty-four years.

"He sounded fine. More gutted to be missing his breakfast than anything. And he spotted one of those falcons he's been looking for. He'll be glad of the coffee and cake." Marianne, whose need to provide food was wired into her DNA, had provided two flasks of coffee, one for Joe and one for Georgie, and a plastic container with sliced banana bread and flapjacks.

The town was quiet under its fine coating of snow, which had failed to settle on road or pavement and contented itself with decorating rooftops and trees. It was the first deep frost of December and much needed after the mild few weeks they'd had, with temperatures as high as eighteen degrees on one day. As they passed the church, Georgie thought it would have looked fine on a Christmas card, although you'd have wanted to get rid of the cars parked outside by the old wall and allow the splendid yew tree that leaned from the graveyard a starring role.

"I'll get out here," Marianne said at the foot of the Burway, as the Land Rover's engine began to growl. "I'll walk up and then you can get on to Joe."

"Two minutes won't make any difference," Georgie said, driving on. "And are you sure you don't want to come and check on him yourself?"

"If you're working, I'm not going to get in the way," Marianne said. "I can help Effie get the lunch and you and Joe can come down when you've finished." She left the '*if you finish*' unspoken, but Georgie heard it nonetheless.

"I'm not on call so in theory, once I've made sure everything's in hand, I can leave." *Unless we find a body in the car.* Like Marianne, she left the words unsaid.

She pulled over to the side of the road, which sloped steeply so the Land Rover tilted towards the bank of white-dusted rose bushes at the foot of Effie's garden. The house nestled at the base of the Carding Mill Valley and was one of the last before the Burway became a single-track mountain road. Fortunately, not the route by which most tourists and visitors approached the Long Mynd.

"Hey, come back here," Georgie said, as Marianne released the door handle and the dogs bounced in the back, anticipating freedom. Marianne's smile didn't quite reach her eyes as she leaned across for a kiss and Georgie took her hand and squeezed it. "It'll be OK," she said. "Promise."

"Who gave you a crystal ball all of a sudden?" Marianne said, but now her smile was genuine and laughter lurked beneath her voice. "I'll believe you because there's nothing I can do about it in any case. Why make things worse by adding worry to them?"

"Buddha and his two arrows," Georgie said. It was one of Marianne's favourite mantras when Georgie was worrying about things over which she had no control, and she laughed as she opened the tailgate to let the dogs out. They pelted up the tree-lined path to Effie's house, barking. "See you for roast lunch and all the trimmings in a few hours. And I'll send Joe back as soon as we're done with him."

As Marianne disappeared between frost-covered birch trees, Georgie let in the clutch and put the Land Rover in gear. She liked the Burway, despite Marianne's misgivings. It reminded her of the roads in her native Scottish Highlands, or of drives in the Alps and Canada when skiing. Where the sight of the hillside falling away in a steep slide of rocks and scrubby grass made Marianne faint, it thrilled Georgie, though she was grateful for the Land Rover's four-wheel drive. The snow, though shallow, added a layer of challenge.

Joe was silhouetted against the bright sky as she rounded a bend. He had tucked his quad bike into the lee of the hill and she eased into the same passing space, pulling in the wing mirrors and cramming the vehicle against the rock wall. He stood on the edge near one of the marker posts so as to be visible to any vehicles approaching from either direction. At least on a day like today, there would be fewer trippers wanting to drive over the Mynd from Ratlinghope or Plowden.

"Have you had much traffic?" she called to him as she pulled on her coat, zipping it up to her chin. Thank goodness she'd remembered a hat and gloves. Despite the sun, the wind had a bite to it. Joe had his padded red Ranger jacket, almost indistinguishable from his Search and Rescue kit, and what looked like ski or snowboard pants.

"A few cars," he said. "One got a bit arsey about me blocking the passing place. Local, so me pulling the National Trust official bit didn't cut much ice. If we want to get the vehicles out of the way, there's a parking area just past the crag. We can walk back down."

Georgie agreed it was a good plan. She followed the quad-bike up the glittering road and across the frozen turf to the right, where the hitherto sheer cliff broadened into a wide, grassy platform, with views that stretched across Caer Caradoc to the Wrekin.

"Your ma sent some supplies," she said when she got out again, handing a flask to him.

He grinned, silver-grey eyes screwed up against the sun. Joe was dark-haired and always seemed tanned. This morning he looked like he'd stepped out of a Winter Sports catalogue. As he unscrewed the flask and poured himself a coffee, Georgie texted her sergeant, Mike Harley, telling him to send any vehicles up to the parking area. If they needed to be nearer the top of Devil's Mouth, they'd have to close the road. Better to check things out before taking any drastic measures.

Once she had her gloves on again they set off down the road, feet crunching on the snow, keeping to the outside of any bends in case of approaching cars but careful not to step too close to the edge.

"The good thing about the weather is that any cars will only be doing about twenty miles an hour," she said.

"You hope," said Joe. "There." He stopped abruptly and pointed down a gully between rocky walls, carved by a stream no doubt. Lower down, it widened into a narrow valley, twisted hawthorn and myrtle clinging to its steep sides. Too steep for the wild ponies that roamed the Mynd, but there was a line of sheep tracks descending beside the stream. They always headed for lower ground if snow came.

From the edge, they could see down to the surfaced bridleway that led from the National Trust centre up the Carding Mill Valley. Early as it was, there were only one or two brightly coloured jackets on it. Later, despite the snow, or even because of it, there would be hundreds. If she and Marianne did go for a walk, it would be away from the crowds, perhaps up to the Bodbury Ring.

"What do you reckon?" Joe said. "Safe to climb down?"

"Mike Harley's called Search and Rescue," she said. "And I know you volunteer with them, but they'd be the first people to tell you not to climb down without the proper kit, wouldn't they?"

Joe grinned.

"Fair enough. I bet you're itching to, anyway."

He wasn't wrong. In her younger days Georgie had done a fair amount of climbing, but in her forties she seemed to have developed a sense of caution. Or perhaps it was just that life was now so much more worth living that she didn't want to risk it.

"Can't see if there's anyone in it," she said.

"I shouted a few times," Joe said. "And I've tried looking from different angles but there's no way of seeing through the windscreen with the sun on it like that. Most likely someone parked up and forgot to put the handbrake on."

Why, though, wouldn't they have reported it?

There was no body in the vicinity as far as she could see. Something to be thankful for. And if there was anyone in the car they must be unconscious or they would have heard Joe's shout. With luck, whoever had driven off the road had walked or at least limped away. Besides being crumpled where it had jammed between the rocks the car didn't look too bad. The numberplate was hidden by a fuzz of gorse bushes.

"Nothing we can do until Harley's here with the rescue guys, anyway," she said. "Why not have a bit of that cake in the meantime?"

Joe, who'd already jammed a flapjack in his mouth while they were walking down to the hollow, took the plastic box from his bag and handed her a piece of banana bread before taking one for himself. The taste took her back to the first day she had met Marianne, over at her bunkhouse in the valley beneath the Devil's Chair. She had been searching for another missing person then, a young woman. Anna Price had turned up dead in the Devil's Pool. She hoped they weren't going to find another young person in Devil's Mouth.

"Why's it called the Devil's Mouth, anyway?" she asked.

Joe shrugged.

"It's not the valley," he said and pointed up the steep hillside.

"It's that crag up there. And that plateau the road cuts across is an Iron Age earthwork. Devil's Mouth Cross Dyke. No one's sure what it was for. Managing east-west access to the hill maybe. It's not defensive, anyway. Might just have been a status symbol. You know; if you're an Iron Age chieftain and you can get people to build something that massive you must be pretty powerful."

Georgie didn't know many twenty-five-year-old young men but she couldn't imagine DC Hallam, who'd been on her team for her last murder investigation, talking earnestly about Iron Age earthworks. He'd be more likely to talk about rugby or films.

Sun flashed on metal further up towards the Mynd's summit where the Burway joined the road that ran up from Plowden past the gliding club. Not Harley. He would be coming up from Church Stretton. The blue four-by-four slowed a little as it passed Georgie's police Land Rover. Descending towards where they stood at the side of the road above the precipitous valley, it slowed again and a middle-aged couple peered out, presumably noting Georgie's hi-vis police jacket.

"Is there a problem?" the man asked, then swore as he noticed a pickup coming up from the Stretton direction. "Better get into that passing place, I suppose."

Georgie waved him on. As the pickup drew closer, she recognised Mike Harley's grizzled head in the passenger seat. The DS was older than her and solid as a rock, with twenty-five years of Shropshire policing under his belt as opposed to her eighteen months. The bulk of her experience had been in the Met.

"All right, boss?" he asked as the truck drew level. "This is Cal Innes, West Mercia Search and Rescue. DI Fraser," he said to Cal. Cal said good morning to her and nodded at Joe, with a grin of recognition. He was dark-skinned and good-looking, with a mop of dreadlocks held back by a wide headband. About ten years younger than her, she reckoned, with the look of someone who spent most of their time outside.

"I'd better put my truck in here," he added, indicating the passing place "we're going to need some of the kit in the back. Not the first time we've had to pull a car out. People park up by the cross dyke and forget to put the handbrake on. You'd be surprised how often."

As well as the climbing equipment they would need to access the vehicle, Harley had brought SLOW signs to put further up and down the road, alerting drivers to a police operation. Georgie helped him position them, considerably warmer once she'd hiked back up to Cow Ridge and down again.

"I checked the number plate for the lad's car," Harley said as they met once more by the pickup.

"Great," Georgie said. "That'll be the first thing when you get down there," she added to Cal Innes, who was stepping into a climbing harness. "Once you've checked there's no one in the car, of course." She wondered on what she'd based her assumption that the car was empty. Perhaps the stillness. Or the intactness. The driver's door was half-open but no limbs protruded. There was no sign of either life or death.

Innes threw a harness to Joe and fetched a couple of helmets from the back of the truck.

"You good to come down with me?" he asked, and Joe nodded. Georgie remembered her promise to Marianne that she would send Joe back to Effie's once she'd finished with him. Watching Cal secure nylon ropes around a sizeable boulder and check safety routines with Joe, she felt strangely left out. As the two of them disappeared over the edge of the hollow, she thought of Marianne again and called out a reminder to be careful.

"Teach your grandmother," Innes called back up, and she laughed.

3

By the time Joe and Cal Innes had reached the car, more vehicles had arrived; a police car with a pair of uniformed officers and a tow truck with a winch on the back, bringing two more of the Search and Rescue team.

"If we're lucky we'll get it up with this," the older man said. "If not, we'll call a heavy duty one later."

"Always supposing we don't need to preserve this as a crime scene," Georgie said. "DI Georgie Fraser," she added, holding out a gloved hand. "And you already know DS Mike Harley, I think." If she remembered correctly Mike had been an active member of West Mercia Search and Rescue for years. He still helped out on the fund-raising side.

"Malcolm Tucker," the older man said.

The younger of the two rescuers shook her hand. "Andy Morgan. I think we've met before. I'm a firefighter. From Shrewsbury."

"That's right," Georgie said, whose inability to match names to faces was becoming well-known to her team. "You came out to that farm fire near Minsterley."

"Bad, that one," Morgan said. "Won't forget that in a hurry."

He joined Malcolm Tucker who was peering down into the gully. "See you've got young Joe down there. Did he come with Cal?"

"He works on the Mynd," Georgie said. "Conservation ranger for the National Trust. He was out looking for peregrine falcons this morning and spotted the car."

Georgie sent the uniformed officers to close the road where it split towards Plowden on one hand and Ratlinghope on the other. Harley slung a couple of POLICE: ROAD CLOSED signs over one shoulder and walked up the road to fetch Georgie's Land Rover. It might not take much to walk down to the foot of the Burway but climbing back up would be a slog he didn't need. As he left, a shout from down in the hollow reached them.

"Empty!" Both climbers had reached the car and it was Joe who called up to them, Cal's head and shoulders invisible as he leaned in through the open driver's door. As they watched, he emerged and said something to Joe who relayed the message. "All clean. No blood or sign of injury."

Georgie felt her shoulders drop. Although, if it was the car that had disappeared with Sam Gray, it being empty prompted as many questions as it answered.

"Registration number?" she called back. Joe had his phone in his hand and was texting. Seconds later, her phone beeped.

-TF68 YXX. Silver Vauxhall Corsa. Craven Arms Motors sticker in back windscreen.

Georgie showed the message to Mike Harley.

"That's the one," he said. "Belongs to a girl called Jessie Pritchard. One of the kids Gray was partying with when he went missing."

There had been a group of them on top of the Long Mynd the previous Wednesday night. Late teens and early twenties. Bored with the usual party venues, they had decided to have an illicit camp-out – more like a rave according to the local team –

at the shelter just down from the summit. Marianne called the place Pole Cottage after a long-demolished house whose ramshackle outbuildings had been there when she first moved to the area. The outbuildings had been dismantled since and the Trust had fenced off the surrounding trees in an enclosure for the use of school and adventure groups, with a three-sided wooden shelter in the middle. Not a place Georgie would have chosen for a party on a December night but, if she remembered rightly, the weather had been mild still. According to the other partygoers, an argument had broken out and Gray had stormed off, taking the girl's car. He hadn't been seen since.

Georgie hadn't worked the case. Missing persons were in the remit of the local Church Stretton team, but she'd been aware of it. Her Rural Crime Unit covered a wide variety of happenings and was often consulted when incidents occurred in the hill country, even when the offence itself didn't fall under the descriptors of rural crime.

Andy Morgan had called Cal Innes and was discussing how best to recover the car.

"Have you got a spare harness for me?" she said, to Malcolm Tucker, suddenly making up her mind. "I want to take a look before you winch it up."

"Are you...?" He didn't finish his question but looked her up and down.

"I'll be fine," she said. "Could do a grade 5C in my sleep." She smiled. "A few years ago, anyway. I'll be fine," she said again. "If one of you's going down, I'll go with you. There's a missing boy," she added. "I want to see the car and I need photographs."

She couldn't remember the last time she had put on a climbing harness. Given her assurances to the rescue team, she was glad that muscle memory took over, threading the rope in its figure eight knot through the loop and testing it. She was glad too of her walking boots and waterproof trousers, as well as her neoprene gloves which would keep the wet snow out but still give her grip.

As she went over the edge, sitting back into her harness, she was glad of Andy Morgan a few feet below her, calling out foot holds while Tucker belayed her rope from above. Halfway down, her foot slipped on an ice-covered rock and she swung, bashing her elbow before she could regain a half-decent abseil position. When she reached the others, she was out of breath and the grin she gave Joe was at least half relief.

"You ok?" he asked. "Been a while since you did that, I reckon."

Georgie rubbed her elbow and released her rope a little so she could approach the car. Besides its rear windows which had shattered in a series of spider-web cracks, and some serious-looking scratches, there was little obvious damage.

"What have we got then?" she said, before remembering that neither he nor Cal was on her team.

"No sign of anyone," Cal said. "If there were any tracks leading away from the car, the snow's covered them. Might see something when it melts but unlikely, I reckon."

"Any idea how long the car's been here?"

"Not more than twenty-four hours, I reckon," Andy said. "You can't see it from the road and it might blend in with the rocks without the sun on it but it would have been busy here yesterday. Someone would have noticed it. When did the lad go missing?"

"Not been seen since Wednesday. What's at the bottom of this valley? Past the trees."

"Houses. The ones just up from the National Trust centre." Joe knew this area better than the others given that he spent many of his work days roaming it. "Holiday lets. Just below the reservoir in the Carding Mill."

"Anyone in them at the moment?"

"Dunno. Think they're booked out most of the time."

"If anyone did get out, they'd be better off going down than up," Cal said. "They could walk along that fence line there past those conifers."

"That'd take them into New Pool Hollow – where the lower reservoir is," Joe said.

Georgie looked around her, puzzled at the position of the car, which was jammed between two craggy boulders, its nose pointing back up towards the road. Though crumpled in the mid-section, it wasn't damaged enough to have flipped over on the way down, and surely no one would have survived such a fall. Not so as to be able to walk away. It fitted with Innes's story of idiots forgetting to leave their handbrakes on. Only the last person to use this car had been the missing boy. Placing her feet carefully, she edged closer, holding the open driver's door to crane in. The firefighter, Andy Morgan, was on the phone to Malcolm Tucker above, discussing how best to get the car out.

Inside, the Corsa was tidy. Georgie sniffed, wondering if she imagined the smell of cleaning fluid. Perhaps her nose, confused by the freezing air, was picking up the scent of the air freshener which hung, shaped like a Christmas tree, from the wing mirror. The keys were still in the ignition. On the back seat lay a rolled-up pink umbrella of the kind that could fit into a handbag. In the door pocket was a plastic disposable lighter and a pack of king-size rolling papers. She wanted to check the passenger side and the glove box but, as she leaned further in, one knee on the driver's seat, the car groaned and shifted. Someone grabbed her climbing harness from behind and pulled her clear as, with a scraping screech of metal on rock, the Corsa sank a few inches.

"Sorry," Joe said. "Don't think Ma would forgive me if I let you get dragged down there."

From above came a disembodied wail, and Georgie looked up to the edge of the road. Andy Morgan grinned.

"It's the winch. Always does that when it starts. We need to get the car secured even if you don't want us pulling it up yet."

A steel cable was snaking down the valley, fed past the rocks at the top by her sergeant, Mike Harley.

"No, you're all right. If you can all stand back a bit. I'll just take some pictures."

The three men clambered out of the way as she photographed both the interior and exterior and Joe scrambled further down with her phone to take some shots of the back of the vehicle, the yellow number plate cracked and hanging loose at one side.

"Take it up when you're ready," she said to the rescue team. "And you'd better get yourself back to Effie's," she added to Joe. "I promised your ma I wouldn't keep you." Ma was his name for Marianne, since the name Mum was already taken.

"I'm going to stay and help with the search," he said. "Make it OK with Ma if you're heading back, will you?" he asked, tightening the rope through his climbing harness, as Andy Morgan secured the steel cable to the tow-ring of the car. "Or will you have to work? Do a search and whatever?"

"Not my case," Georgie said, with a twinge of regret. Curiosity was her besetting sin and the discovery of the car, abandoned with no trace of its runaway driver, was sparking myriad questions in her mind. Where had the boy gone? And, if he'd taken off the previous Wednesday night, four days ago now, where had he and the car been in the meantime?

4

They had just finished lunch when Mike Harley called to say that Search and Rescue had found a body in Callow Hollow.

"Drone spotted it but nothing picked up by the thermal imaging so likely to be deceased," he said.

Beata, Marianne's lodger cum foster daughter, had arrived fresh from her café shift at the Chalet Pavilion in the Carding Mill valley with news that hundreds of volunteers had arrived to join the search. Joe had stayed out on the hill with the Search and Rescue team.

"Couldn't be worse," she said, taking a pile of plates from Effie to ferry them to the sink. "That valley's completely inaccessible."

"Which one's Callow Hollow?" Georgie asked. "Do you have a map, Effie?"

Marianne suppressed a sigh. She ran the tap until the water gushed out hot and set the roasting tin to soak, squirting detergent into it and watching its residual film of grease disperse to the edges, leaving the water clear. Behind her, Beata and Georgie discussed the pros and cons of OS maps on a phone screen – too small, Georgie said, to be useful in a landscape of the Mynd's size. If she wanted to get a real sense of the scale of the place, she needed a proper map. The door creaked as Effie left the kitchen to find one. At the scrubbed oak table, Beata's white-blond head bent over the too-small smartphone next to Georgie's.

So much for their leisurely Sunday. Joe finding the car had been bad enough. But now, the discovery of a body. Twice since she had met Georgie, violent death had dominated their lives. The first time had been a murder at Marianne's bunkhouse, the business she had owned jointly with Effie. Georgie had been the investigating officer and Marianne, if not a suspect, then a person of interest. The second, a brutal killing at the Shropshire Geoscience Trust in the village where Marianne lived. Since then, almost nine months ago now, she had thought they were free of it. Georgie might have been a murder detective in the Met but now she headed up West Mercia Constabulary's Rural Crime unit, based in Shrewsbury. Stolen tractors and sheep rustling, Georgie always said, when people asked what constituted rural crime. Her last job had been investigating a hare coursing ring based around Clun and Bishop's Castle, and, before that, the vandalism of several Bronze Age barrows for reasons that had never been established, even when the perpetrators had been caught. Violent death was not common in rural Shropshire. Marianne felt that they had had more than their fair share.

Of course there was nothing to hint at foul play in this instance. A young lad had gone missing and now, a week later, his body had been found. Still, it hung around her neck like a dead weight, pulling her down and pressing into her belly. Presumably this young lad's mother loved him as she loved Joe. Losing your child, the pain of it, was unimaginable. She had only known Joe for eighteen months, as long as she had known

Georgie, but to lose him would destroy her. How must it be for the mother of this young lad? Sam Gray, she thought his name was. It had been on the news and the local Facebook group. Someone had put a missing poster up in the Geoscience Trust tearoom where she worked, with numbers to call if the boy was spotted anywhere. Now, both he and the car in which he had gone missing had been found. And the finding would bring joy to no one.

The door creaked as Effie re-entered the kitchen with a map. Her house at the foot of the Burway was an old Victorian pile, resembling a rectory, although it was too far from the church ever to have been one. The rooms were spacious and high-ceilinged, a contrast with Marianne's cottage, a converted seventeenth century stable block, with low ceilings and heavy beams. Marianne put the kettle on and filled the base of the Bialetti jug that Georgie favoured for coffee. Although she had recently converted to decaf, she still liked it strong enough to stand a spoon up in. Effie was spreading the orange OS Landranger map on the table while Beata talked, smoothing it out to better show Georgie the body's location.

"Callow Hollow's over here," Beata said, "between Ashes Hollow and Minton Batch. There's a bridleway goes up from Little Stretton to the top of the hill. My mum used to run it," she added, her words leaving a pool of silence. Klaudia, her mother, was nine months into a life sentence for murder. With luck, she might be out in fifteen years. The girl was coping admirably, Marianne thought, but memories like these could sometimes send her into bouts of quiet depression.

"We've walked it," Marianne said to Georgie, turning reluctantly into the conversation. "Do you remember? Past Ashes Hollow campsite at the foot of the valley and then up that very steep bridleway? There's a bit where you round a bend and the wind slams at you, where the track's quite narrow. You can see down into Callow from there."

She remembered Georgie commenting on it when they had walked that way. Looking down and reflecting that it must be one of the least accessible parts of the Mynd and that no one in their right mind would go down there without climbing gear. What had the boy been doing there? Had he fallen? Lost in the snow? But no. He had been missing for several days, well before the snowfall. Had he been lying there all that time? Again, she felt a pang of sympathy for his mother.

"Will you need to go out?" she asked Georgie, doing her best to keep her voice light and natural.

"Local team, I'd have thought," Georgie said. "Mike Harley's there with Search and Rescue but it's not a case for rural CID. Yet," she added. "That doesn't mean it won't become one. For the moment, though, it's still my day off."

Was that an attempt at reassurance she heard in Georgie's voice?

The dogs, who until then had been lying in contented bliss on their mat in the corner of the kitchen, sated with scraps from a roast chicken dinner, now scrambled to their feet barking. Beneath the volley of noise Effie's doorbell chimed, a classic ding-dong that reverberated through all three floors of the house. Effie's hearing was not as good as it had once been.

"Niamh," Beata said, getting up and following the dogs out into the hall. "She texted me. I think she hoped Joe might be back."

"Did you know she was coming round?" Georgie asked Marianne, who shrugged. She'd never admitted to anyone that she sometimes found it hard to share her newly discovered son with his girlfriend, but no doubt Georgie had found her out. There was not much that they didn't know about each other.

Niamh's dark hair was decorated with flakes of snow when

she came into the kitchen. She had classic Irish Rose colouring, and her pale cheeks were flushed pink with the cold.

"It's snowing again," Beata said, and Marianne wondered that none of them had noticed it falling into Effie's garden beyond the kitchen window.

"It's only light still," Niamh said, "but it's meant to get worse later. Not good for the Search and Rescue team with the body recovery."

Georgie looked up sharply and Niamh held her hands up in mock surrender.

"Joe didn't tell me," she said. "It's all over social media."

Georgie muttered under her breath, taking out her phone and swiping at the screen.

"How did they even find out about it?" she said, scrolling furiously as Marianne offered Niamh a coffee. The girl accepted with a smile and asked if Marianne wanted any help with the washing up.

"She won't let you," Effie said. "Or she won't let me anyway. Maybe you can do Beata's share," she added pointedly and Beata grinned.

"I'm fine with it," Marianne said, turning down the heat as the coffee pot began to spit and hiss. "Beata's been washing up most of the morning. Maybe someone can dry things if the rack gets full."

She set mugs and coffee on the table, listening as Niamh and Beata discussed the chaos up at the National Trust Pavilion. Niamh worked part-time in the National Trust education centre, leading school visits. Beata showed her pictures of the crowds of volunteers and onlookers who had descended.

"I suppose it's been in the news so much," Niamh said. "Sam Gray being missing. You know, proper news, not just the socials."

"The worst bit was there was nothing for them to do. Search and Rescue had already decided the best bet was to send the drones up. Then a whole bunch got fed up waiting and headed up the footpath to the top. The S and R guys in the Incident Command were really stressed."

Marianne had seen the Search and Rescue's Incident Command Unit at the Geoscience Trust when they'd been searching along the swollen river Onny in the autumn. An elderly woman, apparently suffering from depression, who had disappeared and whose family had reported her missing. Eventually, she had turned up in a hotel near Whitby. All she had wanted, she said, was some sea air and peace from her bothersome relatives. Marianne had been impressed by the professionalism of the search team, all volunteers. Joe was one of their most recent recruits and she was proud, even if she did worry when he was called out at night or in extreme weather.

"Holy shite... excuse me, Effie," Georgie said, as Beata giggled. "You're not wrong about it being all over social media. Some idiot's even put a call out for 'everyone who held Sam dear in their hearts' to go to the Carding Mill and see him brought home. If they'd held him a bit dearer in their hearts when he was alive, maybe he wouldn't have disappeared in the first place."

"Well, if they're all at the Carding Mill, they'll be well out of the way," Effie said, her voice redolent with practical common sense. "They'll be coming down the bridleway into Little Stretton if they're bringing him from Callow." For years, her home had been the manor house at Little Stretton, only minutes' walk from the track which led up to the Mynd. Briefly, there was quiet and Marianne wondered if everyone's thoughts were occupied as hers were, with images of the boy on a stretcher, borne down from the hill by the rescue volunteers.

Georgie's phone broke the silence, loud and shrill.

"DI Fraser," she said as she picked it up, snapping immediately into work mode. From halfway across the room, Marianne distinguished the deep bass of DCI Pickthall, or Pitbull, as he was known to his team. Niamh and Beata continued to talk in low voices, Effie making the odd interjection. Marianne wiped down the surfaces, her heart sinking as Georgie's side of the conversation progressed in clipped monosyllables. There was only one reason that Pitbull would call. When Georgie put the phone down, her face told Marianne all she needed to know.

"Afraid it looks like I'm going out after all," she said. "The Pitbull's just made me SIO. Sorry," she added, and Marianne wondered if her apology was for the change to their plans for the afternoon or for the fact that for the foreseeable future, Georgie would be engaged in a high-stress investigation. Conspiracy theories about the boy's disappearance had dominated not only social media but the local news, even featuring in the national bulletins.

Niamh was busy with her phone.

"Bad news," she said, as Georgie got up from the table. Marianne automatically transferred Georgie's coffee to a travel mug. "Looks like someone's got hold of the find at Callow. There's a call out for people to head over to Little Stretton."

5

—————

Snow was falling faster as Georgie headed the Land Rover down Church Stretton's High Street, past Housman's bistro where she and Marianne had stopped for lunch a few weeks earlier. The wipers scraped and swished across the windscreen, crushing fat flakes into solid pillars to frame each door. Any more snow and the body recovery might have to be abandoned. In extreme weather, Search and Rescue might not be willing to risk their volunteers' safety and with only one police rope access team across three counties, it might be a long wait before they were able to reach the scene.

Her phone rang as she left the village, passing a terrace of dull, 1970s redbrick houses that sat on a bank above the road as it snaked on towards Little Stretton. Pitbull.

"Sir?" she said, swiping her finger across the screen.

"You there yet?"

"Five minutes tops."

"The campsite has said you can park inside their gate. DC Corby's there waiting for you. Village is chocker by the sound of it."

Even on quiet days there were few places for walkers to park in Little Stretton, only room for five or so cars on the verge at the side of the campsite's lane. The village was a largely linear settlement, with only one or two narrow lanes off the main road. As she neared the timber framed church, Georgie noticed cars crammed along the pavement, and groups of people in outdoor gear all walking in the same direction. Muttering under her breath, she indicated right by the Ragleth Inn and turned down the single track lane to Ashes Hollow.

"Uniform have stationed a few of theirs at the foot of the bridleway," Pitbull said. "They've blocked the gate at the bottom but there's a bit of a crowd. You and Corby should be able to push through together."

So many cars had colonised the grass verge that the sign requesting space to be left for emergency vehicle access was leaning at an angle towards the stream, a blue van's bumper tight against it. Georgie made a mental note to get uniform to ticket it. They might not need ambulances or fire engines but the undertaker's van would need to get through later. Which reminded her to ask Pitbull.

"Has the PolSA got an undertaker on the way yet? If we've got a crowd to deal with, we want them here as soon as possible, even if they have to wait."

"On it," he said. "You've got bigger worries, I'm afraid. The lad's mother's there. Someone gave her a lift over from the Carding Mill. She's on at the bobbies to let her through. Deal with her tactfully though. Grieving mother and all. I can't have you doing a Harkness."

Sam Gray's mother, as Pitbull had told her when he'd called after lunch, had been less than impressed with how DI Harkness, the local CID officer in charge of the case until now, had co-ordinated the search for her son over the past four days. His view had been that the lad had gone off in a strop after falling out with friends and was lying low somewhere. He'd also bought into the view, aired on social media, that Sam had been part of a county line and had disappeared to save his skin. To top it all, Mrs Gray had witnessed the inspector describe her as hysterical when talking to a colleague, unaware that he was overheard.

Pitbull rang off as she crawled the Land Rover through the ford, deeper than usual after winter rains, and along the fence of Ashes Hollow campsite, passing a few groups of people in outdoor gear. Someone thumped the side of the car and shouted something that she couldn't make out.

"Same to you, mate," she said, as she caught sight of Ali Corby by the campsite entrance. Her DC opened the wooden gate to let her through, closing it swiftly behind her. In the half-light, rendered dim by the snow, the place looked beautiful. A small field at the foot of a valley, with a chattering stream, protected on both sides by steep hills and tall trees, and space for about twenty-five pitches between April and September. For most of the year it was lush green but now it stretched like an expanse of white velvet on a dressmaker's table, utterly unspoiled.

Georgie climbed down from the Land Rover, tugging on her hi-vis jacket and pulling a beanie over her hair.

"It's been bonkers," Corby said. "I've had to turn about ten cars away. And one of them nearly ended up in the stream when it was turning round. If I hadn't pointed out that emergency vehicles needed to get through, I'd never have got rid of them."

"What about the Kings?" Georgie said, pointing to a seventeenth century cottage crouched against the hillside where the campsite owners lived.

"I've checked on them and they're OK. Staying inside and keeping the door locked. They've given me a key for the gate."

Another group of people passed as Corby was locking the gate behind them and they followed them up the narrow track that led to the bridleway, past the cottage and across another stream. Corby's hat had ear flaps and she shoved it further onto her head as they passed below the branches of overhanging trees, their shelter keeping the ground free of snow, almost dark enough for twilight. A phalanx of bodies stood between them and the gate. Georgie took her torch from her inside pocket and held it high.

"Police. Coming through, please!" It still required effort to raise her voice without it becoming masculine in sound and she was glad when Corby joined in. People moved aside with murmurs and mutterings, some making their reluctance to let them through clear. They stood in rows about five deep from the gate and voices behind them announced the arrival of others to bolster their ranks. Repeating their call to be let through, Georgie and Corby came at last to the wooden five-bar gate, behind which stood three uniformed officers from the Church Stretton neighbourhood team. Their faces were testimony to the patience they were having to exert.

"That's her son up there," a man was shouting, leaning close to a female officer and punching the air. "You've got no right to keep her from him."

As the officer did her best not to flinch from the spray of saliva that narrowly missed her face, Georgie manoeuvred herself between the shouty man and the gate.

"With respect, sir, we have to maintain the safety of a recovery operation," she said, projecting her voice to be audible above the crowd. "The terrain is hazardous, particularly with the weather conditions, and we don't want anyone else getting hurt."

"Who the hell are you?" a woman next to him said, before the man had a chance to speak. Beneath her hood, tight blond curls glittered with moisture, framing a tear-stained face.

"Detective Inspector Georgie Fraser from Rural CID. This is DC Corby. You're Mrs Gray?"

"My son is up there. You have to let me see him."

"Mrs Gray." Georgie lowered her voice, grateful to Corby who was asking the crowd to move back. Drips from the overhanging trees landed on her face and she wiped them away with the back of her glove. "Mrs Gray, I promise you that the Search and Rescue team are doing everything in their power to bring your son back to you as quickly as they can. Once we've brought him up from the valley and confirmed his identity, you'll be the first to know. At the moment, our priority is to keep you safe which means asking you and your friends to stay away from the rescue site." She raised her voice again. "We understand your concern but the operation may take some time. If you could see your way to waiting in the pub or in your cars we would be very grateful. We need to keep access as clear as possible in case specialist equipment is needed."

One of the officers spoke from the other side of the gate.

"An SAR team's just gone up, boss. And the rope access lot have been on the bridleway about an hour now."

"Great," Georgie said, forcing a smile of encouragement for the distraught mother whose aggression, she felt, was understandable. She might not have children, but if her niece or anyone else in her family was being dragged up out of a desolate, snow-filled valley, having lain there for days, she'd be in a fury. She pulled a card from her pocket. "Mrs Gray, this is my number. I'm not sure what signal we'll have up there but you call me whenever you need to. And I'll have someone come down with updates for you as and when we have them. Ok?" she added as the woman looked about to argue. "I promise, we'll do our best to get him back to you as soon as possible."

Something in her tone must have reassured the woman, or maybe it was the Scottish accent. She'd read somewhere that people found it innately trustworthy. Mrs Gray nudged her friend who was haranguing Corby and he stopped mid-flow, bending close to her. Georgie didn't hear what she said, but the man listened intently, then nodded and straightened up, turning to face the crowd who were pushing uncomfortably at Georgie's back.

"All right, everyone," he bellowed. "Back up a bit and let the coppers through."

As one of the uniformed officers opened the gate just wide enough for Georgie and Corby to slip past, he leaned in and spoke low.

"One hour," he said to Georgie. "You've got one hour or we'll come and get him ourselves."

6

Joe's toes were chilled inside his boots. Out on the hill since sunrise, he was starting to feel both cold and hungry, despite the coffee and cake sent earlier by Marianne. He'd been thrilled to be chosen for the rope access team of four but it was over an hour since they had set off for Callow Hollow, two to a quad bike up the Burway. They'd left the road just after Pole Cottage then headed east across what was usually a wide expanse of turf and heather, now transformed into a glittering Christmas cake. As a relatively new volunteer, he hadn't expected to be included, but climbers were in short supply and with the body located in one of the Mynd's least accessible valleys, they were essential to its recovery. Cal Innes, Search and Rescue's most experienced climber, had driven their quad, saving Joe from the worst of the driving flakes and wind-chill. Andy Morgan had shared the other with a medic called Liz, whom Joe had met once on a training exercise.

The descent had needed careful planning before Cal, as team leader, was prepared to let anyone go down. They had left the quad bikes at the widest point of the bridleway, one turned towards the valley's edge in case its winch was needed.

Around two thirds down the almost vertical slope, the body had snagged against an outcrop of rock, framed with tufts of winter bracken. It was lucky the lad hadn't fallen further. Given the weather, Cal had been in two minds as to whether to OK the operation. Staring down at the prone form, all four had been silent.

"Bloody lucky you were available, Liz," Andy said. "At least we won't have to faff around with CPR."

Recognition of life extinct. In his training, Joe had learned that there were only five, fairly gruesome, instances in which the search team were allowed to make that call without a medic. A decapitated body; one that had been cut in half; one burnt to a crisp; one immersed in water for more than three hours; or one that had already begun to decompose. In all other instances, they were required to carry out CPR until a medic arrived. In this case they already knew the lad was deceased. While the drone operators had spotted the body, its khaki jacket and grey trousers stark against the snow, their thermal imaging equipment had picked up no signal. It was odd that the night's snowfall hadn't covered it more thickly. Perhaps the scouring wind, which screamed up the valley, had swept it clean.

"We can get him from there," Cal said, at last. "Let's not leave the poor lad any longer than we have to, eh?"

With the snow falling ever faster, Cal and Liz went over first, leaving Joe and Andy to attach the plastic stretcher to the winch, ready to lower it once their colleagues reached the bottom. In good weather it wouldn't have taken more than two minutes to abseil down. On a surface made slick by ice and snow, with rocks hidden beneath a white blanket, but no softer or less hazardous for all that, it took more than ten. Joe found himself holding his breath as he watched, relief washing through him when both figures reached the stricken form.

Andy's radio crackled into life, relaying Cal's voice from the valley's side. As Joe began to lower the stretcher on the winch, other voices carried up from below on the bridleway. Another S&R team of four were coming up from Little Stretton, hand-towing a trolley loaded with lights in case the operation went on after dark.

With them was a uniformed police officer, whom Joe thought he recognised from Georgie's investigation at the Geoscience Trust. He was younger than Joe, his face flushed from the steep climb. It might officially be a bridleway but Joe had never seen a horse on it, even the ponies native to the Mynd. Maybe once upon a time, the slope had been more gradual.

Handing the winch controls to the other team's leader, Joe and Andy lowered themselves gingerly over the edge, their ropes secured around the trunk of a hawthorn that clung to the slope as though considering whether to jump. It was old and gnarled, its roots sticking up through the snow like serpents frozen in mid-writhe, more than capable of supporting their weight. As he leaned back into his harness easing out the rope, Joe's boot slid on a hidden rock, pitching him to one side, giving him a moment's fear before he recovered himself. Showers of fine, freezing powder sprayed at him as though powered by a wind machine.

One on each side of the orange stretcher, he helped Andy ease its progress down the treacherous slope until they reached Cal. As Joe's feet alighted on more solid ground, freezing air was sucked into his chest by his relief at having made it without causing the team any mishaps. Liz crouched over the boy's body and Joe saw nothing more than the waterproof clothing on which snow was settling, and a flash of short, fair hair, dotted with white flakes. Fair hair. Pictures from social media nudged at his memory. Fair hair. Hadn't Sam Gray's been dark?

Cal's face was pale, an odd expression on it as he turned to Andy.

"We need to get onto Incident Command," he said. "This isn't Sam Gray."

Andy tugged a radio from his breast pocket with a gloved hand. He flicked his eyes up the slope towards the track where the other team waited.

"You're sure? They'll need to start another search from the last known position."

All those hours wasted, his voice said. Though not for the body that lay at their feet. And if this wasn't Sam, who was it?

"I knew Sam," Cal said, his voice strained. "I worked with him. This isn't him."

Shouts echoed from further down towards Little Stretton. Joe, lost in thought, started as Liz asked for the body bag. Between them they unzipped it and laid it flat. Liz and Cal eased the body gently from its position curled around the rock, laying the young man flat on his back.

"Deceased more than seventy-two hours," Liz said. "Rigor's well and truly gone, and the cold will have slowed things down."

There was something piteous about the thought of him, whoever he was, having lain there undiscovered for so long. Sam Gray had gone missing four days ago. Was this young man anything to do with him? Or was this just appalling coincidence?

On Liz's count of three, Joe and Cal helped her ease the body into its black, plastic shroud. It was heavy and cold but not rigid as Joe had expected it to be. His own fingers were stiff and cramped in his gloves and he had been out in the snow for far less time.

Sadness weighed heavy in his chest. It wasn't the first body he'd recovered. Back in Devon he'd worked as a beach lifeguard and, aged only seventeen, had helped retrieve the remains of a surfer who had got into difficulty on a riptide. And on only his second Search and Rescue callout they had brought a suicide in from the Teme around Ludlow. This was different, somehow. A boy, younger than him, but not by much. And not the boy they had been looking for. A stranger. Nameless. Did anyone even know he was missing? Or was some poor family, enjoying a normal Sunday, about to have their lives ripped apart? And what did it say about the lad that he could be lying out in the open for days and have no one report him missing?

Perhaps it wasn't so unusual. In the year before he'd found Marianne, when he was a student, he might well have gone that long without anyone knowing where he was, out of contact with friends and loved ones just because he felt like it.

Joe was struck by the respect, bordering on reverence, with which the team lifted the body bag onto the stretcher, strapping it in place. It would be a job to climb back up supporting it, but easier than with a live casualty when every effort had to be made to keep the stretcher horizontal, using a technique the team called toe-nailing. Joe still hadn't worked out why. Maybe because the climbers had to cling on with their toenails.

They climbed in silence, each supporting the stretcher with one hand or sometimes even a shoulder, their ascent accompanied only by the hum of the winch which took most of the weight. Snow coated his right cheek, blown by the wind and, when he looked across the stretcher towards Cal and Andy, he saw their faces too were caked. As they neared the top, arms reached down to lift their load over the edge and Joe heard Georgie's voice amongst those who welcomed them back up.

"Been a long day for you," she said, finding him as he freed the rope from his harness.

She wasn't wrong. With the relief of bringing the young man to the top without mishap, tiredness was seeping through his veins. The snow was falling more thickly and light was leaching from the sky, leaving only a rim of pale grey behind Packetstone

Hill. Above was a thick, anthracite blanket, that dropped fat, feathery flakes.

"How come you're back?" he asked, remembering the DI who had been in charge when his team had left the Carding Mill Valley. He stepped out of his harness and thanked her when she handed him a flask.

"Apparently there's been bad blood between DI Harkness and Sam Gray's mother," she said. "Pitbull thought a clean slate was the best idea. Especially now we have a body."

"Have you heard?" Joe asked, wondering if the news that Andy had relayed to the top had reached her.

"That it's not the body we were expecting?" Georgie said. "Aye. And I'm hoping Sam Gray isn't still out there. Not sure what the search possibilities are with snow and dark coming in. The Police Search Adviser's just chatting with your lot now."

The occasional shouts that had been drifting up from the foot of the bridleway were becoming louder. An image of an angry mob with flaming torches surfaced in Joe's mind. Were they going to have to manoeuvre the stretcher with its sombre load through a mass of people?

"What the hell's that?" Joe asked as the noise below swelled to a rumble and then a roar.

"Shit," Georgie said, as her radio buzzed. "Shit. They've broken through."

Far below, through a curtain of swirling flakes, Joe saw moving figures surging up towards them, like a pack of wolves.

7

"I wouldn't have thought Church Stretton even had a rough end," Georgie said, as Corby turned the Land Rover into Attlee Close just before nine on Monday morning. Blocks of identikit box-like houses, rendered with honey-hued pebble dash, squatted on each side, given variety only by the cars on their drives and the straggling shrubs in what passed for front gardens. Several had snowmen, each surrounded by scrubby white through which showed patches of green where the snow had been harvested for their construction.

"It's all relative, isn't it?" Corby said. "I mean we're not talking rough like parts of Brum or Kidderminster, but everywhere's got the bits people only live in because they can't afford anywhere else."

Georgie had read somewhere that almost twenty percent of Church Stretton's population was retired. It had grown as a Spa town in Victorian times, nicknamed Little Switzerland owing to the landscape, and now was a haven for walkers, with quirky shops and several good places to eat. Definitely middle class. Not so Attlee Close.

Number twenty-three was easy to identify, even as they turned the corner of a sharp dog-leg into a further stretch. Outside the low garden gate stood a crowd in brightly coloured winter wear, most carrying cameras or phones. In front of the picket fence a reporter was doing a piece to camera, microphone clutched in a gloved hand, her face earnest and pink with cold beneath a suede, fur-trimmed hat.

Corby parked a few houses along in the only available space. As she locked the Land Rover, the door of number seventeen opened and an elderly man came out, pulling on a quilted coat.

"Have you come to move them on?" he said, opening his gate and stepping onto the pavement, blocking Georgie's way.

"Morning," she said, summoning her best smile. The man was unimpressed.

"It's bloody ridiculous. We've had them camped out here ever since her lad went missing. Parking all over the place, dropping their litter, taking pictures. And not just of her house. The whole street. Enough's enough—"

"We'll have a word," Georgie said. "And I'll send a couple of officers down. Do you know the Grays?"

The man raised a bushy eyebrow. His skin was mottled around rheumy eyes. In his eighties, Georgie would have put him, but full of vigour still. He'd probably been on his way to move the crowd on himself when she and Corby turned up.

"Michelle Gray's lived there ten year or more," he said. "But I wouldn't say we know her. Kids are always in mischief and that new fella of hers isn't the type we'd welcome as a neighbour. Not that I don't feel sorry for her," he added. "Heart goes out to anyone in that situation." He took a handkerchief from his pocket and wiped his nose which was dripping in the cold.

"Understood, Mr...?"

"Conway, Tony Conway."

"DI Fraser," Georgie said, handing the man a card. "And this is DC Corby. Get in touch anytime."

As they walked towards number twenty-three, Corby raised an eyebrow.

"Anytime?"

"You never know who'll have useful info," Georgie said. "And I reckon not much goes on in this street without Mr Conway noticing."

Moving the crowd by the gate was no easier than pushing through the volunteers at the bottom of Ashes Hollow had been. Questions soared through the air, shouted while phones were held aloft, no doubt filming their arrival to post on true crime social media pages. At least the reporter from *Midlands Today* had the grace to look a little shamefaced when Georgie asked her to please have a little respect for the family and grant them some privacy in what was by anyone's standards a difficult time. Chelle Gray's eldest son had been missing for four days. She had faced the news that his body had been discovered, only to learn that the body was that of someone else's son and there was still no trace of hers.

"Any news on Sam?" an anonymous voice shouted. Georgie scanned the crowd but none of the faces, pinched with cold beneath woollen hats and gortex hoods, rang any bells.

"We began a new search operation yesterday in conjunction with West Mercia Search and Rescue. If anyone can offer any information as to Sam Gray's whereabouts we'd be grateful but for now, we'd like to talk to his mother in peace."

Eyes scorched their backs as they made their way up a snowy path to the front door. A lack of footprints showed that no one had left the house yet that day.

"About bloody time," said a deep voice. The door was opened by the same man who had been shaking his fist at the bridleway gate. In the morning light, Georgie got a better look at him. All she had registered before was his height and build, the proverbial brick shit-house. Now she saw that he wasn't bad-looking. His face carried thuggish charm with a hint that violence lurked just beneath the surface. He wouldn't have been out of place in a TV soap as a gangster who excelled at conveying menace.

Along with Corby, she held out her warrant card.

"I remember you," the man said, turning his back and beckoning them in, leaving Corby to close the door. The cramped hall was dark, boots and shoes scattered along one wall, entangled with a couple of skateboards and several bags. A mirror shaped like the sun, with shards of glass forming rays, bore a long horizontal crack and a vase of drooping flowers was crammed onto a shelf too narrow for it. The house smelled of smoke and stale air, overly warm after the chill outside. Georgie unzipped her jacket and shrugged it off her shoulders as their new friend led them into a small sitting room.

Chelle Gray sat hunched on a battered sofa, her feet tucked up beneath her and a box of tissues by her hand. She wore a pink towelling dressing gown that hadn't seen a washing machine for a while. Her eyes, puffy and red, met Georgie's as they entered the room.

"Mrs Gray, how are you this morning?" Georgie asked.

The woman shrugged and made a face.

"Sod all sleep. But then, what d'you expect?"

Georgie nodded.

"Sit down if you want. Clive, put the kettle on, will you?"

Georgie took a threadbare armchair, sitting a little sideways so that she looked at Sam's mum rather than the widescreen TV which formed the focal point of the room despite being switched off. Blue flames danced across a coal-effect gas fire and Corby took off her jacket before sitting down next to it.

"Clive is your partner?" Georgie asked as the big man let the door swing shut behind him, his footsteps loud on the wooden floor of the hall as he went to the kitchen.

"My fiancé. Supposed to be getting married next month. Not that I feel like it now."

"Do he and Sam get on?"

"Oh, don't start that." Chelle Gray turned an exasperated face on Georgie. "I've already had all of that from that DI Harkness. Sam and Clive get on just fine and there's no way Sam left home because of us. Something's happened to him and every bloody second your lot waste trying to dig up dirt on my family isn't helping to find him."

"Mrs Gray, I'm sorry," Georgie said. "That wasn't what I meant. I suppose I was just trying to gauge the family dynamic. I've read all the notes from previous interviews but it would be helpful to get a picture of Sam. I don't mean a photo," she added, as the woman reached a hand up to the windowsill beside her where there were several framed school photographs. Georgie recognised one from TV news bulletins. "I mean an idea of the real him. Not that rubbish that's been all over social media."

She wondered as Mrs Gray talked, how any mother made sense of the disappearance of their child. Surely their first instinct was to feel guilt, however misplaced. As those who are left behind by suicides forever examine their actions for anything they could have done to prevent the loss. Sam had, apparently, been a very easy child, her first and only until his younger brother had come along. It had been just the two of them until she'd met Danny's dad when Sam was six. Sam's dad had been some fly by night who hadn't stuck around. No hard feelings and he'd died not long afterwards. Danny was now twelve and presumably the owner of at least one of the skateboards in the hall. The two boys got on well by all accounts, close given the age gap, and there had been no trouble until things had turned sour between Chelle and Danny's dad.

"He was a bastard," she said, taking a vape from a wooden box on the coffee table. "Of course, I only found that out after I bloody married him. Started off sweet as candy. Until he knocked me about. You try to keep it hidden but Sam knew. Came in on it one night and tried to help me. Got the shit kicked out of him instead." She exhaled a cloud of strawberry scented vapour. "I left him after that but I reckon it was too late."

That was when Sam had started getting into trouble with the police. Nothing too major to start with. Shoplifting. Antisocial behaviour. A bit of joyriding. And then at fourteen he'd been involved in an armed robbery. Not guns or knives. A hammer and an adjustable spanner. And it hadn't been Sam wielding them. He'd only been lookout for some older boys. Got community service.

"Turned him round, didn't it?" Clive said, coming in with a tray bearing a teapot and mugs, a plastic carton of milk dangling from one finger.

Georgie knew Sam's record, of course, but it was interesting to hear it told by someone who loved him. On paper he had been just another troubled adolescent.

"How did it help him?" she asked.

"It wasn't the community service, exactly," Sam's mum said. "Although he made some friends there. He got assigned a youth worker. This support programme for young offenders."

Georgie exchanged a look with Corby at mention of the youth programme. Something she already planned to flag up at the team briefing later.

"They did outdoor stuff," Chelle Gray went on. "You know, climbing, kayaking, that sort of thing. And he loved it. After he left school he got a job at the outdoor shop on the high street. He was doing well."

Her story didn't tally with the rumours that had been rife on social media. Tales of drugs and county lines. Sam had bought a rundown motorbike when he was seventeen and, rumour had it, had used it to courier cocaine and cannabis all over Shropshire.

"Tell me about his friends," Georgie said.

Having poured tea and handed mugs to Corby and Fraser, Clive sat down on the sofa, making it creak and sag.

"Good bunch, aren't they?" he said, reaching out and squeezing Chelle's hand. "Most of them, anyway."

"Would they be the ones he was with on the night he went missing?" Georgie asked. "The party on the Mynd?"

"It wasn't a party," Chelle said. "I told you, he was into all that outdoor stuff. Camping and that. But yeah, they was most of his friends."

Somewhere in the case notes was a list of the group that had been up at the shelter that night. Not a big crowd. Eight as far as she remembered, a mix of boys and girls. All had been interviewed but she would need to speak to them again. One name – now significant – had not been on the list.

"Mrs Gray," Georgie began and Sam's mum interrupted her.

"You can call me Chelle, you know. Mrs Gray makes me feel about ninety. And I feel old enough as it is." She inhaled on the vape again and puffed out a stream of fruity vapour.

"Chelle," Georgie said, relieved to be met with less hostility than she had expected after the breakdown between the family and the previous investigation into Sam's disappearance. "Do you know a lad called Davey Whelan? Was he a friend of Sam's?"

Chelle and Clive exchanged looks. Georgie tried to read their faces, aware of the scratch of Corby's pen as she made notes.

"They knew each other," Clive said, in the end. "Not best mates but they hung around sometimes."

"From community service," Chelle said. "And then that youth programme. Davey was into all his outdoor stuff too. Survivalist, Sam called him. Used to like going off into the wilds and living rough. Why?" she asked, her face suddenly brighter. "Do you think Sam is with him?"

"No," Georgie said. She certainly hoped not. "I'm afraid it was Davey Whelan's body that we recovered from Callow Hollow yesterday."

8

———

They had found his bus travel pass in his pocket. No wallet or phone by which to identify him. Had it not been for the sorry little rectangle of laminated card, they might have taken longer to find his name. No one had reported Davey Whelan missing.

Georgie held her first team briefing at Shrewsbury's police station in Monkmoor. While DCI Pickthall and much of West Mercia's CID worked out of HQ in Worcester, the Rural Crime Unit, of which Georgie was senior officer, was based in Shrewsbury, a shiny new-built station designed by award-winning architects, all open modern spaces and bright, primary colours. For the moment, it was her team and the community officers from Church Stretton. Once it was established how Davey's body had come to be in Callow Hollow, Pitbull might send in the big guns but for now it was her game.

Cupping her hands around a steaming mug of coffee as the meeting room seemed to be struggling against the sub-zero temperatures outside, Georgie waited for quiet before she spoke.

"First of all, to let you know that we've just come from Sam's home. His mum's in pieces as you might imagine. We didn't see the little brother – staying at a friend's she said, to get away from all the ghouls outside the front door – but apparently he's coping OK."

"Any news on the search, boss?" Mike Harley asked. "I called the PolSA but she said it's too early to say."

Joe had had some choice anecdotes about police search advisers when he'd got home from his stint at Callow Hollow. Not about the one running the current op but gems he'd gleaned from his Search and Rescue colleagues. Word had it that in their five days of training PolSAs spent all but one day on counter-terrorism searches, hunting for Sim cards in warehouses as Andy Morgan had put it, leaving little time for missing persons. Often they bowed to the greater experience of the Search and Rescue teams when making decisions.

"They started a new one just before sunrise," Georgie said. "Had to call it off yesterday once it got dark. It was a proper blizzard up on top of the Mynd by all accounts. They've completed the first 300 metre diameter search centred on the car so they're starting the wider circle now. Green zone is it?" she added to Mike Harley who nodded. "Let's hope they find him before we get to the purple." The third and final search area. Could Sam Gray have survived the night out there? Or was he safely holed up somewhere hiding from a rival gang as some of the social media detectives believed, while the search volunteers risked their safety hunting for him?

"For the moment we have two prongs to our enquiry," she went on. "To find Sam Gray. And to find out what happened to Davey Whelan. Probability says that the two are linked. They were friends. It's straining coincidence a bit far to think that they might both have gone missing on the Mynd without there being any connection." She turned to one of the constables from the Church Stretton neighbourhood team. "PC Holton, have we had any luck in tracing Davey Whelan's family?"

"He doesn't have one, ma'am," the officer said, blushing a little as so many eyes turned on her. "Not one living relative that we know of. He grew up in care after his mum died when he was nine. His next of kin is listed as a Mrs Rose Ellis but when I contacted her she said she hadn't seen him for about three years. She was his foster mum from when he was thirteen to when he was sixteen."

"The golden years," Mike Harley said, with a wry smile. "Worked up quite a record between 2017 and 2020. Starting with shoplifting and petty theft. Moved on to arson, possession with intent to supply, possession of a weapon. Several weapons in fact. Seems he was a bit of a collector."

"We'll come back to that," Georgie said. "For the moment, I'm stuck on why no one reported him missing. We haven't had the PM results yet but early indicators suggest he's been dead since Wednesday night at the latest. How come no one noticed? Where did he live?"

"A caravan up on Trevor Hill, in the woods above the golf course," PC Holton said.

"Alone?"

"Yes, ma'am." Clearly no one had yet told PC Holton that Georgie hated being called ma'am. In her London days, just after her gender transition – or correction, as she preferred to think of it – too many colleagues had addressed her that way with lashings of sarcasm.

"Did he have a job?"

"He worked at the timber yard – Pritchard's, on the industrial estate by the A49. Apparently when he didn't show up for work last week, they thought he'd gone off on one of his wanderings."

"That was usual for him, was it?" Georgie asked.

"Not unusual," PC Holton said. "I spoke to John Pritchard this morning. Seems they gave him a job almost as a charity case. Zero hours contract and they paid him when he showed up. He was there most days but sometimes he'd just go off – liked living off-grid. It's a family business and I got the impression John's wife Sarah had been a friend of Davey's mother. Tried to give him a bit of stability."

"And he met Sam Gray on community service, according to Sam's mum," Georgie said.

Mike Harley raised a hand to interject. "And through the young offender programme."

Georgie nodded and drained the last of her tea.

"Which brings us onto Cal Innes."

A layer of awkwardness settled over the room. Four of the officers present were part of Church Stretton's Safer Neighbourhood team. A team which had worked closely with Time Out, the youth programme for which Cal Innes worked.

"Do any of you know him well?" Georgie asked. "Socially, I mean, as well as through work." Church Stretton wasn't a big place. To her surprise it was one of her Rural Crime officers, Simon Thomas who raised his hand.

"We're in the same running club," he said. "I've known him for a few years."

"And?" Georgie said. "What do you make of him?"

PC Thomas had the kind of complexion that flushed easily and now his cheeks suffused with red, making him look like Enid Blyton's Noddy illustrations.

"He's a good bloke," Thomas said. "Sound. Did a degree in social work at Birmingham and worked there for a few years afterwards. Specialised in youth work and moved here about five years ago."

"I'm curious," Georgie said, choosing her words carefully. If there were friends of Cal's amongst them, she didn't want to alienate any of her new team. "Why didn't he recognise Davey Whelan? Or tell us that he knew Sam Gray until the body turned out not to be his?"

PC Thomas shrugged.

"Maybe he didn't get a good look at Whelan. It was snowing and getting dark when they retrieved the body."

"Maybe," Georgie said. "But what about Sam? Innes worked with him on the young offender programme. Why pretend he didn't know him when he came up yesterday morning to help retrieve the car? You were with him, Mike. Did he say anything to you?"

Mike Harley shook his head.

"Maybe he felt it wasn't relevant. Or he was trying to give Sam some confidentiality. If Sam had been successfully rehabilitated, why bring up the young offender angle?"

"Hmmm…" Georgie tapped her pen against her nose absent-mindedly. There was an undefined itch that came over her whenever Cal Innes was mentioned. And up on the bridleway, once he and Joe had brought Davey Whelan's body up out of the valley, he hadn't said a word about knowing him. She would have to wait to scratch it until she interviewed him. Mentally, she put it on her list for her and Corby to do that afternoon.

Outside the window it was snowing, the sky swirling and grey. Another obstacle to the search on the Mynd. Once again, she hoped Sam was holed up somewhere safe and sound, smoking weed and playing 'Call of Duty'. His mum had said it was his favourite game.

"Ok, let's move on to Sam's friends, the ones he was up on the Mynd with on the night he went missing. Ali, have you got the file?" Harkness's team had passed on all the relevant notes and Georgie had asked Corby to collate them.

Ali Corby flipped open an iPad case and picked up the remote for the Smartboard.

"I expect you already know all of this," she said to the local officers, "but just to get the rest of us up to speed."

A list of names showed stark against the board's backlit white background.

"I'll just do a quick run through," she said, "and maybe chip in if I miss anything important."

Sergeant Carradine, who headed up the Safer Neighbourhood team and had spent most of the briefing looking as though he was sucking on a wasp looked marginally less pissed off.

"First, we have Jessie Pritchard," Corby said, and a picture of a dark-haired girl, perhaps eighteen or so, flashed up on the board. "As I understand it, she's interesting for two reasons. She was Sam Gray's on-and-off girlfriend and her parents run the timber yard where Davey Whelan worked."

"Three reasons," Bob Carradine said. "It was her car that Sam disappeared in."

Corby smiled.

"Right, three. Next." Another headshot appeared on the screen, a striking girl with slanting almond-shaped eyes and afro hair scraped up into twists on top of her head like the leaves of a pineapple. "Alisha Johnson. Good friend of Jessie's. They went to the sixth-form college in Shrewsbury together and she now works at the big Boots on the Meole Brace estate. Part-time make-up influencer on Instagram."

More photos followed. Seth Glover, also from the sixth-form college who now worked at the golf club; Lily Morpeth, who'd been at school with several of the others; Bryn Morgan – no relation to Andy Morgan from Search and Rescue, Mike Harley clarified – and Alfie Rickard.

"Alfie Rickard who used to work at the Shropshire Geoscience Trust?" Georgie asked.

"That's the one," Corby said. "He's at the garden centre now."

Georgie remembered him well from when she had investigated the murder of Dr Neil Traynor at the GT the previous spring. Both Joe and Beata knew Alfie too and had worked with him there. She wondered if either of them was still in touch with him.

"And last but not least," Mike Harley said, with an eye on DC Corby, "my nephew. Lucas."

Corby smiled a little awkwardly and flashed the final photo onto the screen. Georgie could see a resemblance between Lucas and his uncle. The same thick dark hair and solid shoulders, the same steady brown eyes.

"He was at school with Sam and they'd done some climbing together," Harley said. "Lucas is having a year out before uni. He's working at the garden centre too. Saving to go travelling in March. The usual stuff – Vietnam, Cambodia, Thailand."

"Ok, thanks, Mike," Georgie said, with a smile. "I appreciate this might be tricky for you so just let us know if you need a bit of distance, ok?"

"Just one thing that came up when I went through the interviews with these kids," Corby said, as Georgie made signs that she was about to move on.

"Go ahead."

"If you read their transcripts, boss, their accounts of Wednesday night, when Sam disappeared, are almost identical."

Bob Carradine shifted in his seat.

"Well, they would be, wouldn't they? They were all together."

Corby nodded with a half smile.

"I appreciate that." She turned to Georgie. "But it's like you always say, boss. If you ask four people to give an account of an identical event they all attended, each one will tell it differently. They'll have noticed or remembered different things. This lot, the way they tell it is practically word for word the same. Like they learned it."

Georgie tapped her pen against her cheek this time.

"Interesting," she said, letting her gaze wander over the eight photos on the board. "Well, I suppose we'll have to talk to them all again, then. See if Davey Whelan's body turning up changes their memories at all. None of them mentioned him being there, I suppose."

Both Carradine and Corby shook their heads.

"No boss," Corby said. "It was just the eight of them. And Sam."

9

"Jesus, you wouldn't get up here without four-wheel drive, would you?" Georgie asked, steering into the bend as her rear wheels slid on a patch of frozen snow. On either side of the single-track road, trees reared up on tall banks, affording some shelter. The snow was less deep than on the more open roads, but slippery and treacherous, hard-packed where local 4x4s had braved the run down into Church Stretton and the residual slush had re-frozen overnight.

"I don't think I've been up this way before," she said to Corby, who, as always when Georgie drove, was gripping the door handle. "I was expecting more of a village."

They had turned off the old Shrewsbury Road and up Castle Hill into the upper hamlet of All Stretton, a series of dwellings spread out along a steep winding lane which climbed to the eastern edge of the Long Mynd. Most of the village was below on the Shrewsbury Road with a pub, The Yew Tree, and a small church.

"Quite a few of these are holiday lets, these days," Corby said as they passed a long, low building that might once have been a small farmstead. "I suppose most people don't want to be so isolated."

Isolation didn't seem to bother Cal Innes. Georgie had had to use *what3words* to locate his cottage, Mytton's Fold, which was up an unsurfaced track just past a sign to the Drover's Rest holiday cottages. As they bumped and skidded between ranks of fir trees, a cottage, invisible from the road, seemed to grow out of the land. It was built from huge chunks of rough-hewn stone, interspersed with almost flat horizontal pieces to fill in the gaps. Presumably there was some mortar in there too, but the whole had the look of a drystone wall. The roof was slate, patches of moss and lichen showing through where the snow had melted, and smoke curled upwards from a cowled chimney stack.

Cal's blue pick-up was parked against the wall of a stone outbuilding with a corrugated roof, from which hung icicles, small droplets clinging to them in the afternoon sun. The temperature had climbed to the dizzy height of one degree above zero and all around were the sounds of nature rejoicing in the cessation of the snowstorm, drips from the trees and a chorus of birdsong.

"Blue tit," Corby said as she climbed down from the Land Rover, causing Georgie to raise an eyebrow.

"Josh is into birds," she explained. "He's got some app that tells you what bird you can hear and whenever we go for a walk we have to stop every five metres to identify it. He even gets phone alerts when the migration season starts. If I hadn't already agreed to marry him I might be running for the hills," she added, not fooling Georgie for a moment. She had only recently met Corby's fiancé, a bright-eyed, rugby-playing man mountain with a roaring laugh and what seemed like boundless enthusiasm for life.

"He went to school with Cal," she said, as the door of the cottage opened. "I only found out yesterday."

Cal Innes didn't look pleased to see them. Zipping up a blue fleece jacket, his feet jammed into unlaced walking boots, he crossed the snow-strewn yard to meet them.

"Were you going out?" Georgie said, looking down at his boots.

"No, I..." he hesitated. "I heard the car. I don't get many visitors up here."

"I can imagine. If it starts snowing again, we might have to stay the night." Georgie smiled. The man definitely didn't look welcoming. "Are we OK to come in for a minute?"

Cal looked around as though searching for a reason why they should not, then shrugged and turned back to the door. His dreadlocks were held back from his face by a rainbow-striped bandana and he wore a fleece buff around his neck, above a Bob Marley sweatshirt and black combat trousers. Despite the fluid energy with which he moved, he reminded Georgie of stoners she'd known at uni and she wondered if he might have a secret cannabis farm somewhere about the place. It would explain his uneasiness at their unannounced visit.

In the small porch they took off their jackets and boots, then followed Cal into a warm kitchen, heated, Georgie supposed, by the Raeburn that stood against the far wall. The quarry-tiled floor was chill beneath her feet and she was glad of her thick wool socks. Marianne had bought them for her the Christmas before and she still got a glow of pleasure whenever she put them on. Their first Christmas together. Soon it would be their second, but their first living together. Eighteen months into their relationship, they were still finding firsts.

"Amazing place this," Corby said, taking in the view from the window beyond the sink. Beneath a razor blue sky, the Long Mynd stretched upwards away from them, rolling in soft, white folds. "My Josh would love it. I think you know him," she added.

"Josh MacArty, Church Stretton School. He'd have been a couple of years below you."

Cal frowned, picking a kettle up from the Raeburn and taking it over to the sink. Then he nodded.

"Big bloke. Played rugby."

"Still does," Corby said. "Semi-pro these days. Nat 2 West or whatever."

Georgie blessed her inwardly. Corby had a gift for making people feel at ease, one of the reasons Georgie chose her for company when interviewing witnesses. Cal's body language was softening with every word, and soon he was making tea and fetching a scratched McVitie's biscuit tin from a corner pantry.

"So, how are you?" Georgie asked, once they were sitting around the table with mugs of tea. "The PolSA said you were out on the hill again this morning."

"Started at seven," Cal said, "then swapped teams at two so they sent those of us that were out yesterday home. Your friend Joe was with us again. Mind you, I suppose he works on the Mynd so he'd probably have been there anyway."

"Any news?" she asked, though she imagined she would have been updated if there had been any.

Cal shook his head and picked up his phone which lay on the table close to his hand. He swiped and turned it around, showing them a map with three concentric circles in different colours.

"I've been keeping an eye on things. They've searched all three zones using the car as last known position, but no joy. I think the plan's to take Pole Cottage as the new LKP – given that that was the last place he was known to have been before he went missing but that was four days ago so it's a long shot. He left there in a car that only turned up yesterday. Why would he be out somewhere on the hill?"

"You think the search is a waste of time?" Georgie said, stirring milk into her tea.

"No, of course not. But none of it makes much sense." He took the phone back, re-positioned it next to his hand as if its presence gave him security.

"I understand that you knew Sam Gray, from the Time Out programme." From the corner of her eye, Georgie saw Corby slide her notebook onto the table and take out a pen.

"Yeah," Cal said. "A few years ago now, but he came back sometimes to help out."

"You didn't mention that up on the hill yesterday."

Cal shrugged.

"Didn't think it was important."

Georgie smiled. "Maybe it isn't. But it must make the search harder, when it's someone you know."

"It's not like we were best mates," the youth worker said. "Just through work."

"Did you have each other's phone number, social media, that type of thing?"

"Why's that matter?"

"I'm just trying to work out the relationship," Georgie said with another smile. If Innes had been a porcupine, every spine would have been standing to attention. "At this stage, everything that we can find out about Sam is important. Anything might help us locate him."

Cal pushed back his chair and got up, moving over to the window as though he thought Sam might suddenly appear in the snowy wasteland behind his house.

"I've been out looking for him for twenty-four hours on and off. If I knew anything that would help find him, do you think I wouldn't have used it by now?"

Georgie took a sip of tea, wondering at his defensiveness. Guilt that, with all his knowledge of the area, he hadn't been able to find him? Or perhaps it was what is often said about a life saved being of more value to the person who saves it than the one who is saved. Bearing in mind the job he had chosen, Innes must have some sort of crusader zeal, a need to redeem. Maybe, having seen Sam transform from petty criminal to outdoor enthusiast, one soul recovered, he couldn't bear the idea of that soul being lost.

"When did you last see Sam?" Corby asked and Cal turned from the window to lean against the wooden counter.

"I don't know. I can check work records to see when he last came in to help."

"Did you ever see him apart from work? Just bump into him, like? Church Stretton's not a big place."

He seemed less rattled by Corby's questions and nodded.

"I've seen him when he's at work. Mountain Pursuits – on the High Street. My mate Tom runs it so I pop in sometimes. But I don't know when the last time was."

"Rough idea," Georgie said. "Two weeks? Six months?"

"Probably about a month."

"And how was he?"

Cal made a face. Irritation. Georgie would have reckoned him a good-natured soul. Perhaps the two days of fruitless searching had taken its toll.

"Fine. Normal. I don't remember."

"And you hadn't heard anything on the grapevine – through your work? You must pick up bits of gossip."

He shook his head. Unzipping his jacket he came back to the table and his mug of tea.

"None of that stuff on social media was true, as far as I know. Sam had turned things round. Yeah, he liked a party but who doesn't at that age?"

It was a fair point. And there was a big difference between liking the odd drink or spliff at a party and couriering drugs around the county. Time for the second part of their enquiry if he had nothing to tell them about Sam. Georgie chose a chocolate biscuit from the tin.

"Can you tell us anything about Davey Whelan?"

This time Cal almost grinned, although there was no humour in it.

"I can tell you lots about Davey Whelan but I don't reckon any of it would have a bearing on how he died. He reckoned himself a survivalist. Liked to go out and live rough on the Mynd – challenge himself for how long he could be self-sufficient up there."

"And you think that was what he was doing when he died?" Corby said.

"How else could it have happened? He was an odd one, Davey, but everyone liked him. I don't know of any beef with anyone. And you're right, I do hear talk. If Davey was still up to his old ways, I reckon I'd have heard." He picked up his tea and frowned as Corby made notes. "Actually there was one rumour, but I don't think anything came of it. That fire over at Minsterley. The farm blaze that got out of control."

Georgie nodded. The firefighter, Andy Morgan, had reminded her of it only the day before.

"Someone reckoned Davey started it but it can't have gone anywhere. Your lot should know if he was questioned about it."

Interesting. Worth looking into, at least, although she wondered that no one on the local team had mentioned it once Davey's body was identified.

Corby looked at her watch and raised her eyebrows. They still had one more interview before the evening briefing and with the amount of snow on the roads, it was going to take them longer than usual to get down off the hill and into Shrewsbury.

"May I just use your bathroom, Cal?" Georgie asked. It wasn't entirely an excuse for a look around Cal's house. She did genuinely need a pee but usually avoided using other people's toilets, scarred by the early days of her gender correction and the extreme anxiety she had experienced then.

Cal pointed her up the stairs to the first door on the right. The bathroom was small and clean, but cold, with only a bar electric heater on the wall. A damp towel hung on the back of the door and moisture lingered in the air as though he had recently had a shower. Perhaps when he came in from his search. As she washed her hands, her eyes ran over the shelves, clocking two toothbrushes in an enamel mug. Did Cal have a partner who stayed over? She'd seen no other signs of anyone sharing the house.

At the foot of the stairs, she peered around the open living room door. On a wooden coffee table was an ashtray holding more than a few white spliff ends, a tin with a cannabis leaf design and a packet of tobacco next to it. At least that explained why he hadn't been keen to let them in. A blue sleeping bag was folded on the end of the sofa, which faced the TV, and a video game console sprawled on the carpet, handsets discarded at its side. Embers glowed in the wood-burner, but she reckoned the nights would be cold in a house like this, however much fuel he heaped into the stove. Maybe he'd chosen to camp out downstairs after the stress and cold of yesterday's search.

Corby and Cal were still chatting when Georgie put her head around the kitchen door.

"We'll leave you to it, then Cal," she said. "You must be knackered. Thanks for your time."

He hardly seemed sorry to see them go, watching from the doorway as they climbed into the Land Rover and Georgie executed a five-point turn in the yard, unsure what lay beneath the lumps and bumps in the snow.

"Interesting snippet for you, boss," Corby said as they headed back down the treacherous track towards the Shrewsbury Road. "That firefighter who was on the search team yesterday with Joe. Andy Morgan."

Georgie nodded, switching on her lights as they came between the tall banks of trees. "What about him?"

"Only reckoned it was Davey started that fire. Reported him to the local cops, apparently."

"Interesting," Georgie said.

"And, according to Cal, he's up on the Mynd at night sometimes. Keen photographer. Runs a Facebook group showcasing gorgeous Shropshire pics – quite a few of stargazing."

"Doubly interesting," Georgie said. "And Cal told you that, did he?" Now why would he do that?

10

Marianne brought a leftover lasagne back from work for supper. Joe had said he would come over and sometimes he brought Niamh with him. Then there would be Beata and Georgie, who would be shattered after a day on the case – and it couldn't have been easy going to see Sam Gray's mum. However busy their days, they always exchanged messages but today's had been few, peppered between interviews in Georgie's case, and short. Marianne's days at the tearoom were always busy but pleasantly predictable, the lunchtime rush between twelve and two a time when her phone had to be ignored. Since the brutal murder of Neil Traynor, footfall to the Trust had increased substantially and it had re-established itself, not only as a geoscience and conservation centre, but also a food hub selling local produce through its shop and tearoom. Marianne was glad of its success and not for her own self-interest. She liked and respected the people who worked there and who hadn't deserved their project to fail because an arrogant predator had brought tragedy to them.

Beata was home first. Marianne had just got in after feeding the donkeys and Josephine the goat when she heard the chug of her 125cc Honda. A present for her seventeenth birthday from her mother, who, despite being detained at His Majesty's pleasure at Eastwood Park in Gloucestershire, had arranged the gift through Marianne. Headlights swung over the snow-capped garden hedge, briefly illuminating the apple tree and the wooden frame of the vegetable patch, all outlined in white.

Minutes later the dogs – never allowed in the kitchen – exploded into a flurry of barking in the living room. Beata called a hello from the porch and Marianne opened the kitchen door to see her, motorcycle helmet hanging from her arm as she closed the front door on an icy wind. She blew Marianne a kiss as she began to strip off her leathers.

"How were the roads?" Marianne asked.

"Fine. The A49 was gritted. Snow piled up at the sides so easier for a bike than a car, I think. And fine in Ludlow."

"And college?"

Beata hung up her jacket and shoved her feet into pink suede slippers.

"Same as." She took her phone from her bag and followed Marianne into the living room where the dogs greeted her in a blur of fur and tails. "How was the tearoom?" Once upon a time, Beata had worked there with her.

Marianne smiled. "Same as," she said. "Tea?"

"Please. And can I light the fire? Then I'll come and help you."

"No help needed. I've got a spare lasagne in the oven."

Ten minutes later, they sat with tea, Beata cross-legged in front of the log-burner watching it as though it was television, waiting until the first flames died down so she could put some larger logs in.

"I talked to Alfie today. Remember him?"

"From the GT?" Marianne asked and Beata nodded, blowing

at her tea. Marianne remembered. Brown-haired and stocky – not the sharpest tool in the box, the director of the GT had always said about him – but he was good-hearted and hardworking.

"He's at college one day a week for his horticulture course. I saw him at lunch."

"How is he?" Marianne asked, suspecting there was more to Beata's story than just the fact that Alfie had been there.

"A bit weirded out." Alfie, it transpired, had heard that Georgie had taken over responsibility for the search for Sam Gray.

"How on earth did he know that?" Marianne asked.

Beata wiggled her phone at her.

"Everyone's talking about it. You know Alfie was there the night Sam went missing?" To hear Beata talk, it had given Alfie a bit of celebrity status around the college. He was a year or so younger than the others who had been on the Long Mynd but knew them through Lucas Harley, from his job at the garden centre.

"I think he wants to talk to Georgie," Beata said.

Marianne thought it more than likely that Alfie would be talking to Georgie whether he liked it or not, or at least to one of her team, if he'd been up at the camp-out on the Mynd last Wednesday night.

"Do you know what about?" she asked.

Beata shrugged.

"He just kept asking what it was like, living with her. Then he asked if he could have her number. I said he could get her work number but he said he didn't want to contact her through the police. And of course, I can't give him her private number." Although born in Poland, Beata had lived in England since she was a baby and even had a faint Midlands accent. Sometimes though, her Polish origins came through in her speech patterns, the emphasis that she placed on words. She and her mother had always spoken Polish at home.

Marianne sat back in her chair, stroking her big dog, Maggie, who had laid her head on her knee. She'd be in raptures later with both Georgie and Joe for company. Beata knelt in front of the log-burner and opened its door, letting out a hiss and crackle of sparks on wood. Using her hands rather than the tongs – learning bad habits from Georgie – she placed a larger log into the heart of the glowing embers.

"I think it might be serious," she said, her back to Marianne. "And Georgie definitely needs to know. Should I tell her?"

"Tell her what?"

Beata sighed and sat back on her heels, then swiped across her phone screen, scrolled for a few moments and passed it to Marianne.

"Look. He sent me these later."

Marianne ran her eyes over the text conversation.

A- *what happens if u lie to police?*

Beata had replied with a string of question marks.

A- *if u lie 1st but then say truth*

Then came Beata's reply.

B- *tell them before they find out...cos they will*

Marianne almost flinched. Beata was, after all, speaking from experience. Both she and her mother had lied to Georgie and her team in the Neil Traynor investigation.

From the time stamps at the bottom of the messages, Marianne saw that an hour or so had passed before Alfie sent his last message.

A- *thing is i know he was rite til satday cos he was texting then it all went quiet*

Again there was a time-lapse. Marianne imagined Beata, head bent over the phone which in Marianne's imagination she held under the desk, while she should have been concentrating on a psychology lecture. At 14:32 she had replied.

B- Do you want me to tell DI Fraser?

Alfie had ended the chat with a shrug emoji.

BEATA WAS in the shower when Joe arrived. Charcoal semi-circles lurked beneath his silver-grey eyes and he yawned as he took off his jacket and boots, fending off the dogs' overenthusiastic greeting.

"Sweetheart, you didn't have to come over if you're so tired," Marianne said, hauling Maggie off him by her collar. "Down, you silly dog, he's here all evening, you know."

Joe pushed Pip gently aside with his foot and wrapped his arms around Marianne.

"I'm fine. Although I might crash here if it's OK. It's all starting to freeze again. I wanted to see you," he added, squeezing tight. Marianne gasped and laughed as he let her go. Had the search for Sam unsettled him? Surely the finding of Davey Whelan's body must have done. And perhaps hearing about Davey's origins had made him think of his own uncertain start in life, though he'd been settled enough until he decided to look for her. His adoptive parents had always been open with him. He didn't remember a time when he hadn't known that he had another mother somewhere out there. And they had found each other. Or rather he had found her.

"When's Georgie home?" he asked when they were back in front of the fire, Joe sprawling on the sofa with a bottle of low-alcohol Peroni and Pip on his lap. Marianne was in Beata's place, adding another log to the blaze.

"Not for a good half hour, I don't think. Maybe more. Last time I heard, she had one more interview and an evening briefing."

Joe nodded. He looked pre-occupied, frowning a little as he stroked Maggie's head. Both dogs were his devoted followers and, though Maggie was not allowed on the sofa – there would be no room for anyone else – she pressed as close as she could to his legs.

"How was the search today?" Marianne asked.

Joe lifted one shoulder in a half-shrug. The summer that she had first met him, she had noticed it as one of his characteristics. He had been a man of few words then. This evening, he seemed to have reverted to old habits. It made her want to reassure him, though with regards to what, she didn't know.

"Didn't find anything," Joe said. "If he's out there in this weather, we're not going to find him alive, are we?"

"I don't know," Marianne said. "There's that story of the old parson who was on his way over the Mynd to Ratlinghope when a blizzard struck. He made it. They used to have his boots at the Carding Mill. Before you worked there."

Joe took a sip of beer, still stroking Maggie's head. His gaze was far away, looking out through the un-curtained French windows, though she was fairly sure he wasn't seeing the snowy garden.

"Are you all right, love?"

He lifted one shoulder again, eyes still on the darkness outside. Then he looked at her without speaking and away again. One finger tapped on the beer bottle.

"I wanted to talk to you about something. Without Georgie or Beata."

"Ok," Marianne said, wondering why her stomach flickered with anxiety. "Beata won't be down for a bit. She'll be doing her yoga if she's out of the shower. What's up?" Did she want to know? Had the events of the past two days made him re-think his decision to live and work in Shropshire? Was he missing his beach life in Devon? He'd come across bodies there too, of course.

Whatever it was, he was finding it hard to say. He put his bottle down on the floor and sat up a bit, hoisting Pip into a more comfortable position on his lap.

"It was something Niamh was asking me. The other day."

Nothing to do with searching on the snowy hills then. Marianne waited. Like her, it was best not to hurry Joe if he had something to say. The second hand ticked loudly on the mantelpiece clock.

"About my father," Joe said, at last. "Niamh asked if I know anything about him."

Nausea slammed Marianne hard beneath her ribs. The smell of salt and sweat. A dark night in the dunes. Crushed into the sand, unable to move, unable to fight. As now, she was unable to respond. Five men, one after the other. She focused her attention on the seconds ticking by, counted them, waited for her heart rate to slow just a little, waited until she was sure she wouldn't throw up.

"What did you tell her?"

His strange eyes, his father's legacy, grazed hers.

"Nothing. I said I didn't know."

Didn't know what? Who he was? Neither did Marianne. But how could she ever explain that to her son? She had talked about it with Georgie of course. Discussed how she might tell him a watered-down, less unpalatable version of the truth. But he had never asked and she had never told.

"Thing is," he said, "I know it can't be good. Or you'd have told me about him." He picked up his beer again and took a swig, then gave a half-laugh. "I used to tell myself that you'd had a teenage romance – like a holiday one or something – but you didn't have mobile phones back then so maybe you lost touch and he never knew about me. But I know it wasn't that," he added, his voice flat again. "Because you'd have told me. And because of what happened after."

How much of that did he know? Some of her story was available online and she was realistic enough to know that he would have searched for it. After the murders at her bunkhouse in the shadow of the Devil's Chair, a true crime website had splashed the story of her conviction for murder and the fifteen years she had spent in prison. They had made much of her history as a homeless, drug-addicted sex-worker, somehow making it seem fitting that murder had followed her to her new life of redemption in the Shropshire hills. That her victim had been a rapist and she had acted in self-defence had gone largely unmentioned. At the thought that Joe must surely have read all of that, saliva surged in her mouth again and she turned away, swallowing hard.

"Ma? You ok?"

She nodded, not trusting herself to speak. She should be the adult. The parent. Reassure him. It must be harder for him than it was for her. Only when her teeth began to chatter, did she realise that she was shaking.

"Ma?"

As she felt Joe shift on the sofa, the dogs erupted towards the door, barking and scrabbling until Joe opened it for them. Marianne sat, statue-like before the fire, arms wrapped tight around her knees. As though through fog, she was aware of Joe going out into the porch with them. Of his voice and Georgie's low tones, masked by the dogs' delight in Georgie's return.

She should move. Get up. Smile. Make supper for everyone. Her limbs were locked. Nothing would move.

A draught of cold air brushed over her as the door opened and closed again. She clutched herself tighter and buried her face in her knees. If Georgie touched her, she might break apart.

She heard a creak and a click as Georgie knelt beside her,

smelt her faint perfume, felt the coldness of her cheek as she pulled Marianne into her arms.

"Shhh..."

She hadn't even realised she was crying until she heard Georgie's murmurings, the soft soothing sounds you made to a distressed child.

"I can't ..." The words stumbled past her lips and ground to a halt.

"It's OK," Georgie said. "It's OK. He gets it."

11

Tuesday dawned dry and cold, the snow crisp underfoot as Georgie crunched through Marianne's garden to her Land Rover. She had been living in Onnyford for more than six months now, but still she thought of it as Marianne's garden. Her only contribution was occasionally mowing the lawn and she barely knew a weed from a wisteria.

No dawn as such, yet, but there was a gleam of pale gold light above the Iron Age hill fort at Norton Camp, its trees like black paper cut-outs against the sky. Marianne had left twenty minutes earlier to walk the dogs by the fast-flowing river, still quiet, her eyes haunted. She could struggle to sleep at the best of times and last night had not been one of those. Poor Joe. The lad had well and truly wrenched the lid off the can of worms. And though she and Beata had done their best to keep some semblance of normality, dinner had been an uphill struggle.

Over the washing-up, Joe had asked Georgie what he should do. Was there any way he could find out about his father without having to put Marianne through agony?

"If you're asking me to tell you, Joe, I can't," she'd said. "Or not without Marianne's permission. But, if you want me to, I can ask her. It may be that she just can't talk about it. And to you least of all. As you said last night, you already know it's not a happy story."

The boy had nodded, rubbing a hand across his face, shattered both by two days of searching in the snow and having devastated his mother.

"I understand you wanting to know," Georgie had finished. "And so does she. She always knew this day would come. But give her a bit of time." And tell Niamh to back off with her questions, she had almost added but had bitten her tongue just in time.

Tired as she was, Georgie felt energised by the prospect of the morning briefing. And by the day ahead. The previous day they had broken the back of the necessary re-interviews and got to grips with the early investigation. Their final interview of the day, at Pritchard's timber yard, had killed two birds with one stone. John Pritchard had been able to tell them more than anyone else had about Davey Whelan, and they'd also managed to catch a chat with his daughter Jessie.

Interestingly, her account of the night that Sam had last been seen had tallied almost word for word with the statement she'd given the previous week. Georgie's thumbs had pricked and she had remembered Corby remarking on the uncanny similarity of all the other accounts. Add that to what Beata had said about Alfie and she felt a good line of enquiry was shaping up, one that might advance both cases. For the moment, Pitbull wanted a joint enquiry, feeling, as she did, that the death of Davey and the disappearance of Sam must be linked, but they would need to make progress quickly if she were to keep charge of both investigations.

There was little traffic until she hit the Hereford Road roundabout where she turned right on Shrewsbury's bypass. Passing along the Abbey Foregate ten minutes later, she looked towards her old house on the edge of the Abbey Meadows and felt not one twinge of regret for her move. Living with Marianne in Onnyford might mean a longer commute to work but it was worth every second. The only thing she missed was next-door's cat who had adopted her. She wondered if he still visited whoever had moved in in her place.

The briefing was scheduled for eight forty-five which gave her an hour to prep her notes from the day before. By the time she reached the incident room, the team were gathered and she was pleased to see that DS Chowdhury, who was based at Worcester HQ with the DCI, had joined them.

"I've brought Hallam with me, boss," he said, pointing across the room to a tall officer with floppy blond hair. Someone had set out tea and coffee, and a plate of wrinkled croissants had been purloined from the canteen, adding a warm, patisserie smell.

"Great," she said, wondering if she really meant it. DC Hallam had lost some of his sharp edges over the course of their last joint investigation but she wouldn't have chosen him for her team. Even if he had saved Marianne's life.

"Ok, everyone," she said once they were all seated, looking at her expectantly like a class of eager primary school children. Nothing like the beginning of an investigation; give it a few days and they'd be yawning and slumping in their chairs, muttering to each other when they thought she wasn't looking. "We had a good day yesterday and we need an even better one today. Everyone at one hundred percent. Let's get this done as efficiently as possible and then we can get on. Mike," she said, turning to DS Harley. "Where are we with the Long Mynd search?"

"Done, boss." He put down his mug and made an apologetic face as though the decision had been his. "Search and Rescue carried out three full concentric searches starting from both

Sam's possible last known positions and from where Davey Whelan was found. They also carried out drone searches over the whole Mynd. No sign of him. Which in one way is good news," he added. "If he was up there, the likelihood is that they'd have found him."

Georgie nodded. "Ok. So we pursue our investigations on the assumption that Sam is still to be found. Holed up safe and warm somewhere. I've had some informal intel – to be confirmed later – that Sam texted one of his mates up until Saturday, suggesting that he was alive and well then. We'll follow that up today." She turned to DS Chowdhury, who had been charged with liaising between HQ and the local team. "Any news from the PM?"

Chowdhury flipped open his tablet.

"Preliminary findings are interesting, boss. Davey Whelan's body showed evidence of extensive contusions and fractures consistent with a fall. But," he hesitated a moment as though waiting for a drum roll, "the pathologist reckons that several were post mortem. And not all occurred as a result of the fall. She reckons he was in a fight, an hour or so before he fell. And that he might already have been dead when he sustained some of the fall-related injuries."

"So, it wasn't the fall that killed him?"

Chowdhury shrugged.

"Broken neck, she reckons; but the heart showed abnormalities that need further investigation and she said you'd asked for a tox screen, so obviously those results won't be through for a bit. He might have been dead before he fell and the neck broken post mortem."

"What's her evidence for the fight theory?" Georgie asked.

Chowdhury pressed the remote, firing the Smartboard into life and, at the touch of his tablet, several photographs appeared on the screen. One showed very clearly the imprint of a clenched hand around what looked like an upper arm, a thumb-shaped bruise on one side and four reddish finger marks. Another, on a larger, flat area of cold white skin made a set of purple knuckles and folded forefingers. An x-ray showed two broken ribs.

"The bruising on these injuries is more advanced than on some of the others, suggesting that they were made well before death."

"He also had a couple of cracked ribs adjoining the sternum. The pathologist said that if she hadn't had the report from the search team, she would have thought that they'd done CPR. Clumsily."

"Interesting..." Georgie's thoughts began to spiral, threatening to take her far away from the meeting. She pulled herself back.

"DC Hallam," she said, and the young detective, graduate entry and only nine months into CID, sat up like an overeager Labrador. "I think we could use some of your tech expertise. PC Holton here has Sam Gray's laptop. It's already been looked at but I'd like you to go through it with a fine-toothed comb. Get DS Morgan from HQ on board, if you need to. Take it to pieces. We need his email, his social media, everything he deleted or might have wanted to hide. Sergeant Carradine ..." She turned to the Church Stretton community sergeant, wracking her brains for his first name. "We need a search of Davey Whelan's caravan. If there's a laptop there pass that on to DC Hallam too. Anything you can find out about friends, hobbies, places he liked to go, we need. Get your team to find us as many details of Davey's life as you can. Ok?"

The grizzled sergeant nodded, mollified, it seemed, by being given responsibility for what was undoubtedly an important task. The last thing that Georgie wanted was for the local team to have their noses put any further out of joint by the arrival of yet more CID officers parachuted in from HQ.

"DC Corby and I will talk to all the youngsters who were up at Pole Cottage on Wednesday night. We had an interesting chat with Jessie Pritchard last night. And by chat I mean a verbatim recital of her original statement. Something's not right. I'm considering getting them all together but we're going to talk to Alfie Rickard first. He's my bit of informal intel," she said. "Great then, if there's nothing else, let's get to it. Mike, you're manning the fort here, ok?"

DS Harley nodded and gave a thumbs up, uncomplaining about spending a day in the warm after two days supporting Search and Rescue.

Once the rest of the team were dumping their mugs on the tea trolley, she stopped by his desk.

"I wondered," she said, making sure to keep her voice below the hum of talk, "if you'd had a chance to chat to your nephew."

Harley shook his head. "I've had my sister-in-law on the phone. She's worried about him. Says he's not sleeping. Uncharacteristically moody."

"He's on my list to talk to today. Do you want to come with us? I know he's too old for an appropriate adult but he might feel easier if you're there."

"It's good of you..." Harley hesitated. "Probably best not. If there is something going on, he'd be worried about anything he said in front of me getting back to his mum and dad. Thanks, though."

Georgie smiled and gathered up her jacket and phone.

"Boss," Harley said, just as she and Corby were heading for the door. He got up and came over to them. "It might be nothing, but Suse – my sister-in-law – said she was worried that Lucas had been fighting. She saw some bruises on his torso when he came out of the bathroom and he got really mad at her when she asked how he got them. He's not the fighting type, Lucas. Not at all. Peacemaker. But still..."

The spiral of thoughts that Georgie had been keeping in check since Chowdhury's postmortem report swept up Harley's words greedily. Thanking her sergeant, she followed Corby out into the corridor, and let them take flight.

12
___

At the garden centre, they found Alfie Rickard outside among the Christmas trees, dressed as one of Santa's elves. He was serving a middle-aged couple, taking trees out of the serried ranks and showing them off to their best advantage, discussing their pros and cons in terms of longevity and needle drop. When he saw Fraser and Corby, his cheerful expression wobbled and a red that wasn't entirely due to the cold stained his cheeks.

'Winter Wonderland' blared tinnily as they waited until the couple had chosen their tree and Alfie had fed it through the wrapping machine, encasing it in a fine white net. He came over to where they stood amongst small potted Nordmann firs, a sheepish grin faltering every few seconds.

"Inspector Fraser?"

"Alfie," she said, showing her warrant card for form's sake. "You remember DC Corby?" The boy nodded. "We're sorry for coming to see you at work – I'm sure you know what it's about."

"About Sam," Alfie said. "Yeah, Jessie texted last night to say you'd been round to hers. Thought you'd probably want to talk to the rest of us."

"We need to talk about Davey Whelan too," Corby said, ignoring Alfie's double take. "Your boss said there was a staffroom we could use. Bit blooming chilly out here, isn't it?"

Alfie was still looking at them like a confused cartoon character, the bobble on the end of his elf hat bobbing.

"What about Davey? I mean, I don't hardly know him even."

If he was going for innocently confused, he was failing so miserably that Georgie almost smiled.

"Inside, eh?" she said, rubbing her gloved hands together. "Your manager said you'd put the kettle on for us."

The staffroom was at the rear of the garden centre, behind the café, from which issued a smell of fried food and coffee. It was lit by a fluorescent strip light that bathed its off-white walls in a greenish glow broken only by a noticeboard covered in health and safety notices. Several foam-cushioned easy chairs that had seen better days crowded around a cheap pine coffee table, marked with the rings and stains of years of spilled drinks.

Georgie took her jacket off in the sudden warm and unwound her scarf from around her neck, before she sat down. Corby joined her while Alfie poured water onto teabags and asked them if they took milk, his hands shaking as he shovelled sugar into his own drink.

"So, Alfie," she said, as he joined them, "I've read your statement about last Wednesday night when you were up on the Mynd with your friends." Alfie nodded. "The night Sam was last seen." He nodded again. "As I'm sure you appreciate, this is a new investigation for us, so we just wanted to talk to everyone again, clarify a few details. You know how it is."

Alfie nodded for a third time, his eyebrows furrowed. It wasn't the first time he'd been questioned by the police. As a young member of the grounds staff at the Geoscience Trust, he'd been interviewed over the murder of Neil Traynor. If Georgie remembered rightly he'd been far more relaxed then. Presumably, because then, he'd had nothing to hide.

"I wondered," she said, "if there was anything that you wanted to add to your statement. Anything that you forgot to tell the officers who spoke to you last week."

"Like what?"

The flush on Alfie's face could have been the result of coming from outside into a warm room, but she thought not. Time to go in hard, maybe. After all, enough time had been wasted since Sam had gone missing. And there was the small matter of another lad's death that no one seemed too bothered about.

"Like the fact that you lied to the police, Alfie. You and all the others."

The boy put both hands up to cover his mouth, again reminding Georgie of a cartoon character, though she couldn't give it a name. Perhaps it was just the elf costume.

"You – all of you," she went on, "lied about who was there that night. Didn't you?"

Beside Georgie, Corby took out her notebook and pen, giving Alfie a reassuring smile which seemed to confuse him as much as the question.

"I don't know what you mean," he said, at last.

"I mean, Alfie, that Davey Whelan was up at Pole Cottage with you on Wednesday night. A fact that none of you mentioned when questioned. Given that we found his body on Sunday and no one appears to have seen him in the meantime, I'd suggest that you and your friends were the last people to see Davey alive. Which means you need to start telling us the truth."

It was no accident that she had chosen to talk to Alfie first. Even without Beata's information he would have been her first choice. Well-meaning and friendly, as easily influenced by her as by his friends.

He said nothing, staring into his mug as though the answers might be found in the depths of hot tea. Then he looked up.

"How did you know?"

Georgie smiled. "I'm afraid we have to keep our sources confidential. But, given that we do know, I'd like you to tell me about the evening as you remember it. Not," she said firmly, "the story that you cooked up between you. Tell me what really happened."

Much of Alfie's story matched the statements given on the Thursday, when it first became apparent that Sam was missing. The group had gone up to the National Trust shelter on the site of the old cottage in three cars: Alisha and Alfie in Lucas Harley's Toyota Corolla; Bryn, Lily and Seth in Seth's dad's Volvo; and Sam with Jessie in her silver Vauxhall Corsa, the one that had been found by Joe in Devil's Mouth Hollow.

"Whose car was Davey in?" Corby asked, pen hovering over her notebook.

Alfie hesitated, biting the end of his thumb.

"Jessie's," he said. "With her and Sam."

"Ok. Good," Georgie said. "What then?"

They had made a fire in a pit behind the shelter, cooked some food, had a few beers.

"Just beers?" Corby asked.

Alfie shrugged.

"Alfie," Georgie said, "I'm sure you know that there has to be a post-mortem examination of Davey's body. That will tell us if he had anything apart from beers that night. You could help us out a lot. Save us some time," she just held off from saying *win yourself a few brownie points*, "if you tell us what else people were taking. Spirits? A bit of MDMA? Weed? Coke maybe?" It was just a hunch and so far she had nothing to substantiate it but both Davey and Sam had had previous convictions for possession. It seemed unlikely that this had been the clean-living camp-out that Sam's mum had claimed.

"Not all of us," Alfie said, looking miserably from one officer to the other. Georgie reckoned his greatest fear was of being found out by his parents.

"Go on," she said.

"We all had some beers and a smoke. Weed. Except Lily. She doesn't like it," Alfie said. "And some of the others had ... Alisha brought some coke. And Davey. He deals a bit. Sorry, I mean ..." For the first time, the boy looked scared.

Georgie gave him her best reassuring smile.

"It's OK. Go on."

"I think everyone had a few lines. Except me and Lily. And maybe Bryn. He'd brought some vodka up and we had that. And Jessie'd brought some tequila, so some of them had that too."

"Sounds like quite a party."

Alfie nodded, morosely.

"It was. And we were having fun. Seth had his speaker so we had some tunes. It was cool."

"Until?" Georgie asked. Alfie's tone had made it very clear that what had started off as cool had not stayed that way.

The boy stared at his un-drunk tea, elbows on his knees. He put the mug on the table and sat up, running his hands through his hair and pushing back the elf hat so that it fell to the floor behind him. He looked from Fraser to Corby and back again.

"There's an old film. *Fight Club*. Have you seen it?"

Corby looked blank but Georgie nodded. She remembered watching it as a teenager. Fifteen or so she would have been, too young to watch it officially, so it must have been a DVD at some-one's house. Twenty-five years ago and so old that to Alfie it might as well have been in black and white.

"They – Sam and Davey – watched it a few weeks ago," Alfie said, "and they were telling us about it. And then there was this argument. I can't remember how it started or even what order things happened in ... I'd had a bit to drink ... and a smoke." His eyebrows creased again, presumably as he wondered if his parents would ever find out the detail of his statement.

"They were arguing about Alisha," he went on. "Sam and Jessie used to go out but they split because Sam got with Alisha. And then they got back together but they weren't exclusive anymore. Or Sam wasn't anyway. I think he carried on things with Alisha and Jessie was really pissed off. Only Alisha had been seeing Davey too and he and Sam started arguing about it. And I can't remember if it was before or after that but someone said why not have our own fight club. And it seemed like a laugh." As he remembered it, Alfie looked more like he wanted to cry than laugh.

"I didn't do it," he said. "I was feeling sick. Too much vodka. But Seth did. And Lucas. I think Bryn had a go with Seth too. But they was just messing. You know, like wrestling. It was a laugh."

"And then?" Georgie prompted when the boy had been quiet for a while.

"Sam and Davey started. Only it wasn't funny anymore. They got really serious. Like really going for each other. Hurting each other." Bewilderment sounded in every syllable. "And I don't know what happened but it was like Davey suddenly collapsed. Just keeled over. He had his arm back to punch Sam, and Sam was on his knees and then Davey just crumpled. Fell right over. Hit the ground like a tree."

As Corby scribbled the detail of the scene in her notebook, Georgie followed it in her imagination. Alfie's telling transporting her to the enclosure which surrounded the wooden shelter, almost at the summit of the Mynd. She could see the wide, star-strewn sky, purple fading to blue, the vast expanse of moorland, the boggy pool beyond the fence.

They had thought Davey was messing around at first. Then the panic had set in. Scrabbling to find a pulse, horror when they couldn't, frantic attempts at CPR though no one knew what they were doing. Then the flood of relief when they realised he was breathing, a pulse, however feeble, going in his neck.

"We got him in Jessie's car. Sam was going to drive him to A&E in Shrewsbury. Not go in or anything, just dump him outside. So he'd be looked after. And they went."

Silence fell across the room. Corby's eyes met Georgie's. Alfie's were far away.

"And do you know what happened next?"

"Sam called Jessie. He was really panicked. He said Davey had like suddenly woken up. And he'd gone mental. Like super-human. Hitting Sam and trying to get out of the car. He ran off. Sam followed but he couldn't find him."

"And?" Georgie prompted as the silence threatened to stretch on.

"Sam never came back. And we were all waiting. He didn't call or nothing. Not till after we'd gone home."

"What did he say?"

"He called the group chat," Alfie said. "Said Davey had disappeared somewhere on top of the Mynd. And he reckoned he ought to lie low for a few days. Didn't say where he was. Just thought he and Jessie's car should disappear until Davey turned up. Only he never did."

Georgie let the story sink in, feeling detached compunction for the boy who looked ever more as though he might cry. He was barely eighteen and just holding on, perhaps thrown by the relief at sharing the burden he'd been carrying for days with an adult, someone who might take charge.

"So you all made a plan to tell the same story?" she said after a while.

Alfie nodded.

"Sam said we had to. So no one ever knew Davey was there. Sam said he was staying with a friend and we mustn't tell anyone we'd heard from him."

"And you all went along with it? Even though you knew his mum was worried sick?" Despite the police investigation and a social media frenzy? she didn't add.

The silence ticked along, disturbed by the faint hum of 'Feliz Navidad' from the café. Alfie rubbed his eyes.

"Davey didn't show up," he said. "And he wasn't answering his phone. Then his phone was dead." He sighed and when he next spoke it was as though he was dragging the words up out of his belly. "So we knew Davey must be dead too. But we didn't know where. And we had to keep quiet or Sam would get in trouble. Everyone would think he killed Davey. With the fight." The words seemed to strip away his years, and Georgie could see how he must have been as a small boy, hesitant and always seeking reassurance.

"Have you told anyone else the truth, Alfie?" Corby asked. "Your parents, maybe?"

Alfie shook his head.

"Do they have to know?"

Georgie smiled, offering the only reassurance she felt able to give.

"It's bound to come out, Alfie. Even if it's not until this case comes to court – which it will eventually. And it would be much better for your parents to hear it from you."

The boy swallowed hard. "Are you going to tell the others it was me told you about Davey?"

Georgie picked up his elf hat and handed it to him as she stood up.

"Like I said, Alfie. We already knew. You just filled in a few details for us. And the others will do the same."

13

On the way back to the car park, Georgie spotted Lucas Harley.

"Interview number two," she said, tucking her scarf inside her coat. "Lucky that manager's eager to please or he might not have given us access to two of his staff when it's this busy. Makes you wonder if he's running a money-laundering Christmas tree racket."

Stocky, with thick, dark hair and square shoulders, the boy was shifting bags of compost from a trolley to form a large stack near the front doors, arranging them alternately parallel and perpendicular to the pallet to stop them slipping.

When she stopped and said hello, he looked up with a frown which cleared as he clocked Corby's police jacket.

"I'm DI Fraser," Georgie said, "and this is DC Corby. We work with your uncle."

Lucas nodded, taking off a glove and wiping his forehead which glistened with sweat despite the cold.

"We've just been having a chat with Alfie about last Wednesday, when you were all up on the Mynd."

"Right." The boy looked from one to the other but didn't seem to feel the need to speak.

"Would you have time for a quick word?"

"Maybe." He looked at his watch. "I'm on my break in five minutes. Not in the staff room though," he added, looking around. "It'll be busy."

Georgie said that they'd wait for him in the Land Rover.

"Might have to say sod the planet and run the engine, just to warm it up a bit," she said to Corby, as they crossed the rutted car park, avoiding patches of frozen snow that had escaped the scattered grit.

"Don't let Marianne hear you say that," Corby said.

"Or Joe," Georgie agreed. "Or Beata for that matter. I'm surrounded by eco-warriors. So," she said, pulling open the car door and climbing into the driving seat. "Where next after Lucas?"

Corby pulled her beanie down over her ears and put her gloves back on.

"We need to talk to all of them, I suppose," she said, "but that Alisha sounds interesting. Carrying on with both Sam and Davey, dishing out the coke. Funny Jessie didn't mention anything."

Not funny at all, Georgie thought, when you considered the fact that she was protecting her sometime boyfriend from a charge of manslaughter. While they waited, Corby phoned Alisha's mobile and arranged to meet the girl on her lunch break. There was no point in making the visit a surprise. Their visit to Alfie and Lucas would have spread through the group before they had even left the garden centre. With luck, the other three wouldn't have had time to synchronise new stories by the time she caught up with them that afternoon if they were at work or college. She would have to get back to Jessie Pritchard too. Once they'd heard what everyone else had to say.

Just as Lucas put his trolley away and started towards them, she remembered Cal Innes' story about firefighter Andy Morgan being up on the Mynd that Wednesday night. If Sam had been pursuing Davey across the hill in the small hours, might Andy have seen something?

Corby opened the passenger door for Lucas, then clambered through into the back so that he could sit up front. Noticing their breath forming semi-crystalline clouds, Georgie turned the key in the ignition and whacked the heater up full, silently promising Marianne that she would make sure she didn't forget to turn any lights off for the next month. If she kept her eyes on Lucas, she might not even notice the exhaust fumes billowing out into the frozen air.

"Can we be quick?" Lucas asked, checking his watch again. "I've only got fifteen minutes and I want to get a coffee before I start back."

"Quick as you like," Georgie said, with a smile. "We just need to clarify a few things." She explained that they were aware that Davey Whelan had been with the group on Wednesday night and that an impromptu Fight Club had started.

Lucas said nothing but stared through the frosted windscreen. 'Frosty the Snowman' sounded merrily from the Christmas tree area and Georgie wondered if Alfie was back out there in his elf hat.

"Were you involved, Lucas? In the fight?" She decided not to ask a policeman's nephew if he'd been taking cocaine. He could have that conversation in private with his uncle.

Lucas shrugged.

"It was a laugh. Seth and Bryn to start with. Then me and Seth, cos he was the winner. Even though Bryn's really big. Like I said, just a laugh. No one got hurt."

"How about later, when Sam and Davey started? Was that still fun?"

Lucas looked out of the passenger window, letting Georgie see little more than his ear and the side of his head.

"Dunno. They started off like it was a joke but ... there was some kind of beef going on with them."

"About Alisha?"

"Dunno. Maybe."

Lucas's reluctance to talk reminded her of Joe when she had met him as a suspect in her first Shropshire murder investigation. She wondered if it was in part embarrassment, knowing that she and Corby worked with his uncle. That his uncle, even if not his parents, would now know everything that he had got up to that night.

"Davey liked her," he said. "And she was like egging them on, saying whoever won got her as the prize."

Georgie wondered how Jessie Pritchard had felt about that. Her best friend, offering herself as a prize to someone she still regarded as a boyfriend.

"I don't think she was interested in Davey. She was just having a laugh," Lucas said.

"Do you think she was more interested in Sam?"

Lucas's head moved a fraction in what might have been a negative.

"Not really. She likes stirring things up."

Georgie moved her questions on to Davey's collapse. Lucas's account was less emotional than Alfie's, as though he'd been watching from the sidelines, not actively involved.

"Who gave him the CPR?"

"Bryn," Lucas said, easier now that they were no longer discussing the fight. "He works down the leisure centre. Lifeguard and trampolining and stuff so he knows first aid."

"Did you help to get Davey in the car?"

"Not really. Everyone was like falling over each other. Panicking. I was trying to calm Alisha down with Lily."

"And after Sam drove off to the hospital what did you do?"

"Dunno. Drank a bit more. We were all well freaked out. We had to stay cos no one was fit to drive."

Sam hadn't been fit to drive either of course, but she supposed they had regarded his going as an emergency. To think that someone off their head on vodka, tequila and cocaine might be capable of driving down the Burway was enough evidence of the fact that none of the others had been thinking clearly. And yet, Sam must have managed it. Because, even if he had lost Davey, there was no way that silver car had been up on the Mynd for three days before it was found. Someone would have seen it. So where had Sam been in the meantime?

"You didn't go looking for Davey?"

"We wandered about shouting for a bit. But like we were going to find him if he didn't want to be found. Or if he'd collapsed again. It's massive up there."

Lucas got his phone out and checked the time.

"Just one more thing, Lucas," Georgie said. "When did you last hear from Sam?"

"I dunno. Friday. Maybe Saturday. On the group chat. I can check."

Georgie smiled.

"If you wouldn't mind."

He unlocked his phone and scrolled through a few messages.

"Here," he said, passing the phone to her with a chat called Hebduz open. "Friday night – well, Saturday morning."

"Hebduz?" Georgie said.

"Just some shit joke of Sam's from school."

Georgie looked at Sam's last messages, sent in response to messages from Bryn, Seth and Lily discussing where he might be.

- told u im safe yeh so quit chatting

- with a friend ;) might head off til all gone quiet

"And that was the last you heard from him?" She passed the phone back to Lucas and he nodded, then checked the time again.

"Ok, well thanks, Lucas, you've been very helpful. If you think of anything else, give us a call, ok?" She handed him a card. "Listen, it might be worth having a chat with your parents. Let them know the real story. You don't have to tell them all the details. But the truth about Davey and Sam is going to come out. Best they hear it from you, maybe."

The boy turned his head and gave a brief smile as he opened the passenger door, letting a wave of icy air into the car. Georgie had almost forgotten the engine was running, pumping fifteen minutes' worth of diesel fumes into the atmosphere.

"Yeah," he said. "Thanks."

They watched him as he passed the trolley park and shouldered his way through the doors, hands firmly in his pockets.

"Bit of a dark horse," Corby said, clambering through from the back. "Wonder what Uncle Mike's going to make of all that."

SHREWSBURY'S SUPERSTORE branch of Boots was in the Meole Brace Retail Park, nestled between Superdrug and Next.

"I always wonder why you get that," Corby said as they crossed the car park. "Two places that sell exactly the same stuff next to each other."

"Competition?" Georgie said, avoiding a suspiciously yellow patch of banked snow by the curb.

As they passed through the sliding doors, simultaneous blasts of warm air and dense, cloying perfume hit them. Brightly lit cosmetics stands jostled for space with the cheaper make-up racks and a well-stocked fragrance counter. Further back in the store were the pharmacy and toiletries sections.

Michael Bublé was singing 'Have Yourself a Merry Little Christmas'.

"Is that her?" Georgie asked, her eyes falling on a striking girl in a make-up artist's tunic, who was painstakingly stippling powder onto the cheeks of a middle-aged woman. The woman sat on a tall stool in front of a high-end cosmetics counter, a brand that Georgie only bought if she was feeling particularly flush.

The girl, whose afro hair was pulled up into the same high ponytail as in her headshot on the interview room Smartboard, caught sight of them and waved the little finger of the hand that held her palate.

"Be with you in five," she said, as though they might be her next clients. "Is that ok?" Compared to the two lads they had seen earlier, Alisha Johnson seemed entirely at ease with her visitors.

"No problem," Corby said. "We can do a bit of shopping while we wait."

It was ten minutes before she was ready for them, by which time Corby had bought some new make-up brushes and Georgie had found her favourite mascara half-price. She celebrated by buying two bottles.

"Do you mind if we pop over the road and get some lunch?" Alisha said, pulling a coat out from beneath her counter and wrapping a long, woollen scarf around her neck. "Right bunch of gossips in here so I asked my manager if I could take my break late." She propped a *Back At...* sign with a little clock set for forty-five minutes' time against the stand's logo and led them out of the store, every inch the hostess.

"I usually go over there," she said, pointing to the Marks and Spencer store opposite which boasted a café. "The coffee's OK."

While Corby found them a table near the condensation-clad windows, Georgie ordered drinks and Alisha got herself a baked potato with cheese, announcing to Georgie, as though they had been friends for years, that she was starving.

"I'm sure it's the cold that makes you want to eat all the time," she said, as she sat down. "You not having anything?"

Wanting a chance to observe the girl, Georgie let Corby take the lead on the questioning. She smiled as Corby bemoaned the police canteen, which in reality was very good, and said that they might grab a couple of M&S sandwiches to take back with them.

"So, I expect you've heard from Jessie and co that we've been catching up with all of you," Corby said. "Since Davey Whelan's body was recovered at the weekend," she added, and Alisha's fork paused for a fraction of a second on the way to her mouth.

She ate a mouthful of baked potato, her almond eyes wary, and nodded.

"Jessie said last night," she said. "But not about Davey. About Sam, I thought."

"It seems," Georgie said, happy to play bad cop to Corby's friendly questioner, "that the statements you gave after Sam's initial disappearance were lacking some crucial information. i.e. Davey's presence at your party. So I'm afraid we need an updated version."

The girl let her eyes rest on Georgie while she ate another mouthful and then turned back to Corby.

"What do you want to know? I mean, I guess if you've talked to the others, you already know Davey was there."

Again, Georgie was impressed by her self-possession. Almost insouciant.

"Could you tell us about your relationship with Sam?" Corby said.

Alisha shrugged.

"I wasn't in a relationship with him."

"I just mean what kind of friendship did you have? Were you close?"

"Not really. I met him through Jessie. We were at school together and she and Sam were going out – for a couple of years, I suppose."

"They're not anymore?"

Alisha smiled and sipped her drink, some sort of matcha tea which looked to Georgie far too thick and green to be appetising.

"Never know with those two. They split officially but ..." she let the sentence tail off, leaving possibilities dangling.

"And there was never anything between you and Sam?" Corby persisted.

Again, the slanting almond eyes, subtly made-up for gentle enhancement, rested on Georgie. She returned the look, keeping her face as blank as possible. The girl's attitude was intriguing. Was it Lucas who'd said she liked to stir things up?

"Nothing serious," she said.

"What about with Davey?"

She shrugged again.

"You weren't in a relationship with him?"

This time, Alisha laughed.

"I hooked up with him a couple of times. That doesn't mean a relationship."

Georgie was reminded of a previous case where a suspect had mocked her generation's need to believe they were in love before they had sex. Her eyes met the girl's and Alisha said: "Would you have that expression on your face if I was a guy, inspector?"

"You might be misreading it, Alisha," she said evenly. "I was intrigued, rather than implying any judgement."

"How did Jessie feel about you and Sam?" Corby asked.

"What's that got to do with anything?"

Corby looked towards Georgie who answered.

"We're trying to establish the dynamic that was going on on Wednesday night. There was a fight between Sam and Davey that apparently started as a laugh but changed. They took off together and neither was seen again, until Davey turned up dead. Jessie's car has been found with no sign of Sam. You'll understand why we need to make enquiries about their relationships, whether serious or not."

Alisha pulled a face that suggested she thought Georgie was taking life a bit too seriously.

"Sam and Davey fighting was nothing to do with me. It might have been about Jessie. Or just something else. They were all fired up about that movie."

"Were they good friends?"

Alisha sucked up more of her matcha tea through a straw. She'd left half the baked potato uneaten, her knife and fork neatly to the side of her plate.

"Hard to tell. Sometimes. They pissed each other off. Quite a lot, recently."

"Since when?"

"Don't know. October maybe. They spent a lot of time together but there was some sort of shit going down with them. I wasn't that interested to be honest."

Interested enough to offer herself as the prize for whoever won their fight, though, Georgie remembered. If Alfie was to be believed, at any rate. She thought that Alfie had been too wound up at their meeting to make things up. Or had it been Lucas?

"I understand," she said, "that Sam and Davey met on a young offenders programme."

Alisha's eyes gave nothing away as she picked up her fork and took another mouthful of potato.

"I also understand," Georgie went on, wondering how hard she would have to poke to get beneath the girl's polished surface, "that you and Davey both had some cocaine with you on Wednesday evening."

"Says who?"

"I'm not really interested in whether you did, Alisha," she said. "But I am interested in whether Sam or Davey might have been involved with dealing recently. You'll be aware of the rumours that have been spreading on social media since Sam went missing. Was there anything in them?"

The girl's expression was dismissive.

"All that stuff's just people chatting shit. Sam might have sold a bit a couple of years ago but not anymore. And Davey just liked a good time. He always knew where to get it if you wanted some but he wasn't a dealer."

"Did you get yours from him?"

"You're assuming that whoever told you I had some wasn't lying," Alisha said.

Georgie smiled. The girl was what? Nineteen, at most? Her self-possession was extraordinary.

"Did you like Davey?" she said, keeping back some of the questions she would have liked to ask. *Did you keep him dangling because he was useful to you? Getting your cocaine and weed on the off-chance that you might sleep with him again? Did you like Sam? Or did you just like them fighting over you?*

Alisha made a face.

"He was all right."

"If you don't mind me saying so," Georgie said, "you don't seem particularly sad that he's dead. Or worried by the fact that Sam is missing."

The girl shrugged and sucked up more of her matcha tea through her straw.

"Probably because I'm not. It's not like they were my soulmates. I hung around with them because they're a laugh – for something to do. If you grow up in a dead end like Church Stretton, which is basically like a retirement home, you're not exactly spoiled for choice. I'm having a bit of fun while I earn enough to get out of here. What's wrong with that?"

Nothing, Georgie supposed. And there was something refreshing about the girl's honesty, however hard it might seem.

"Did you see anyone else up on the Mynd that night?" she asked, forgetting that she had meant to leave the questioning to Corby. The DC didn't seem to mind though, unlike DS Chowdhury who would have been bristling if she'd stepped on his toes in the same way.

"Like who?" Alisha asked.

"Anyone. People go up at night for stargazing, don't they?"

Alisha finished her tea but her eyes suggested she was considering Georgie's question.

"Yeah," she said. "Maybe. When we were looking for Sam and Davey. After Sam had called to say he'd run off. There was some guy taking photos with one of those big lens cameras. Just down from Pole Bank. He was sitting on that cairn at the top of Ashes Hollow. You know, where people piled up all those stones."

Georgie knew the place. And she'd have to go back and look at a map but unless she was mistaken it was only a few hundred yards from the track that led over Cross Dyke towards Callow Hollow. Interesting. Very interesting.

14

"It's a bit weird that she wouldn't tell you anything," Niamh said, unhooking her arms from around Joe's waist and climbing off the quad bike. He felt an absence of warmth where she had been pressed against his back. Or perhaps her words had caused it. He had hoped the subject of his parentage was closed, at least for a while. Opening it with his mother had unleashed a torrent of feeling that he'd rather have kept tightly buried.

Leaving the bike in gear, he switched off the engine and swung his leg over the back, tucking the keys into the zip pocket of his jacket. The last thing they needed was for him to drop them in the deep, drifting snow that covered the summit of the Long Mynd. Or a few metres down from the summit. Walkers had reported that part of the National Trust shelter's roof had been damaged by a fallen branch and Joe had been asked to take a look, with a view to either making it safe or fencing it off pending repair.

Only the day before the shelter had formed the epicentre of the search for Sam Gray, a long shot, given that more than five days had passed since he had last been seen there but, after completing the search centred around the car as his last known location, none had been ready to give up. In such severe weather, everyone had felt the need to pull out all the stops to find him, and Search and Rescue volunteers had shown a willingness to put their own comfort and safety to one side, well beyond the call of duty.

Now, the tracks left by the searchers had been filled by more overnight snow, leaving only undulations that might as easily have been caused by drifts. Yesterday, the shelter roof had been intact. This afternoon, a crack rent its corrugated metal roof and the thin branch of a silver birch pierced through to its dark interior. A line of fallen snow marked the extent of the break on the ground within, which was otherwise clear. The wind must have been coming from the west behind the shelter, driving the snow before it.

"Definitely not safe," Niamh said. "There must be about a ton of snow on the roof. No wonder it broke when the branch fell."

The corrugated metal panels of the roof and walls had been recycled from the derelict outbuilding that had once stood there. God alone knew how old they were.

"Looks like the rest could cave in any minute," Joe said. "Tree doesn't look too clever either."

The branch that had broken the roof wasn't the only one to have fallen. It was a young birch and three of its four lower branches had spit from the trunk, hanging suspended like greenstick fractures. Like as not the whole thing would have to come down. For the moment, though, the best they could do was padlock the gate to the enclosure and rope off the shelter to further deter anyone who might climb over.

Joe had always thought of snow as a bringer of beauty. On the Devon coast they had never had much. Some on the hills above Woolacombe, maybe, but where he had lived, in Croyde, the bay had been too temperate for snow to last. Here it had transformed the hills into a dazzling Alpine range but had brought destruction and disruption in its wake. He was only glad that, after a thorough search, no trace had been found of the missing boy. The likelihood was that he had taken off somewhere before the snow had fallen and was alive and well, hiding out at a mate's house.

Between them they unloaded the quad's trailer, Niamh taking tools and the nylon rope, and Joe the posts and mallet. On the road and in the gateway, where the snow had compacted, it crunched underfoot. Once through into the enclosure though, their boots sank deep, reminding him of wading through the sand dunes at Braunton Burrows, effort required to lift each leg for the next step. While Niamh ferried the posts to near the shelter, Joe fetched the drill and fixed a DANGER sign to the gate.

Beneath the snow, the ground, usually soft, was frozen and he needed first to break it, bringing the mallet down hard on a metal spike before there was any chance of getting the posts in. Niamh held them in place as he battered them, occasionally cursing him as the mallet grazed the air near her cheek.

"You get that any closer and you'll be taking another corpse off the hill today," she said and he tried to laugh. The memory of hoisting that frozen body up the steep sides of Callow Hollow had haunted his dreams the past two nights. When he'd not been lying awake asking himself why he'd been so stupid as to broach the subject of his father with Marianne.

With the last post in, they took an end of the rope each and wound it around the stakes, double-threading it so that it would stay fixed even if the wind picked up. Despite the sub-zero temperature, Joe was too warm and unzipped his jacket, loosening the buff from around his neck, while he took another look at the tree.

"Time for a break?" Niamh said, appearing from the other side of the shelter with the flask they had brought.

Joe nodded.

"Thought I might just trim that branch off," he said. "If the wind gets up again, it might pull the whole shelter down, stuck like that." There was a small electric chainsaw in the trailer, along with safety kit. Better to finish the job properly.

While she poured the coffee, steam rising into the frozen air, he found his helmet, goggles and chainsaw gloves, wondering how best to reach the point where the branch had splintered from the trunk. Swallowing the scalding brew, he thought again of Marianne and wondered how she was feeling now. Last night it had been as though an empty shell sat at the table in her place.

"You don't want to talk about it, do you?" Niamh said, brushing the snow off a tree stump and sitting on it, snug in her snowboard pants and down jacket.

"Not much."

It was a running theme in their relationship. She liked to talk about feelings and he didn't. He tried. And usually he appreciated her efforts to draw him out, tacitly agreeing that bottling things up did no one any good. Today, though, he wished the subject of his father had never been raised. Not by her, and not by him to Marianne.

"You must look like your father," Niamh said. "I mean, you look like her a bit – your hair and the shape of your face – but your colouring, your eyes, they're nothing like hers. So they must be like him."

Joe said nothing, hoisting himself up onto the beam that supported the rear wall and roof of the shelter, checking it was stable before he put his full weight on it. From there, he could reach out a leg to rest his foot in the fork of the tree and was almost as steady as if he'd been on the ground.

"You'd think that would help her remember who he was," she went on and Joe almost smiled at her persistence. Almost. Why did she think it would be good for him to know his origins? Niamh came from a warm, close Irish family – three siblings and parents who had been childhood sweethearts – even if she had chosen to cross the Irish Sea and study in England. Did it bother her that he had been given away as a baby by a mother who was too young to raise him? Not given away, Marianne would have said. Taken away.

Apologising for the noise he was about to make he started the chainsaw and, bracing his foot to keep himself stable, sliced through the branch fibres that still attached the broken limb to the tree's body. It was easy and, while he was there, he severed the other damaged branches as close to the trunk as possible, leaving only a few wiry pieces of young growth sticking up like a bad haircut.

"Pass me up that bit of rope," he said when he was done, thinking he'd attach it to the end of the branch and use it to drag it free of the crack in the metal sheeting. Niamh left her tree stump and grabbed what was left of the neon orange rope. As she came towards the back of the shelter, she stumbled suddenly and shrieked, her foot disappearing through the powdery snow until one leg was submerged to above her knee.

"Ow, Jaysus, that hurt!"

"You OK?" Joe asked. He laid the chainsaw on the edge of the beam and clambered down. Niamh still had one leg buried beneath the snow and couldn't get purchase to free herself.

"It's like it's stuck down a hole or something," she said, half laughing but with a wobble in her voice that wasn't like her. "There's something scratching my ankle and it hurts like bejesus when I try to move it."

"Hang on," Joe said. "Stay still, just in case there's wire or anything down there." He fetched a small spade from the pile of tools that they had left at the side of the shelter and knelt beside her. While he dug the snow away from her leg she leaned her hand on his shoulder, teasing him for still having his chainsaw helmet on. Again, her way of dealing with things, rattling off jokes and laughing to hide what he guessed must be considerable pain. As he dug down towards her boot, the snow was stained red.

"Don't move," he said, jettisoning the spade and digging with his gloved hands until he'd scraped away the snow from the ground surface. Her foot had gone down a hole which was surrounded by blackened earth and charred sticks. From beneath a chunk of soil and organic matter, a gleaming shard of metal protruded, its tip millimetres from Niamh's ankle. As her foot had gone through the snow and earth, the force of it must have pushed the leg of her snowboard pants up above her boot and the blade or whatever it was had cut deep, slicing through her sock. Trying to wiggle her foot free couldn't have helped.

"Ok, you're bleeding a bit," he said, keeping his voice even, glad that the breadth of his shoulders and his helmet would be hiding it from her view. "Stay really still while I get the first aid kit and don't look if you think it'll make you faint."

"Make me faint, my arse," she said. He should have known telling her not to would be like a red rag to a bull and a few seconds later she said, "Oh shit, that doesn't look good."

"It'll be OK," he said. "We'll clean it up a bit and stop the bleeding. Get you down to the pavilion. You might need a stitch or two."

He made the hole in the earth bigger, easing the shard of metal away from her, and helped her to sit down in the snow before gently freeing her foot. The boot was intact so the cut ended just above the ankle cuff, a good thing too, she said, as there was no bloody way she was taking her shoes off when it was minus two. Joe removed his gloves and snipped the top off a sachet of saline, sluicing her leg and washing away the blood until the edges of the wound showed clearly, like two thin, angry lips either side of a dark red mouth. Blood began to well again and he tore open a clean cotton pad, pressing it to the cut and telling her to hold it in place.

"Pressure," he said, taking a roll of white bandage from the kit.

"I know, I know, I've done my first aid." Her tone held most of her usual humour but when he looked up, her face was pale. She might have scoffed at him for suggesting she might faint but she didn't look too far from it now.

"Reckon you fell through into their fire pit," he said, diverting her attention to the charred sticks as he wound the bandage around the cotton pad. Pinpricks of deep red were beginning to appear on its surface and he wondered if he'd be able to elevate her leg on the quad bike.

"Whose fire pit?"

"That lot the other night. When they had the party up here."

"What the hell's the metal thing, then?"

His bandage finished, Joe secured it with tape and eased her trouser leg down over it. He had cut away most of her sock and now stuffed it with the saline pouch into the bandage wrapper, using it as a rubbish bag. The cold saline had made his fingers itch and he pulled his gloves back on as Niamh manoeuvred herself onto her knees, her injured leg sticking out behind her as she examined the hole in the ground.

"There's something else down there," she said, reaching in with a gloved hand.

"Careful," he said, though he needn't have worried. She was approaching it with all the care of a forensics officer extracting evidence.

"It's a top or something," she said, pulling a corner of silver fabric free. "Look, there's the arm." As more of it emerged above ground, the bundle unravelled and the metal that had cut her leg was revealed. A knife, like you'd find in most kitchens, the blade around six inches long and a black handle. Where the metal met the plastic was something reddish-black and sticky, like resin. Niamh kept pulling until the fabric was clear and laid it flat on the snow. A thin silver jacket like someone might wear for cycling after dark, its zip and pocket details fluorescent green. A dull russet patch stained it on both sides of the zip.

Blood began to thud in Joe's ears.

"Why do you think they buried it?" Niamh said, poking in the hole to see if anything else lay there. "I mean, I get them filling in their fire pit, even if they didn't do it very well. Leave no trace and all that. But why bury the jacket and the knife?"

Joe's tongue was stuck to the roof of his mouth. He took off one of his gloves and pulled his phone from his pocket.

"Joe?"

"It's the description they gave us when we were searching for Sam Gray," he said. "Blue trousers and a hi-vis silver jacket."

15

Georgie arrived back at the station in Monkmoor to find Andy Morgan waiting for her in reception.

"I can wait if it's not a good time," he said.

"Looks like you've been waiting a while already," she said. He didn't look cold enough for a recent arrival. "Come in."

She and Corby had eaten their M&S sandwiches in the Land Rover and the sudden warmth of the station corridors after a morning in and out of snow was enough to make anyone feel drowsy. She needed coffee.

"We can use one of the small meeting rooms," she said to Corby, adding to Andy that her rural crime office was so far from reception that it wasn't worth the journey. There was no way she could take him to the incident room. He might be a fellow member of the emergency services but given that he was a person of interest in the enquiry, they couldn't risk him seeing the noticeboards detailing the investigation so far.

The room they chose was one usually used for interviewing minors with either social workers or family present. Unlike the formal interview rooms, it had brightly patterned curtains framing the window, with a matching sofa and chairs. On a counter in the corner were mugs and a kettle and Corby offered to make drinks, then put a tin of biscuits on the coffee table in front of the sofa.

"So what can we do for you?" Georgie asked, taking off her jacket and scarf and unlacing her boots which were damp and starting to feel tight. "Or is it more that you can do something for us?"

"Cal came to see me. Cal Innes," he added and Georgie nodded to show she knew who he meant. She had only seen Andy Morgan outside before, the first time at the farm fire in Minsterley when he'd been head to toe in fireproof clothing, and the second on the Long Mynd in deep snow. In the comfort of the meeting room he looked smaller, though still solid and well-built. Clean cut, with a neatly trimmed beard and light brown hair shaved close to his head. If she hadn't known his profession, she might have put him as a teacher or a nurse, perhaps. He had that easy air of comfortable communication.

"He had a bit of a go at me. Said I should come and talk to you."

Georgie took the mug Corby handed to her and thanked her. "Ok," she said. "What about?"

"I do a bit of photography. A side hustle, I suppose you'd call it. I have a Facebook group for showcasing pictures of Shropshire. Landscapes and wildlife. Other people can contribute. Like a community I guess. And I sell calendars and postcards online."

"Oh, I think I've seen it," Corby said. "Is it Wild Shropshire? My Josh likes it. He's into birds and all that. I think he submitted a photo he took. A buzzard. You could see all the wing feathers from underneath."

Andy smiled. "Sounds familiar. Yeah, a few people upload stuff." He took a sip of tea. "Anyway, sometimes I go up in the hills at night. It started out of the Search and Rescue stuff.

Noticing how clear the sky and stars are. We're pretty much free of light pollution in some parts."

"Where do you go?" Georgie asked, feeling that he might need a little shepherding to get to the point.

"Caer Caradoc, Brown Clee sometimes. The Long Mynd mostly because I live over near Woolstaston." Corby offered him the biscuit tin and he took a custard cream, turning it over in his fingers. "I was up on the Mynd the other night. The night those kids had their party." He took a bite of the biscuit and chewed while Georgie waited. Some people couldn't be hurried. "That's why Cal had a go. He said I must have seen something if I was up there."

"And did you?"

Andy gave a grim smile.

"I heard them before I saw them. They had some music system up there and you could hear it from miles away. They had a fire going behind the shelter. I could see it from Pole Bank." He put the remains of the biscuit in his mouth. "I was on my bike, looking for somewhere to stop. I use the shelter some-times but obviously it was out with them there. I went over to Packetstone Hill, past the gliding club, to get away from their noise."

Georgie could imagine the frustration of seeking peace and solitude beneath the stars and finding it violated by a bunch of young partygoers.

"You didn't think to tell them to put the fire out?"

"You're joking, aren't you? One of me and however many of them. I could see they had it contained so I just thought I'd call young Joe in the morning and tell him there was probably some mess to clear up."

"And did you?"

Morgan nodded and Georgie made a note to check that with Joe later.

"I was up by the Packetstone for an hour or so, then I went back towards the top of Ashes Hollow. Where that cairn is." For the second time in only two hours, Georgie nodded her recognition of the cairn's location. "The music had stopped by then but the fire was still going and I heard shouting and saw some of them running up and down the road."

"Did you hear what they were shouting?"

Andy Morgan shook his head.

"I suppose they were shouting for Sam – or that Davey lad – but at the time I didn't know what it was about. I didn't care to be honest."

Georgie took a sip of tea.

"Did you see the car that Sam was in, heading from the shelter down the Burway?"

"No. He must have gone before I got there. I wouldn't have seen anything from the Packetstone."

"And you didn't see Davey Whelan running towards Callow Hollow?"

"Do you think I wouldn't have said something before now if I had?"

Georgie smiled. "I don't know," she said. "Why did Cal think you should come and talk to us?"

Andy shrugged.

"Anything to do with you having a problem with Davey Whelan?" she asked and almost laughed at his look of outrage.

"Where the hell did you get that idea?"

"Wasn't it you who reported him as a suspect for starting the fire at Minsterley Farm?"

"Yeah, but ..." Morgan looked from her to Corby, who was sitting in one of the easy chairs, notebook on her knees. It seemed he hoped that at least one of them would support him. Corby dipped a ginger nut in her tea and raised her eyebrows for him to go on.

"Look, I told you I live at Woolstaston, not far from there. And I've got friends in Minsterley. They rent one of the cottages on the farm."

"So the fire felt personal?" Georgie said. Like the search must have felt for Cal, given that Sam had been on his young offenders programme. No matter how well trained you were as a member of the emergency services, it was always hard to stay objective when people who mattered to you were involved in an incident.

"Yes, I suppose but ... it wasn't that. Davey had been hanging around there. He had a thing for one of the girls who worked in the farm shop. But she wasn't interested and in the end Annette – Annette Evans, she and her husband Tim own the farm – asked him to stay away. And he got shitty with her so Tim got involved and warned him off. Then a week later the barn gets set on fire. And, not being funny or anything, but Davey had convictions for arson so ..."

"So he seemed the likely culprit?"

Andy Morgan nodded. He looked suddenly deflated and took a gulp of tea.

"Look, I was wrong, ok? I reported it, your lot investigated and there was no evidence to tie him to it. Fair enough."

"Didn't someone get hurt in the fire?" Corby said, leaning forward, frowning. "One of your fire crew."

A frozen expression came over the firefighter's face.

"Jayne Bennett," he said, after a while. "She lost her sight."

"And she was a friend of yours?" Corby persisted.

"Yeah. She was. She is."

"So it *was* personal?" Georgie said.

Morgan put his mug down on the coffee table with more force that was necessary and sat up, looking as though he might get to his feet and stride out of the room. Then he sighed.

"Yeah. It was. But I didn't see Davey Whelan up on the Mynd and seize the opportunity to throw him down Callow Hollow."

Georgie smiled. She hadn't thought that he had. Her desire to talk to him had been born out of the fact that he might have seen something that would help them unpick the night's events. As it was, if he could remember timings, he might at least be able to give them an idea when Sam had driven off down the Burway which might help them to narrow down the time he had got into Church Stretton. With a more precise time, maybe they'd be able to jog someone's memory, someone who might have noticed the silver Vauxhall Corsa driving through the village in the small hours. If they knew what direction he had taken and could trace him to the outskirts of Shrewsbury or Ludlow, Bridgnorth even, he might have been picked up on a camera.

Probably owing to his Search and Rescue experience, Andy Morgan had good recall of the time that he had first passed the shelter on his way to Packetstone Hill, how long he had stayed there and when he had come back to set up camp at the top of Ashes Hollow. Corby made a note.

One other thing was prodding Georgie's curiosity.

"Before you go," she said, as he thanked Corby for his tea and picked up his jacket. "Why do you think Cal Innes is getting so involved?"

Morgan looked puzzled.

"How do you mean?"

"Well, he pressured you into coming to talk to us. He'd also already told me that you were up on the Mynd that night." At his expression, she felt a flicker of guilt for perhaps sowing seeds of trouble between friends but not enough to bother her. She had one missing and one dead young man to fight for. "It seems Sam's disappearance matters to him."

"I don't know. Sam was part of his Time Out programme, wasn't he?"

"So was Davey," Georgie said. "It seemed odd to me, when you brought Davey's body up out of Callow Hollow that Cal didn't identify him."

"Maybe he didn't recognise him. It was getting dark and it was snowing. The boy had been dead for a while. What are you trying to say?"

Georgie smiled.

"Nothing. I'm just curious as to why Cal seems to be much more concerned about Sam Gray than about Davey Whelan."

Andy Morgan got to his feet and shrugged himself into his jacket.

"I can't help you with that, Inspector Fraser," he said, suddenly formal. "You'll need to talk to Cal. Thanks again for the tea."

Georgie thanked him for having come in and held the door open for him, watching as he strode off down the corridor without turning back.

"What was that all about, boss?" Corby said, as she gathered the mugs off the table and put them on a tray to take to the utility room behind the custody sergeant's office.

"Just a pricking of my thumbs," Georgie said, taking her phone from her jacket as it buzzed loudly. She held it to her ear. "Hi Joe, what's up?"

16

Georgie's evening team briefing started late. After Joe's call, she and Corby had headed back to the Long Mynd, leaving Chowdhury and Mike Harley to keep her appointments with the remaining partygoers, Lily Morpeth, Bryn Morgan and Seth Glover.

"And push them hard," she'd said, as she left the office. "If what Joe's found up by the shelter did belong to Sam Gray, then it doesn't fit with any of the stories we've been told so far." Along with the excitement of new evidence and a possible new lead, had come a wave of irritation at the thought that the second lot of stories they had been told by Alfie, Lucas and Alisha hadn't contained all the facts. At no point had anyone mentioned a knife. Maybe she should have got them all together. Which was still an option, of course.

Joe hadn't been at the Pole Cottage shelter when they had arrived. Instead they had found his boss, the Area Ranger Dan Edwards, a big man with a beard and a genial air of solid competence.

"Joe had one of our volunteers with him," he'd said. "Injured herself. In fact that's how they discovered it, she put her foot down the hole so he's taken her off to get it seen to. Nasty cut."

Everything had been left exactly as Joe and Niamh had found it, except that the jacket and knife were no longer down the hole. Georgie had arranged for a couple of SOCOs to meet her up there. Of course the place had been searched once already but that had been by Search and Rescue looking for signs of a missing person. No one had thought they would need to dig below ground.

Not that the SOCOs had been encouraging. With the snow, the likelihood of them finding trace evidence of any sort was pretty small. Suited and gloved, they had first photographed the charred earth and sticks in the area that Joe had cleared of snow, then begun to dig through it. To everyone's relief, there had been nothing but the remnants of the fire. No sudden exposure of pale, human flesh. Which didn't mean that Sam Gray wasn't still up there somewhere.

Back at the station in the warmth of the Incident room and hoping that either there would be a thaw or she might find an excuse to stay in her office the next day, Georgie called the briefing to order.

"DS Chowdhury, any luck with those other three youngsters? And let's all be brief, ok? We're late starting – my fault, I know – and I expect you're all dying to get home." Two of the local Church Stretton officers had gone already, citing childcare commitments, and they were left with only Bob Carradine.

"Pretty much the same story as you got from that Alfie," Chowdhury said. "Only not word for word like the first time around. Lily Morpeth got very tearful. We spoke to her and Bryn Morgan together. Seems they're an item, got together that Wednesday night. She went into quite a bit of detail about when they all thought Whelan was dead. Bryn doing the CPR and all that. Don't think she was happy about them all covering it up. Seemed relieved to talk about it."

"Seth Glover was similar," Mike Harley said. "Not tearful," he added with a grin. "Bit of a wannabe tough guy, all groomed beard and man bun. From the way he talks you'd think he was from Jamaica rather than Church Stretton. But he definitely wasn't happy he'd been caught lying. Stressed the whole loyalty to the group thing and then spilled the beans. But nothing about a knife or any explanation for how it got buried. Said they'd just put the fire out before they left, piled earth on it and that. The only knife anyone had was his, a kind of Swiss Army type thing. They used it to open the bottles."

"And did they confirm whether Sam was wearing that silver jacket when he drove away with Davey in the car?"

Chowdhury and Harley both nodded.

"As far as they could remember, yeah," Chowdhury said. "But Glover did say he'd been pretty pissed so he might not remember accurately. Covering his back, I reckon."

"The girl was sure, though," Harley said. "Lily. Silver cycling jacket with green zips."

"Green zips and bloodstains, now," Georgie said. "The question is, whose blood?"

She tapped a key on her laptop and a picture of the jacket, laid out on the snowy ground, appeared on the Smartboard.

"SOCOs have bagged it and sent it off to the lab and I've put in a request for it to be fast-tracked so fingers crossed we'll have an answer to that soon. You can see from the pattern that there's some splatter as well as more solid staining. I'm no forensic scientist but it seems to me inconclusive as to whether the person wearing the jacket was injured – presumably stabbed – or whether they got in a mess when they stabbed someone else."

"But there wasn't any sign of Davey Whelan being stabbed,

was there?" Corby asked. "They'd have seen that straight away in the post mortem."

"Exactly," Georgie said. "We know Davey wasn't stabbed. So the most likely explanation is that Sam was. But it seems odd that no one would have mentioned that. We're not dealing with a bunch of young psychopaths here. Just ordinary kids out for a good night. Which seems to have gone horribly wrong."

DC Hallam raised a hand and Georgie nodded at him to speak. On her previous investigation nine months ago, Hallam had never waited for permission. Now, she almost missed his impulsive need to be front and centre. The reticence seemed artificial.

"So are you thinking that Whelan stabbed Gray? Because if so, how do we explain the car? And the fact that Gray was sending messages to the group chat until Saturday saying he was safe with a friend?"

"Unless Whelan took his phone," Chowdhury said. "Maybe he stabbed Sam after Sam made that call to the others saying Whelan had run off. He lay in wait somewhere when Sam went looking for him and jumped him."

Georgie tapped her pen against her cheek. It was possible, she supposed. DC Corby spoke, articulating the doubting voices in Georgie's head.

"But the pathologist said that Davey Whelan had been dead for at least three days and more likely four. So how could he have been sending messages? And what about the car? He was dead before the car went off the side of the Burway."

"All true, DC Corby. So however unlikely it all seems, I'm inclined to think that Wednesday night happened just as Alfie Rickard described it and that Sam was hiding out somewhere until his messages to his friends stopped on Saturday. And after that, who knows what happened?" She took a deep breath. "I've asked the PolSA to contact Search and Rescue again to organise a team with cadaver dogs. They'll meet us up at Pole Cottage tomorrow morning."

"So you think...?" Corby left the sentence unfinished.

"I don't know what I think," Georgie said. "But we've got a knife and bloodstained clothing belonging to a missing person. We'd be negligent if we didn't follow it up."

Silence settled over the room. Outside it was snowing again, fat feathery flakes falling against an ink-black sky. Georgie was vaguely aware that there was something she had forgotten to raise but her thoughts kept dragging her back to her conversation with Andy Morgan earlier. Somewhere in the back of her mind was an itch that she couldn't scratch.

Bob Carradine cleared his throat.

"Do you want to know about our search of Whelan's caravan, then?"

Georgie's attention snapped back to the room. She should have asked him first, for diplomatic reasons, if nothing else.

"Yes, Bob, of course. Thank you."

The sergeant stood up and came to the front, self-consciously plugging his laptop into the Smartboard. Sam Gray's bloodstained top was replaced with what looked like shots of a ransacked bedroom.

"Bit of a mess, as you can see, the caravan," he said. He scrolled through a few photos. A kitchenette piled high with dirty dishes, takeaway cartons and empty cans. Beneath the counter, a bin was overflowing onto cardboard pizza boxes stacked to one side. In the living area, the table was strewn with books and paper, the lace curtains mottled with mildew. A low mew of sadness settled in Georgie's belly. At twenty, Davey Whelan had been a year or two older than most of the young-sters gathered up at Pole Cottage on Wednesday night, exactly a week earlier. But he'd had no one to care for him, it seemed, since he'd left his foster home at the age of sixteen. How many twenty-year-old men were bothered about being house-proud? Davey had, it seemed, lived hand to mouth, caring for himself as best he could.

"Liked his weed," Bob Carradine went on, scrolling to a picture which showed an enclosed white space, brightly lit, which housed two bushy marijuana plants. "Could smell it as soon as we opened the door. In a cupboard. Hydroponic growing system, lights, the works. Wouldn't have yielded enough for dealing but would have kept him supplied, I reckon."

"Any other drugs on the premises?" Georgie asked.

"Not that we found. Some paraphernalia," Carradine said. "Bong, pipes and what have you. And signs of cocaine use. A cut-off straw and an old library card in a small box, traces of white powder in the cracks. I sent it off to the lab for testing." Georgie nodded her approval and Carradine went on. "Also found a stash of weapons, some improvised, in a bag labelled Zombie Apocalypse. A heavy chain, two hunting knives, an iron bar that looked as if it had broken off something, and a crossbow."

"A crossbow?"

"And a set of bolts, some of which seemed fire damaged. A bundle of rags and a couple of bottles of lighter fuel."

Georgie remembered Andy Morgan's suspicions about the fire at Minsterley. Had he been right after all? The wind was howling now outside, swirling the flakes into a flurry. She needed to get the team off home before the roads became too challenging.

"Did you find a laptop?"

"Passed it on to DC Hallam," he said, and the younger officer nodded.

"Not got into it yet, boss, but DS Morgan's going to have a go at it tomorrow. Quite sophisticated encryption."

"One thing, ma'am," Sergeant Carradine said. Georgie

wondered if he was using the term deliberately, knowing that it set her teeth on edge. There was a slightly arch tone to his voice whenever he said it and he was old school enough to be discomfited simply by her presence. "He liked his writing. And drawing. Poems, cartoons. Looks like he was writing a graphic novel." He flashed another picture onto the board. An elongated head, possibly an alien, with slanting eyes and tall, Spock-like ears, a long sinuous body crouched as though about to pounce. It was captioned with a few lines of upper-case script, too blurred for Georgie to read.

"Talented," she said, again feeling that stab of sorrow.

"And then I found this." Another photo popped onto the screen. The team stared. Corby was the first to speak.

"Is that Sam Gray?"

It was a head and shoulders pencil sketch but startlingly similar to the photo released by the Gray family when Sam had gone missing. Beneath the face was written in the same block capitals as the alien's caption, *MY BROTHER IN ARMS*.

"Seems Sam hung out there a bit. We found a couple of books with his name in them. A notebook with scores for a game, Sam's name in one column, Davey's in the other."

DC Hallam raised his hand with some of his old excitement.

"Sorry, boss, I was waiting my turn but the lab sent over Whelan's phone. Found in the pocket of his jacket. I've been going through his photo library. May I?" he added to Carradine who nodded grudgingly. Hallam pressed a few keys on his tablet and the screen came alive again with photos of the two boys lounging on the caravan's unmade bed, Playstation controllers on the rumpled duvet between them.

"There were these too," Hallam said. More selfies, the camera held in Davey's hand, capturing both him and Sam. They were standing by a gravestone and Sam was pointing at it with an expression of pantomime shock. "There are a few of them. Like it was important for them to get it right. Wasn't posted on either of their socials, though. And then these." The last two were of Sam alone standing on the gravestone. In one he had his arms in a strongman pose. In the other he was urinating on the grave.

"Do we know whose grave it is?" DS Chowdhury asked, while Georgie was still absorbing the pictures.

"Can't make the name out," Hallam said.

"Definitely Greenhills cemetery," Carradine said. "On the Ludlow Road between Church and Little Stretton."

"A job for your team tomorrow then, Sergeant. Find that grave. Great work," she added. "All of you, I know it's not been easy with the weather. Thank you. And pass that on to the rest of your team, would you, Bob?"

Davey Whelan and Sam Gray. Fighting over a girl. Hanging out together in Davey's caravan. Desecrating an unknown grave. Now one was dead and the only trace they had of the other was a piece of bloodstained clothing. Had they been brothers-in-arms? And against what or whom?

17

Marianne had had enough of the snow. The dogs were loving it, true; bounding through the drifts where they were deep, chasing each other with tongues lolling and tails waving. To her left the river flowed almost black between its white banks, swollen and fast, and she whistled the dogs away from it, all too aware of how quickly they could be swept away with the current. Only two weeks ago, Joe had come home with a story of Search and Rescue having recovered a body from the River Teme; a father of two who'd gone in to help his Labrador and succumbed to cold water shock, dragged beneath the surface and held there by the weight of water in his lungs. The dog had emerged from the river a few hundred yards downstream, unhurt.

Of course, when it thawed the river would most likely flood at Onnyford. All that meltwater coming down off the hills, pouring into the east and west branches of the Onny which met just north-west of the village to become one stream. Even so, she wanted the snow gone and soon. It had brought danger and unrest into her life. Not only the investigation into the death of one young man and the disappearance of another, which had Georgie working all hours. When she wasn't physically at work her brain was still churning through possibilities, so she became pre-occupied and withdrawn. Marianne didn't blame her; it was why she was good at her job. But, whenever Georgie was locked into a case, Marianne knew she would have to do without her until it was resolved. When a puzzle took hold of her she couldn't rest until she had solved it.

And then there was Joe and his sudden need to know who had fathered him. Perhaps it wasn't sudden. Perhaps he had always wondered, at least once he had begun his search for her, his birth mother. There would have been no name on his birth certificate which had simply stated 'father unknown'. And in his case that had been no matter of concealment. There had been five candidates from which to choose and only one whose name she had known or could remember. Given that Joe bore no resemblance whatsoever to him, he was unlikely to have been responsible.

Her legs were becoming tired with the endless tramping through untouched white powder and a gunmetal cloud above the village threatened more to come. As she climbed over the stile into the lane, she whistled to the dogs again and waited, holding up the dog-gate to let them through. She passed Alan Ross's static caravan and saw the curtains closed and the lights on, his beloved semi-derelict Onnyford Court – or the Scooby-Doo house as Georgie called it – in darkness. Since sloughing off the ghost of Neil Traynor, whose murder Georgie had investigated at the Geoscience Trust nine months earlier, Alan seemed to have managed to stay on the wagon and slowly, if not steadily, the house was coming back to life.

Hers was the next house before the start of the village proper and the unsurfaced lane had seen little foot traffic and no cars that day. Compacted snow crunched under her feet and she took care, aware that sheet ice lurked beneath it from the rain that had fallen and frozen before the snow had come. Rounding the corner from which her cottage could first be seen, with Onnyford Farm beyond, she stopped. A small car stood on the gravel drive and for a moment she didn't recognise it in the half light.

"Joe?" she said as a figure uncurled from the driver's side, too tall for a Fiat Panda. Then the passenger door opened and a smaller figure got out. The dogs shot towards them, Pip letting out squeaks of happiness.

"Hey, Ma. Niamh and I were just passing. Time for a cup of tea?"

What else could she say but of course? Although her heart sank just a little. Knowing Niamh had first raised the subject of Joe's father, she couldn't help feeling that the girl was judging her. And who could blame her? She had judged herself more harshly than anyone else could have done for the best part of Joe's life. It was only through Georgie – and maybe through knowing Joe himself – that she had begun to heal.

"Did you finish work early?" she asked as the dogs leapt around him and Niamh in demented circles.

"We were in Ludlow," he said, "Minor Injuries. Niamh cut herself. Less of a wait than Shrewsbury."

They followed her through the garden to the front door, Niamh limping a little and leaning on Joe's arm. As they took off their snowy coats and boots in the porch, Joe began the story of Niamh's foot disappearing through the snow and breaking the ground beneath.

"A rabbit hole?" Marianne asked. "I thought you didn't get rabbits on the top?"

"You don't," Joe said. "Soil's too thin above the bedrock in most places. Someone had dug it, behind the shelter. In the old cottage garden."

Marianne sent them into the living room with instructions to light the fire while she made tea. Her cottage had no central heating and was always cold when she came in from work. If Georgie ever got home first, she made jokes about having had to chase the penguins out.

As they drank tea and ate cake in front of the fire, Niamh sitting sideways on the sofa to rest her injured leg on Joe's knee, they told her about their grisly find behind the shelter.

"And you reckon it was to do with the missing lad? Sam Gray?" Marianne asked.

Joe shrugged.

"Fits the description of what he was wearing when he was last seen," Joe said. "Ranger Dan," as he always called his boss, "said Georgie was up there with SOCOs all afternoon."

"And they didn't find anything else?"

"Like a body?" Joe said. "Not as far as I know."

Marianne was quiet, her mind playing over what this might mean for Georgie. DCI Pitbull had been on the phone that morning before Georgie left for work, chivvying her to make progress.

"The social media shitstorm's not getting any calmer," he'd said. "If it weren't for the weather, the place would be flooded with amateur detectives and the true crime lot." Mrs Gray had apparently been on the phone to him several times and he'd had to station officers outside her house where she was almost a prisoner.

"She's got my number if she wants updates," Marianne had heard Georgie say.

"Well, it's mine she keeps using," Pitbull had growled over the speakerphone. "Get onto her today and give her whatever crumbs you've got. And another thing," he'd added. "Someone's started trouble about your ... er ... gender status. On the Friends of Sam Gray feed." Marianne's blood had run cold but afterwards Georgie had shrugged it off.

"It's not my problem. They can think I'm whatever they want. Man, woman or giraffe. I know what I am and the only thing that interests me is getting the job done."

Marianne wished she could summon the same resilience. Later, when Joe and Niamh had left, she busied herself in the kitchen, making a vegetarian ragout for her and Georgie to have with pasta, her mind heavy. How could she help her son without destroying the hard-won peace that she had enjoyed for the last few years? Since leaving prison, she had resolved to look only forwards. Joe's questions, quite justified, risked dragging her back.

It was seven before Georgie was home and the weather worsening. Marianne had been to the field across the lane and furnished the donkeys and goat with hay, mucking out their shelter and laying fresh straw so they could hide out of the weather. The wind was picking up, blowing her across the gravel drive with a coating of snow on her back. Physical work amongst the animals always made her feel better and she greeted Georgie with a long hug, tension easing from both their bodies.

"No Beata?" Georgie asked as they brushed snow off their coats and hung them above the heater in the porch.

"At Meribette's and staying over. Which is good given the roads. They'll probably be snowed in over there."

Georgie smiled.

"Just us. Heaven."

Marianne often wondered if Georgie minded that she had allowed Beata to come and live with them. With her, originally. Beata had moved in before Georgie officially had, desolate after her mother was remanded in custody, seen as too much of a flight risk to be granted bail. At sixteen, Beata had been too old for the formal foster care system and social services had approved Marianne's offer of a home. Meribette Igny, a palaeontologist at the Shropshire Geoscience Trust had also offered but, since her work often took her away, Beata had preferred to stay at Marianne's and visit Meribette from time to time.

"Hey," Georgie said, touching Marianne's cheek with cold fingers. "You know I think Beata's great," she said, displaying that uncanny ability she had to read Marianne's thoughts, "and it's not like she gets in our way. But it's nice when it's just us, too."

Later, as they sat on the sofa in front of the fire, bowls of steaming ragout on their laps, Georgie told her about her day, treading that fine line between sharing her thoughts and keeping aspects of a police investigation confidential.

"Not that there is much confidential," she said, as she checked herself. "I don't know where everyone's getting their information but it spreads like wildfire. You know the latest? Sam and Davey were having a secret gay relationship. We only searched his caravan today but people seemed to know we'd found evidence that Sam had spent time there."

"Neighbours?" Marianne asked.

"He didn't have any," Georgie said. "Caravan's in the middle of bloody nowhere. Up that bank before the golf course. But it's so easy for it to spread without anyone consciously leaking it. Take Joe and Niamh," she said, putting her bowl down on a side table and picking up her glass of cider. "They go off to the hospital. Maybe one of the nurses is asking what happened and they accidentally give a bit too much info. *Foot down a hole? How did you cut yourself? A knife? And where were you? Oh, on top of the Mynd. Where that lad went missing?* And before you know it, we've found Sam's body buried up on the Mynd. I'm not kidding," she added, when Marianne half-laughed. "Corby found a post on that 'Friends of Sam Gray' group."

"I'm sorry," Marianne said. "I know it must be frustrating. But maybe it will throw up some useful information too. Someone must know where he is. If they're in that group, they might give something away without meaning to."

Georgie's phone rang and she rolled her eyes as she picked it up from the arm of the sofa.

"Pitbull. Here we go again." She held it to her ear. "Evening, sir! What can I do for you?"

Marianne gathered up the dirty dishes and took them through to the kitchen, the dogs following her expectantly. They were always fed after she and Georgie had eaten, unless it was unusually late. She heaped kibble into their bowls, not consciously listening to Georgie's side of the conversation but aware that her attention was pulled towards it, however unwillingly.

When she went back to the living room with camomile tea for herself and a decaf coffee for Georgie, she found her sitting in her favourite armchair, legs thrown over the side.

"Breakthrough," Georgie said, taking the coffee and thanking her. Marianne went to put another log on the fire.

"You know I said that firefighter from Search and Rescue came to see us?"

Marianne nodded.

"He helped us narrow down when Sam must have left the Mynd. None of the kids seemed to have any idea. Anyway," she said, holding out a hand and pulling Marianne over towards her chair. Marianne walked to her on her knees and sat back against the firm upholstery. "Turns out the car he was in was picked up on camera going past the golf club at 1.32 am. And if that ends up on Facebook or X or whatever, I'll know it was you because no one else knows yet."

Marianne smiled. Georgie knew very well that she never used social media.

"Will that help you?" she asked.

"Well, it's sparked a little seed in my head," Georgie said. "But I'll need a bit of time to think it through. For now, though, I'd rather talk about you." She tugged gently at Marianne's hair. "What's on your mind? And don't say nothing because I'll only badger you until you tell me and then we'll be here all night when we're both knackered and want to go to bed."

Marianne watched the flames for a while. Maggie had come to sprawl on the rug beside her and she pulled at the dog's soft ears wondering how to formulate her thoughts into words.

"I've been thinking about Joe. And what I can tell him."

"Do you want me to tell him for you?"

Georgie had suggested it before, the day after Joe had first raised it. It seemed cowardly, but perhaps it might be easier for both of them. And Georgie was used to discussing the darker side of humanity, knew how to tell people things that were difficult for them to hear. Joe would not have to consider her feelings when he reacted, as he no doubt must, with disgust. And she, Marianne, would not have to relive her horror and shame. She had only ever told two people the full story. Her defence barrister when she had been prosecuted for the murder of a client who had raped her, and Georgie. The defence barrister had submitted it to the judge who had ruled it inadmissible, meaning that at least Marianne had not had to repeat it in court. But then, neither had it been taken in mitigation of the crime for which she was on trial. Effie knew some of it but not the detail. And therapists had only ever heard a sanitised version. What would have been the point of talking about it? Nothing could have changed what happened.

"I was thinking," Georgie said, "that maybe I could access information. Through the police databases."

It took a while for the words to percolate through Marianne's brain so that she understood their meaning.

"I didn't report it," she said, at last.

"No, I know. But it occurred to me that perhaps you weren't the only one. Maybe there were other girls in your part of Devon back then, who had a similar experience."

It might have occurred to Georgie but never, in almost thirty years, had it occurred to her.

"They were a bunch of surfer boys out for a party and a good time" she said, "not a gang of serial rapists. I'd had too much to drink and they took advantage."

"Or," Georgie said, "they spiked your drink. Deliberately."

Marianne was silent, watching the flames and listening to the big dog's snores. Behind her, Pip scratched noisily in her bed then got up and stretched. How simple life was for dogs. In her next life, she would like to come back as a dog in a good home, with nothing to worry her but when she would next go for a walk.

"Maybe there weren't any similar cases of rape," Georgie said, the word grating on Marianne's skin. "But there might have been complaints of sexual assault. Harassment. I think it's worth checking."

"It was twenty-six years ago."

"And records go back a long way."

Marianne sat forward and Georgie tugged at her hair again.

"Hey." She felt a kiss planted gently on the top of her head. "I'm not going to pressure you. But it might be a way to answer Joe's questions. And to put things to rest properly." Marianne could guess the words that Georgie was omitting. Put things to rest properly rather than just burying them beneath twenty-six years of denial.

"I'll think about it," Marianne said.

Georgie kissed her again and said that she wouldn't do anything, either talk to Joe or start looking at records, until Marianne had made up her mind. The words, intended to reassure, had the opposite effect. What if Georgie had already looked at police records? Wouldn't that be the natural instinct when you had access to them if you thought it would help someone that you loved? Wouldn't she in Georgie's position have done exactly that?

18

"Over here!"

Even without the dog handler's shout, Georgie would have known they had found something. The big animal had let loose a baying that could probably be heard down in Church Stretton. Not where they had expected, though. The enclosure had been searched with no result when the handler had asked if she could take the bigger of the two dogs out beyond the fencing onto the moor behind.

"She's dead set on going out there."

Georgie had watched as the dog, once free of the fenced enclosure, had gone into hunting mode. At a certain spot she had stopped, giving out a great bark and then run back to her handler, jumping up.

"That's how they show there's a find," Malcolm Tucker had said, watching with Georgie. Of the Search and Rescue volunteers she had met so far only Malcolm Tucker, whom she'd met when Joe had first found the car, was present. Without a dog himself he seemed to be there in a team leader role along with two dog handlers, one with a cadaver dog and the other with an air-scenting spaniel, who had been bustling around all over the enclosure and the moor beyond. It astonished Georgie that they could pick up any scents in such cold temperatures. They had found the site of the hole where Joe had pulled out the jacket and knife within seconds.

"Show me," the big dog's handler said outside the fence, stumbling in the deep snow and struggling to keep up as the Malinois, on a long lead, shot off once more.

There, serene and flatly white amongst the undulations where springy heather lurked beneath the snowy blanket, was a wide, boggy pool. It wasn't deep, barely a foot even, and, if what Joe had told her when he first started working as a ranger was accurate, lay on the site of the old house, Pole Cottage.

During the annual Festival of Archaeology a couple of years ago, volunteers working alongside the National Trust archaeologists and Historic England had uncovered the foundations of outbuildings and even the back door of the house itself, suggesting that the pool now filled the space where its robbed-out foundations had been. Evidence for when the house had been demolished was hard to come by and there were suggestions that some old photographs had been faked, shrouding the cottage in an ever thicker layer of mystery. Georgie had a horrible feeling that today they would be adding another tale to the local lore.

"There's ice under the snow," the handler said as Georgie approached.

The dog was still fussing her, jumping up and pawing at her jacket.

"Better clear it to be sure. Can't give her the reward until we confirm a find."

Malcolm Tucker arrived then with brooms and shovels, joined by the other search volunteers. Aware that something must have happened, DC Corby was approaching from the Land Rover which they'd parked to the south of the enclosure, where she'd been making phone calls. Georgie went to meet her.

"Those kids are all set to meet us later, boss," she said. "And Chelle Gray's happy for us to drop by any time. Have they found something?"

"Looks like it," Georgie said. "I don't know whether to feel glad or not." And yet, any news, surely, was better than none. Better for Chelle Gray, although it might be news from which she might never recover. Better than spending the rest of her life wondering, torturing herself with hope. "Oh shit," she said, starting off over the snow-covered heather, like plunging through knee-high treacle that clung and snatched at her legs. The handler had just given the big dog a rubber toy, its squeaks echoing through the still air. The weather gods had furnished a day of beauty after the previous day's steely grey cold. Sun glinted off a landscape so shiny it reflected the blue of the sky and in the distance you could see far into Wales.

Georgie stopped by the edge of the pool as if someone had seized her by the back of her jacket. Just below a thin layer of ice was the shadowy outline of a human form, pale and ghostly. Dark-brown hair framed an ivory face above a grey torso, in the middle of which lay a rust-coloured stain. The arms were spread wide, hands turned upward in supplication. Below the waist, dark trousers blended with the murk of the black water that surrounded them.

"We need photographs," Georgie said. "And we need to call the pathologist and forensics. Ali, would you...?"

"On it." Corby turned back towards the Land Rover, her face drained of colour. Georgie didn't blame her. The photos she would do herself.

Tucker surveyed the scene. "Forensics won't find anything useful in these weather conditions."

"We still have to give them the chance to try. I'll get some uniform officers up here to secure the scene while we're waiting," she said to Tucker. She looked down again at the body beneath the ice, hoping scientific curiosity might allay the terrible pity that seeped through her.

"How do the dogs pick up the scent? Under ice and snow, I mean."

"More scent receptors," the handler said. "We've got five or six million. They've got three hundred million."

Georgie found her eyes drawn to the dog's long nose, trying to imagine the network of nerves that carried scent information to its brain. She could smell nothing but cold crisp air and a faint whiff of horse. One of the wild herds had left droppings not far from where they were standing and a few strands of silver tail hair trailed from the wire fence. If a herd had been here since Sam had been entombed in the ice, they'd have trampled any traces the killer might have left for forensics.

Rather than any elation of a find, a crushing weight settled on her shoulders, so that merely standing upright took all her effort. The group of youngsters who had agreed to meet her and Corby would have to wait. First, she would need to see Chelle Gray. She hoped to God that the pathologists would have him out of the ice and down to the mortuary soon for his mother to identify. Even if they had to bring up lights, he needed to be recovered before the day's end.

"I don't get it," Corby said, as they descended the Burway into Church Stretton. On the left, Effie's house was set back amongst the trees and Georgie wished she were there, just visiting with Marianne, rather than on her way to break news that would change a mother's life forever. "How did the dog manage to pick up a scent from beneath the ice?"

"I was asking one of the handlers about that," Georgie said.

"Tiny holes, apparently. In the ice and snow. If the body was warm when the ice was forming it would have made it fragile compared to the surrounding sheet. And then gases escape from the decomposition. The dog picks them up."

"Grim," said Corby. "Sorry, boss. Understatement of the year. What are you going to tell his mum?"

"That we've found him. She doesn't need the details."

"But you'll tell her where...?" Corby sounded shocked.

"Of course. Just if I was a mum – and I know I don't have kids but I do have an imagination – I wouldn't want my last image of my son to be him trapped under a layer of ice. I won't lie, I just won't offer more than she asks."

Corby seemed to digest this as they rounded the corner onto the Shrewsbury Road towards Attlee Close.

"Did you ever want kids?" she asked. "I mean, I know you can't give birth but you could have ..." She tailed off, perhaps worried that she had crossed a line.

"I would have loved kids," Georgie answered, less awkward than Corby at the turn the conversation had taken. "And yes, of course I could have done if things had gone differently. I wanted to be a mum. But back then, I'd have had to be a dad and that didn't work for me." She laughed. "HR probably wouldn't want us to be having this conversation, you know."

"Sorry." Corby blushed. "I didn't mean ..."

"No, you're fine. But it had better be off the record. I was married before. When I was in London. And we did want kids."

"Were you? I never knew. To a woman?"

"What do you think? I was still living as ... my pretend self, then. Although not very successfully. But I tried. The only problem was that when you know inside that you're a woman, it's practically impossible to have sex as a man." Georgie was glad she was driving. Corby's silence felt contemplative rather than judgmental but you could never be sure, and it was easier to keep her eyes on the road. "My poor ex-wife just thought I didn't fancy her enough."

"You didn't try IVF or anything?"

"That would have meant telling her what the problem was and I was too scared. Things are different now. People are more accepting despite all the online bile and EHCR judgements. And with my job, it didn't feel possible. Until continuing to live as I was felt even less possible."

"So what happened? I mean, when did you tell her that you were…?" Again her words tailed off.

"That I was a woman in the wrong body? About two years after we got together. She knew something wasn't right. I mean, she was a psychologist so you'd think she'd pick up on it. And after I told her … well, she wanted a man and I couldn't be that. It wasn't acrimonious," Georgie added. "Just sad, really." She took a deep breath in as she turned the Land Rover into Attlee Close. "So, no kids," she said. "But I have Joe by proxy, even if he is a grown-up. And Beata. Though officially she's a grown-up too."

"Seventeen?" Corby said. "You're joking aren't you? I'm twenty-six and I hardly count myself a grown-up. At seventeen, I was definitely still a kid. Like those poor buggers partying up on the Long Mynd last week. Two of them dead and what the hell is going on with the rest of them?"

A police car was parked outside the Gray's house and the spaces either side were blocked off with cones. Georgie spotted a few people sitting in parked cars but the ranks of onlookers and reporters outside the house had gone, chased away by either the cold or the police presence. The snowmen in the front gardens seemed to have become a little sadder since their last visit. She tucked the Land Rover into the same space they had taken last time, outside number seventeen. Before she had even got out, the door opened and the elderly Mr Conway appeared, pulling on a coat.

"Bit better," he said, as though they had been in the middle of a conversation. "Got rid of the vultures. Have you got news for her?"

Georgie smiled as she locked the vehicle.

"I'm afraid I can't discuss that, Mr Conway. Have you got any news for me?" she added, more as a pleasantry than anything else but the man looked around as though to check the coast was clear and then leaned towards her.

"I have, as it happens. Was going to call you."

"Oh yes?"

He looked around again, furtive but a little important too.

"That other lad. The one who was found up at Callow Hollow."

"Davey Whelan?"

"He was round here a couple of weeks ago. Three maybe. Anyway, there was a screaming row. Midnight, it was. My wife and I don't sleep well. Watched it all out of the window."

"Davey and Sam were rowing here? On the doorstep?"

Tony Conway shook his head, eyes wide.

"Not Sam. Her. Michelle Gray. Giving that Davey what for, she was, and him giving it right back."

Germs of ideas that had been sprouting in Georgie's brain since she'd seen the photos found on Davey's phone had a little surge of growth.

"That's interesting. Thank you, Mr Conway. Are you on Facebook, by any chance?"

The man looked as though she'd slapped him.

"Can't bear the thing. My granddaughter tried to get us interested but ..." He made a noise halfway between a spit and a cough.

Georgie smiled again.

"Well, I'd be grateful if you kept what you've told me to yourself," she said. "There's enough gossip muddying the waters."

The man touched his tweed cap in what resembled a military salute.

"Don't do gossip," he said, then, as she and Corby set off towards the Gray's house called after them, "Give her my best. Anything we can do."

19

Georgie felt utterly drained after their visit to the Grays. The younger brother, Danny, had been home, the family all together when she had broken the news that Sam would never be coming back.

Had there been relief for them? Not yet, though perhaps there might be in the days to come. First and foremost though, there had been grief. And fury. At the police for not finding him sooner, at his friends because surely they must have known, at whoever had done this to him, had robbed them of their beautiful boy.

Chelle Gray's distress had been such that it hadn't been possible to ask the questions that had originally driven Georgie to make an appointment to see her that day, before they had even found her son. As they were leaving to interview the group of friends with whom the bereaved mother was so furious, Clive cornered them in the cluttered hallway.

"So what's going on, then?" His tone was belligerent.

"How do you mean?" Georgie asked.

Corby's fingers were on the latch when Clive leaned heavily against the door with a meaty hand.

"I mean, what the fuck was going on with those kids? The party lot. You must know. It must be one of them did it."

"We're on our way to talk to them now, Mr ...?"

"My name's Clive as you bloody well know."

"Yes, but I don't have your surname." Though it must have been recorded in the original investigation. The lapses in her memory database were occasionally inconvenient.

"Holyman," the big man said. It seemed thoroughly inappropriate.

"Mr Holyman, I'm intrigued by the relationship between Sam and Davey Whelan. I noticed—"

He spoke over her before she could finish her sentence.

"Don't tell me you've sucked up all that shit on social media about them having some gay bromance. Jesus!"

Georgie smiled. Relentless friendliness, as her first sergeant had taught her so many years ago.

"Not at all, Clive. That isn't what I meant. As you might have heard, we found photos of them together on Davey's phone. It would be helpful to know how close that friendship was and if they had fallen out recently. When we were first here, I thought you and Chelle seemed to find it significant when I asked you if Sam and Davey had been friends."

His face clouded over.

"Don't know what you mean. They were mates, that was all." He pushed past Corby, his bulk too big for the narrow hall when there were other people in it, and wrenched the door open.

"Close mates?"

Clive Holyman stood back, not so much pushing them out of the door as giving them nowhere else to go but into the sunlit, snowy street.

"If they fell out," he said, his voice causing them to turn on the slippery path, "it was because of that girl."

"Alisha Johnson, do you mean?"

"Nah," Clive said. "Never heard of her. Jessie Pritchard. That was the one they were both daft over."

SHE AND CORBY were due to meet Sam and Davey's seven young party companions in Church Stretton's police station at three-thirty, when all had either finished work or were able to get away for an hour or so. Given that all their employers must know they had been in some way involved in Sam's disappearance, after both the local team's enquiries and the relentless media coverage, social and mainstream, she imagined it hadn't been hard for them to arrange the time off. Only Alfie had seemed anxious about his manager knowing he'd been interviewed by the police twice in three days. Lucas Harley had stepped in to reassure him, according to Corby.

"Only helping with enquiries, isn't it? It's not like anyone's going to think you're some kind of psychopath. They'll be talking to all Sam's mates and we was the last ones to see him, weren't we?"

With no time to go back to the office after their visit to the Grays, Georgie suggested coffee and cake at Mr Bun the Baker on Sandford Avenue, just opposite the police station.

"Where's your head going with the whole Sam/Davey thing, then?" Corby asked, tucking into an eclair.

"I'll have a clearer idea when the local team have dug up some info on that name on the grave."

"Colm something ... Doherty, wasn't it?" Corby said, flicking back through her notebook to the record of the calls she had made that morning, waiting in the Land Rover on top of the Mynd. "Died nineteen years ago – so before Sam was even born."

"Not before Davey was, though. Might be a relation. Doherty

and Whelan are both good Irish names. Maybe the families knew each other."

"But Sam's family isn't Irish."

"True," Georgie said, feeling warmth curl down into her belly along with a gulp of coffee. Cell by cell, the sugar from her Chelsea bun and a blast of caffeine was revitalising her. "Like I said, I can't find the connection yet, but my nose is twitching. What was it made Sam and Davey brothers in arms?" She looked at her phone to check the time. "I was hoping we might have time for a trip to All Stretton after our chat with the youngsters but we'll never make it back to Shrewsbury for the team meeting. Have to be tomorrow."

"All Stretton?"

"Sam's car was picked up on that camera by the golf club. If he was going further afield – Shrewsbury for example – why not use the A49?"

Corby swallowed the last of her eclair and wiped a dab of cream from the corner of her mouth.

"Wanted to steer clear of main roads in case he was stopped? He'd been drinking."

"True again. But it also occurred to me that Davey's caravan is up that way. Maybe he was planning to stay there. And there's at least one other person friendly to Sam Gray who lives up Castle Hill." Through the steamy window she saw a familiar figure pass the Mountain Pursuits shop that flanked the police station. The place that Sam Gray had worked. "Someone's early."

Jessie Pritchard reminded Georgie of a young Christine Keeler. Presumably she had consciously adopted that sixties look to stand out in a small town where most people were into their outdoor activities. Now she was wearing an A-line herringbone coat and knee-high black boots, a pale pink scarf knotted around her head.

"Time to go," Georgie said, pushing her chair back and downing the rest of her coffee. Grumbling that Georgie might have finished explaining her theory, however half-formed, Corby stood up too. With a wave and a thank you to the woman behind the counter, they left the warmth of the bakery and headed across the road to the police station.

THEY FOUND Jessie Pritchard in reception, chatting to Bob Carradine who was behind the desk.

"More like being chatted at," Corby said, as she and Georgie headed down the corridor to get the meeting room ready. "She didn't look exactly happy and relaxed, did she?"

"Her boyfriend disappeared a week ago. And now he's dead."

Corby stopped.

"They don't know, do they? None of them. That we've found him, I mean."

"Not unless the Facebook crowd have somehow got it out of the Grays. I wonder if Danny's on social media."

"Bound to be. Probably not Facebook or X though. More like Snapchat or something at his age. And you asked Chelle and Clive to keep it to themselves for a few hours."

The door to one of the offices was open and PC Holton called out to them as they passed.

"I got the room ready for you," she said. "Eight chairs wasn't it? And two for you, of course."

"Thanks, Sharon," Corby said, and Georgie tried to drill it into her mind. Often her only way of remembering names was to construct a story around them. She couldn't think of anything about Sharon apart from a character from *Eastenders* when she was a child. She'd only watched it to annoy her parents. They'd preferred *Take the High Road*. There was a plant in Marianne's garden that she liked, with bright yellow flowers, that she thought was called a rose of Sharon.

"There's a kettle and cups. And I've put some biscuits out."

"That's great, Sharon, thank you," Georgie said. "Any luck with digging up info on the Doherty fella?"

PC Holton stood up behind her desk and came over to the open door. Her uniform was very clean and she smelled faintly of washing powder. Her hair was very clean too, shiny and parted neatly with an immaculate straight line.

"I think I've found him. There was a C. M. Doherty who worked up at the gliding club about twenty years ago. At the south end of the Mynd. An instructor, I think, but no one who works there now remembers him. The manager's going to have a word with some of their older fliers."

"Great. Any connection with the Whelan or Gray families?" Georgie asked.

"Not so far. We have an address on Easthope Road but again it's from twenty years ago so there are unlikely to be neighbours who remember him."

Georgie thanked her again and they went into the meeting room. PC Holton had set eight chairs in a semi-circle with another two facing them.

"Looks like we're about to give a seminar," Georgie said. "I tell you what, if Jessie's here already, why not ask her in? We won't tell her about Sam until everyone's here but we could ask a couple of questions about Sam and Davey's friendship. She seems to have known them better than anyone."

Corby set off for reception and Georgie let her mind free-wheel for a moment. PC Holton's remarks about the unlikeliness of anyone remembering anything twenty years on had reminded her of the enquiries she had offered to make on Marianne and Joe's behalf. Joe was twenty-five. The assault on Marianne had taken place twenty-six years ago. Would anyone remember a group of surfer lads who had spent a summer partying hard in the sand dunes around Braunton Burrows? Maybe they would. Small communities did remember things. Her home on Mull had taught her that. But you had to be in the heart of them to find out.

Marianne hadn't been back to Devon since she had been sent away to the unmarried mothers' home in Worcester when pregnant. She had no idea if her parents were still alive, even. Joe's question had indeed taken the lid off a very sizeable can of worms. Still, Georgie couldn't help seeing it as good thing. Burying her past had not helped Marianne to resolve it. Perhaps the time had come to face those demons once and for all.

The door swung open and Corby came in, followed by Jessie Pritchard. She had unwound the pink scarf from around her head, revealing glossy dark hair held back with a broad Alice band. Her face was pale, eyebrows and lashes accentuated with dark kohl, and she wore a fitted, black dress and a string of pearls around her neck. She looked far too smart to work in a timber yard. Georgie wondered if the black was an indication of mourning.

"I rescued Jessie," Corby said, with her usual smile and easy manner. "Bob's a friend of her dad's. They play golf together."

Georgie smiled, as Jessie rolled her eyes.

"Never understood the appeal of the game, myself. Spoils a good walk, I always think," she said.

"Sam liked it," Jessie said. "He used to play with my dad sometimes."

"How about Davey?" Georgie asked.

"Sometimes. But he got bored. Said it was too slow."

Corby offered Jessie a drink and said she was sure the others wouldn't be long. Jessie thanked her and Corby put the kettle on while the girl hung her coat and scarf on the back of a chair and sat down. She was quiet and self-possessed, seemingly without the need to talk for talk's sake.

"I was hoping you might be able to shed some light on Sam and Davey's friendship, Jessie. Before the others get here. It seems you were the one who knew them best," Georgie said, sitting down opposite her. The girl's smart appearance was making her conscious of her own practical clothes, chosen for maximum warmth and to be worn underneath outdoor gear.

"Davey was like my brother," she said, brown eyes suddenly swimming. "We neither of us had real brothers or sisters. And he spent so much time with us. Especially after his mum died."

"When was that?"

"About ten years ago. And he was round ours a lot before that too. His mum had mental health problems."

"What about his dad?" Georgie asked as Corby handed Jessie a mug of tea.

"Wasn't around," Jessie said, after thanking her. "I don't think he was ever around. Maybe when he was little. I can ask my mum. Davey never had any contact with him far as I know."

"So he and Sam had that in common."

Jessie blew on her tea, then put it on the floor by her handbag.

"How do you mean?"

"As I understand it, Sam didn't know his dad, either."

Jessie considered, her face unreadable.

"He didn't know his real dad. But he had a stepdad. And now there's Clive."

"Did he and Clive get on?" Georgie suddenly noticed her use of the past tense and hoped that Jessie hadn't.

Jessie smiled.

"Yeah. Weirdly." She seemed to think that needed an explanation. "If you've met Clive then ... well, he's not what he seems, that's all. He's kind. Comes over all big man but he's actually quite soft. Sam liked him."

A knock on the door made her sit up and turn her head sharply. Through the wired glass, Georgie saw PC Holton's neat, brown head and behind her several other figures. After a nod from Corby, the door opened and PC Holton stood back to let Jessie's friends through. Georgie hadn't met Seth Glover, Lily Morpeth or Bryn Morgan before but recognised them from Chowdhury and Harley's descriptions. Lily was blonde and petite, holding tight to Bryn's hand. In contrast to her, he was at least six foot two with an athletic build, though one that owed more to the gym, Georgie reckoned, than to the rugby pitch. Mentally she scrolled through her notes. Was he the victor of the first Fight Club round who had then gone on to challenge Lucas Harley? The one who had no doubt caused the bruises that Lucas's mum had seen when he came out of the shower? But no, if she remembered rightly, that had been Seth Glover. He was smaller than any of the other lads, with a wily air, suggesting that if he fought, it might be dirty.

Alisha Johnson strode past them all, going straight to Jessie.

"Where were you, girl? We was all waiting on you."

Jessie shrugged. "I was early."

Was it Georgie's imagination or had she perhaps been avoiding her friends? She watched the group as they helped themselves to hot drinks under Corby's supervision, the boys seesawing between brash, overloud banter and gobbets of awkward silence. Lily said nothing and Alisha, having asked for someone to get her a tea, sat next to Jessie, talking to her in a low voice that Georgie, no matter how she strained, failed to hear.

The group dynamic interested her. Seth and Bryn at the heart of the banter, Alfie joining in nervously as though not sure he belonged. Lily sitting quietly next to the other two girls, but separate somehow. Lucas calmly handed Alisha a cup of tea and didn't seem surprised when he received no thanks. When they were all seated, not far enough from their school-days to avoid reverting to child-like behaviour, Georgie cleared her throat and waited for quiet. The banter petered out, leaving behind a layer of embarrassment tinged with expectation.

"As you know we got you together because further evidence has come to light concerning what happened to Sam."

The group exchanged glances. All except Jessie who stared straight ahead, though Alisha's eyes were boring into the side of her face.

"I'm very sorry to have to tell you," Georgie said, and there must have been something either in her face or voice because Jessie's fists clenched tight and a small sob escaped her.

"Oh no ..."

"We found Sam's body earlier today. It seems he died a few days ago, possibly on Saturday." There had been no forensic evidence yet for this. The pathologist had said time of death was hard enough to determine at the best of times, let alone when a body had been submerged in icy water. Georgie was working purely on when the car had been abandoned and Sam's messages to his friends had stopped.

Murmurs spread throughout the group. Faces blanched while others flushed. Alisha reached for Jessie's hand and the girl let her take it but without any reciprocal clasp, tears brimming from her eyes. Lily buried her head in Bryn's shoulder and he put an arm around her, murmuring into her hair.

"What the fuck?" Seth said, speaking, it seemed, for all of them. "How, man? I mean, where? Where did you find him?"

"Not far from where you last saw him," Georgie said. "On the moorland behind Pole Cottage." There seemed no need to tell them that he had been frozen beneath a sheet of ice. "As I think you already know, we also found a knife and blood-stained clothing belonging to Sam."

"That sergeant told us. And Lucas' uncle," Bryn said. He had a pleasant voice, deep with a Welsh lilt. Corby had taken the chair next to Georgie's facing the group and had her notebook out.

"We're hoping that one of you – or all of you," Georgie said, "will be able to tell us how those items came to be there. And whether there is anything you neglected to mention when you gave statements about Sam's disappearance."

Alfie sat up very tall, his face grey with spots of colour on each cheekbone.

"No way, man. Swear down. I told you the truth. Second time. We all did." He looked to the others, appealing for back-up. No one spoke. Alfie looked at Georgie again and when he spoke his voice was high-pitched and querulous. "Sam drove away – taking Davey to the hospital. Then he called to say Davey had run off. And when he called again he said we all had to keep quiet. He was going to stay with a mate."

"Did he tell you who he was planning to stay with?"

Alfie shook his head and again looked around the group. This time they responded with shakes of the head and muted negatives.

"He didn't tell any of you where he was going?" More head shakes. "And between Wednesday and Saturday when he was messaging your group chat, he didn't tell any of you where he was? Jessie?" she prompted.

The girl was milk pale, trails of black mascara marking her cheeks.

"I don't know where he was," she said, barely above a whisper. "I asked him to tell me but he wouldn't. He said to wait for it all to die down. Or until Davey turned up."

"Do you think he knew Davey was dead?"

The girl dashed a hand across her eyes, smudging the mascara further. Alisha pulled a pack of tissues from her pocket and pushed one into Jessie's hand.

"Of course he didn't," she said, answering for her friend. "What you saying? That Sam killed Davey? No way. Or are you just looking for an easy solution to solve your caseload?"

"Alisha ..." Lucas said.

"What? It would be convenient, wouldn't it? Sam kills Davey and then himself. Everything neatly tied up and Sam not here to defend himself."

Georgie said nothing, letting them play it out between themselves.

Seth pointed out what she did not.

"They found the knife and stuff buried, fam. Not like he could have done that after stabbing himself, is it? Is that how he died?" he added to Georgie.

"It seems so. We've not yet had confirmation."

"So where was he, then?" Alisha glared around the group. "When he was telling us to keep quiet."

No one met her eyes.

"I did wonder," Georgie said, "if he might have gone to someone older. Someone he trusted. Local, maybe." Apart from the odd head shake, no one reacted. When their eyes met another's they looked away hurriedly. "What about his boss at Mountain Pursuits. Tom, is it? Might he have gone to him?"

"Tom's got two young kids," Bryn said. "Like three and five. Sam couldn't have hidden out there."

The atmosphere crackled. Jessie stared straight ahead still, twisting the now damp tissue in her hands. Beside her Alisha seemed to be shooting hard looks at Lucas who looked down at his hands, fiddling with his watch. Someone, Georgie was sure, knew more than they were telling. Aware that she hadn't yet filled Corby in on her hunch, she decided to go with it.

"What about Cal Innes? The guy who runs Time Out." When deliberately blank looks came back at her, she elaborated. "The young offenders programme that both Davey and Sam took part in."

"Guy with the dreads?" Seth asked. "Nah, don't reckon so. Sam thought he was a bit weird."

20

oe was in the workshop behind the Chalet Pavilion helping Ranger Dan transform a fallen tree into a bench, to be placed by the shallow reservoir in New Pool Hollow.

"Weird world we live in," said Ranger Dan, as though a remark of Joe's had led him to conclude so. His enormous hand held a plane, stroking it over the surface of the timber, curled shavings falling to the ground and releasing a scent of green wood.

"What about it?" Joe said.

"Turns out a body being found's good for business. The café's never this busy on a weekday. And in the snow too."

There had been no new falls for twenty-four hours but no sign of a thaw either. Church Stretton had rarely earned its nickname of Little Switzerland so thoroughly.

"Two bodies," Joe said. "That lad from Callow Hollow the other day."

"True enough. Liz had someone asking for the way to where the Gray lad was found along with their coffee. Sent them up the Lightspout waterfall."

"The path's closed isn't it? Because of the ice."

"Ah, well." Dan chuckled to himself. "Get them some exercise at any rate." Liz managed the café and, while she valued the visitors who furnished a good proportion of the Carding Mill Valley's income, had little time for social media tourists. Joe had heard the tale of the TikTok short that had swelled the valley's visitors a couple of years earlier. A video listing the reservoir as one of the top fifty must-see sites in the UK had attracted busloads of tourists whose sole aim was to make content of themselves with the still, green water in the background. "Hey!" someone had shouted at Ranger Dan from a moving vehicle. "Where's your lake? Point us to the lake." Dan had told them to park their car and then sent them in the opposite direction.

Joe finished smoothing the piece he'd been sanding which would make one of the legs of the bench and picked up its twin, setting to work with the sanding block. He enjoyed time in the workshop and Dan's easy company. Dan liked to talk but never minded when Joe didn't and often was as happy whistling between his teeth if Joe was in one of his quiet moods. Today, after an argument with Niamh, he wanted nothing but peace.

She hadn't meant to criticise his mother, he knew, and perhaps had been right to accuse him of being defensive of Marianne. Of course he was. Most of him wished he'd never asked about his biological father. He'd had a perfectly good dad for most of his life. Patrick and Sarah Ingles had given their adopted son the most stable, generous upbringing any child could ask for. And while they'd been older than most of his friends' parents, which had occasionally embarrassed him in his early teens, when, uncharacteristically, he'd cared what his peers thought of him, he'd wanted for nothing, neither material nor emotional. Often, he thought there was a lot to be said for being adopted into a stable, nurturing home. At least you knew you were wanted. That your family had chosen to have you. Not all his friends who lived with their real families had been so lucky. So why did he even need to know his biological father? Niamh had said that one day it would be important to know his genetics. What if he wanted to have kids ever? Wouldn't he want to know what genes he might be transmitting to his child?

Not really, he'd said. He already knew – or suspected, since Marianne hadn't confirmed anything – from information he'd found online, that his biological father had been a rapist. The less he passed on of him the better. He'd talked about it briefly with Effie the night before, after Niamh had gone. She knew Marianne better than most, had welcomed her into her home as a housekeeper when Marianne was fresh out of prison, trusted her and backed her and, she said, never regretted it for a moment.

"I've never known anyone work so hard to make a go of their life," Effie had said. "If Marianne's not telling you, it's for a good reason. I mean a reason that's good for you, not for her. And I can't tell you, because I don't know. Although I would if I could. Things are always best out in the open."

He was so intent on his work, enjoying the hiss of fine grade sandpaper on sleek wood, that he didn't notice the tentative knock on the open workshop door and wouldn't have looked up if Ranger Dan hadn't whistled softly and said, "Visitors for you, I think, young Joseph."

Just outside the tall barn door, a gleam of sunlight caught Beata's white-blond head. Behind her was another shape, taller and stockier, with a shock of brown hair. Joe hadn't seen Alfie Rickard since he'd worked with him at the Shropshire Geoscience Trust, though they'd been in touch on social media, the odd message exchanged. Now Alfie looked nervy and grey, shifting from foot to foot, hands in his pockets.

"Take a break, if you want," Ranger Dan said. "Getting on for lunch. I'll carry on in here for a bit."

Joe thanked him and washed his hands at the sink in the corner before going outside. In the yard, Beata and Alfie stood near the big green tractor hissing at each other in low voices. It sounded very much as though Beata was losing patience.

"All right?" Joe said, and felt the corner of his mouth lift as Beata rolled her eyes.

"Alfie's wetting himself. He thinks Georgie suspects them all."

"I didn't say that," Alfie, said, flushing. "I just said I didn't know how straight to be with her."

"I brought coffee," Beata said. "Just finished my shift. Where can we go that's not freezing?"

She handed Joe a takeaway cup and he suggested the classroom. He knew from Niamh that the week's school trips had been cancelled, more for health and safety reasons than for the two recent deaths on the Mynd, but reckoned it was a good thing, even if the centre would lose much needed income. The last thing anyone wanted was a busload of teenagers with smartphones and social media connections.

"What's up?" Joe said once they were in the classroom, warm thanks to underfloor heating powered by a biomass boiler. He took off his jacket and hat and laid them on one of the tables before sitting on a plastic chair.

"Alfie has something he thinks he should have told Georgie and hasn't," Beata said.

"So, tell her." He liked Alfie but sometimes the lad came across as a few sandwiches short of the full picnic.

"But she already knows I lied once. If I tell her something else she'll think I've been lying about everything."

"You have, haven't you?" Joe said. "Look," he added, as Alfie's face flushed darker. Maybe it was the sudden warmth of the room but he reckoned there was some emotion in there too and he hadn't meant to take the piss out of him. Or not unkindly, anyway. "All DI Fraser wants are the facts. And yeah, she might be a bit pissed off you didn't tell her before but all she'll really be bothered about is if it helps her move things on."

"What about obstructing a police enquiry?" Alfie said. "I searched it up. It's an offence."

"And you're eighteen years old and two of your friends have just died. The whole lot of you are so set on covering your arses that the police can't get on and find what happened to them. Break the mould," Joe said. "Be the big man and tell DI Fraser what's going on. She's not going to charge you if you help her out."

"I told him," Beata said, taking a sip of hot chocolate and wiping cream away from her upper lip. She was sitting on one of the tables, swinging her legs in fur-lined snow boots.

"What's it all about, anyway?" Joe said, curiosity getting the better of his desire not to get involved.

Alfie hesitated.

"Money," he said, after shooting furtive looks at both Joe and Beata, as though they might secretly be recording him. "I heard them arguing. When we was just starting the fire, getting wood and that. Davey said something about when the money came through, then everything would be easy. And Sam got mad and said Davey had better not have told anyone."

"Told anyone what?"

"I dunno. It wasn't just about the money. There was something else. Like, some secret. Davey said he reckoned Sam had told Jessie anyway and Sam said he hadn't but he wouldn't be surprised if she'd guessed. It was some money they were both owed, from someone's will. Davey had been looking into the legal stuff, he said." Alfie rubbed his head and looked up at Joe. "Then they saw I could hear so they started talking about something else. But when they were fighting later and it got vicious, Sam said, 'if I punch you right out, I get it all, man'. And then

Davey said he was the oldest so by rights it should all be for him. And it didn't make sense at the time and I didn't remember it even until yesterday when DI Fraser had us all down the police station."

"So you're OK, then," Joe said. "You didn't lie, you just didn't remember."

"But what if Sam did kill Davey? Because he wanted all the money. Maybe he caught up with him and pushed him over the edge into Callow."

"Maybe he did," Beata said, and it was clear from her tone that she and Alfie had had this conversation several times already. "But it's not like you're going to get Sam into trouble, is it? He's dead. All DI Fraser wants is to find out who killed him. You should just call her now." She looked at Joe, appealing for back-up. Joe had never had any real siblings but Beata felt like a sister to him these days. Now, it was like they'd gained a third and he was being asked to adjudicate between them as the older brother.

"But she's like a DI. And she's busy," Alfie said, in something approaching a whine.

"Oh ffs, Alfie! Then call your mate Lucas's uncle. Or Ali Corby."

"I don't have her number."

"I do," Joe said, intervening quickly before Beata could add to the tally of deaths on the Long Mynd and make it three. "And you'd better call her this afternoon. It might not be important but they need to know as soon as possible. And I'm not going to be the one to tell her. It'll be better coming from you."

21

Georgie hid a yawn as she waited for a few members of the team to be ready. They weren't due to start until nine and, as it was only five to, she was prepared to give them grace, especially since she usually sailed in at one minute to and hit the ground running. This morning though, her eleven o'clock meeting with Pitbull was hanging over her like the charcoal snow clouds gathered beyond the window and she needed a good hour after the briefing to get all her leads together. If the time gods had also allowed her to complete her interview with Cal Innes before she had to face the DCI, she would have been grateful but the man was busy with work and she preferred not to insist he came in until it was convenient. Best not to rattle him too much until she'd got him through the door.

She had been in early that morning and was still feeling the effects of poor sleep. Marianne had been restless, which usually didn't disturb Georgie but, when Marianne had gone downstairs a little after four am, she had found herself annoyingly wakeful. Her brain had been busy, not only with the mystery of what had befallen Sam Gray and Davey Whelan, but also with those five surfer boys and that summer night twenty-six years ago. At six she had got up and, since Marianne was out with the dogs, had downed a quick coffee then headed straight into the office.

With a pressing enquiry underway, she had mixed feelings about pursuing a historic investigation on Marianne's behalf, but a quick half hour trawl through the Police National Database had given her plenty to think about. In the summer of the year two thousand, two girls had reported a sexual assault in the Woolacombe area in a situation that sounded similar to Marianne's. A party in the sand dunes in the small hours of the morning, the girls, fifteen and sixteen, outnumbered five to two by a group of young men in their late teens and early twenties. One of the girls had been sober enough to not only fight off her attacker, but had made enough noise to give her friend's assailant pause for thought and the girls had got away, largely unharmed. A month later, just down the coast at Westward Ho!, a young girl's parents had reported an assault on their daughter at a party on the beach. The girl, however, had refused to co-operate and no charges had been brought.

As the clock had neared seven she had logged out and searched instead for CID contacts in Devon and Cornwall police. To take it any further she would need Marianne to report it officially, but the morning's work had, if nothing else, given her encouragement that there might be an enquiry to pursue. Now, she pointed at the clock as the minute hand lurched towards the hour and waited for her team to settle.

"We have precisely two hours," she said, "to make enough progress to prevent the DCI coming over here and giving us his own peculiar brand of pep talk, so let's get going. Sergeant Carradine, where are we with Colm Doherty and the possible reason for Sam and Davey to be interested in his grave?" Alfie Rickard's call to Corby the afternoon before had reinforced the suspicion in Georgie's mind but, as yet, she had nothing to substantiate it. Maybe Carradine's team would be able to shed some light.

"Died in 2008," Carradine said, stating the bleeding obvious since that was the date on the gravestone, "glider accident. A couple of the older fliers at the gliding club remember him. Apparently he had lung cancer, quite aggressive and no chance of recovery. The feeling at the time was that he went out the way he would have wanted, before the cancer could get him, but suicide was never proven. Coroner recorded an open verdict."

"Family?" Georgie asked.

"Parents and siblings back in Ireland. Not married and no dependants over here. Bit of a player, by all accounts. In his forties but liked his women a bit younger. Charming, good-looking and all the girls love a pilot."

"Ok, good, thank you. We need to explore any possible connection with the Gray and Whelan families. DS Chowdhury, I'd like you to visit Michelle Gray. Take PC Holton with you – if you can fit that around your safer neighbourhood surgery, Sharon." Briefly, she congratulated herself on remembering the PC's name. "You'll need to be sensitive but I want to know if she ever knew Colm Doherty and, if so, what their relationship was."

DS Chowdhury nodded and made a note on his tablet.

"Then I'd like you to visit Sarah Pritchard at the timber yard. She was Sadie Whelan's best friend. Does she know of any acquaintance or friendship between Davey's mum and Colm Doherty? Did Sadie and Chelle know each other? Dig around as much as you can, please."

"Where are we going with this, boss?" Chowdhury asked.

Georgie pulled a face.

"Not going to commit myself just yet, sergeant. Still on the hunch side of things and you know the DCI doesn't approve of that. But the information DC Corby received yesterday from Alfie Rickard," she had shared it at the evening briefing, "got me thinking. We'll know more, I think, when we've spoken to Cal Innes. He should be in at two pm, but ideally I'd like you to have spoken to Michelle Gray and Sarah Pritchard before then."

Chowdhury nodded and Georgie turned to DC Hallam.

"Ben, anything on laptops or phones for us?"

DC Hallam pushed back his hair which flopped over his forehead, despite Chowdhury occasionally suggesting he use a hairband to keep it back. Georgie thought inconsequentially of Jessie Pritchard's Alice band. Hallam exchanged a look with Mike Harley who grinned.

"Ben seems to have solved a bit of petty crime for us, boss," the sergeant said. "You remember that thing with the flags?"

Georgie frowned.

"All those Union Jacks and England flags on the lamp-posts. The roundabouts around Bridgnorth and Telford."

"What about them?" And what possible relevance could they have to the current investigation?

"There were a few nights when a load of them were set on fire. Local stations couldn't work out how. Did someone climb the lamp-posts to torch them and all that?"

Georgie nodded, her memory waking up. She had driven one day via Bridgnorth, taking the Corvedale Road back to Onnyford, and been surprised at the number of posts adorned with flags, though amused that most seemed to be flying at half mast, as though whoever had attached them had run out of strength halfway up. It had made her think of climbing ropes in primary school gym lessons. She had always been good at it but some of her bigger, heavier peers had struggled.

The flags had made her feel depressed, a sign that she and her kind, anyone foreign or a little different were not welcome, and she had been irrationally cheered by a rainbow painted on the back of a road-sign. A little beacon of hope, evidence that not everyone felt that way. It was easy to see the flag-wavers as a majority, when in fact they were just more bullish in spreading their message of exclusivity. Most people she encountered seemed to deplore the climate of intolerance.

"You remember Bob's team found a stash of weapons in Davey Whelan's caravan?" Harley continued. "A couple of knives, small crossbow etc? Well, in the plastic bag with the crossbow bolts there were also some rags and a couple of bottles of lighter fuel."

"Davey filmed himself," DC Hallam said. "Or someone filmed him. I found the videos on his TikTok. Soaked the rags in lighter fluid, attached them to the crossbow bolts, then lit them and fired them at the flags."

"Bloody idiot," Mike Harley said, though not without some admiration. "He could have burned his face off before he managed to shoot them if the wind had got up."

Not for the first time, Georgie wished she could have met Davey Whelan.

"Also found some emails to a Shona Doherty that you might find interesting. Not blackmail as such but mentioning money owed. He seems to have deleted the earlier ones in the thread so I'm not sure who she is but DS Morgan and I are on to tracing them."

Georgie thanked him and nodded towards DS Chowdhury who'd raised his tablet, indicating that he had more to contribute.

"Email from the lab at Birmingham Met, boss. Final post-mortem report on Davey Whelan and preliminary findings on Sam Gray. Thought you might want to go through them before you talk to the DCI."

"Good thinking, Haris. Headlines? If you've had time to read them, of course."

She knew that he would have done. DS Chowdhury was always ahead of the game and where she had once resented what could present as pushiness, she now appreciated his value to her team.

"Sam Gray is largely as expected. He was stabbed; a single wound to the torso which pierced the aorta causing catastrophic bleeding. Likely made with the kitchen knife recovered with his clothing. He had no defensive injuries and so far no DNA recovered from beneath fingernails and so on. Still waiting on a tox screen. Time of death most likely on the Saturday or possibly early hours of Sunday morning."

Georgie nodded. Nothing much of use so far but then she hadn't expected there to be. It was unlikely that anything the pathologist might find could indicate where he had spent his missing four days.

"Final results from Davey Whelan's PM," DS Chowdhury continued, "show that he'd consumed significant quantities of vodka, cocaine and cannabis in the hours before his death. Essentially, he died of a massive heart attack."

Silence echoed in the wake of Chowdhury's words. DC Hallam broke it.

"He was twenty. What's he doing having a heart attack?"

"It happens," Georgie said. "You hear of it sometimes in young, fit people. Sports people, often."

Chowdhury consulted his tablet. "Dr Sinha – pathologist – reckons he had two cardiac events. The first was quite minor but it would explain why he collapsed during the fight when the others all thought he was dead. It's possible his heart did stop and that the CPR revived him, but it might also have done some damage. The second event probably occurred when he was running away from the car. With the amount of drugs and alcohol in his system it would have been like being on rocket fuel and, if his heart was weakened by habitual cocaine use, it might have just given out."

In her mind's eye, Georgie saw a figure with a crossbow at a darkened roundabout, shooting fire at flags that swung in the breeze. A young man who loved to climb and hike, to live in the outdoors. A young man who, by all accounts, had embraced life with gusto. Not murdered. But dead nonetheless. And what about his death had sparked the murder of Sam Gray? Because, where Davey's death might have been by misadventure, someone had knowingly plunged a knife into Sam Gray's chest and dumped him in a moorland bog to lie undiscovered for days.

22

Cal Innes dressed no differently for work, it seemed, than for his days off. He wore the same rainbow bandana around his hair and had swapped his Bob Marley T-shirt for Che Guevara, beneath his blue fleece jacket.

"Thanks for coming in," Georgie said, shaking his hand, the fingers long and cool. Cold, more accurately, but then whose wouldn't be? There had been more snow that morning, nowhere near the weekend's blizzard but in contrast to the previous day's sunshine it was gloomy and chill. Marianne's little menagerie of donkeys and goat was getting fed up, as was their owner. Georgie had spoken to her briefly at lunchtime, catching her in the field as she'd nipped home from work to replenish their hay. It hadn't been the right time to tell her about her morning's enquiries into the Police National Database but perhaps there might be time in the evening if she could persuade Beata to make herself scarce. To be fair, the girl was very sensitive and adored Marianne. If Georgie hinted at a need for time alone with Marianne, she would no doubt find some college work to do in her room.

"I should have asked," Cal said, as he followed her and

Corby along the corridor to the interview room, "should I have a solicitor or something?"

The jauntiness of his loose-limbed walk, habitual, she suspected, was belied by lines of anxiety around his eyes.

"Not unless you think you need one," she said. "This is a voluntary interview and you're free to leave whenever you want to. There's just some background I think you can help us with." Probably not the background he would think she meant but, as far as she was concerned, background that would cast a new light on the whole investigation. She had shared her suspicions with Pitbull earlier and, while he'd been outwardly sceptical, she'd sensed curiosity beneath his scoffing.

Rather than the gentle space to which she had taken Andy Morgan, she led Cal Innes to a formal interview room.

"You'll understand if we record this, Cal?" Georgie asked as he settled himself on one side of the table, opposite her and DC Corby. "Keeps you safe as well as us, makes sure we don't put words in your mouth." Corby had her notebook out, her pen laid neatly on top. Back-up in case the recording equipment failed. Without explicitly trying to intimidate him, Georgie was quite happy to make Cal Innes uncomfortable

"Yeah, sure. Whatever ..." He wiped his upper lip and tightened his bandana.

Georgie sat back in her chair and smiled.

"So, Cal, I called you in because I think it's about time you told us where Sam Gray spent the last few days of his life."

The youth worker's skin was usually the colour of taupe. Now it flooded darker along each cheekbone.

"What do you ...? I mean ..." he stammered. He looked from one to the other. "What makes you think ...?"

"I don't think, Cal. I know. But I'd rather hear it from you. If you make me dig too deep, I'm going to think you have something to hide, aren't I?"

Innes rested his elbows on the table and put his head in his hands.

"Jessie Pritchard's car, driven by Sam Gray," Georgie said, "was caught on camera last Wednesday night passing the golf club in the direction of Castle Hill. Where you live." She held up a hand and ticked each piece of evidence off on her fingers as she spoke. "Sam told his friends he was staying with a friend, somewhere no one would think to look. When we visited your house, there were two toothbrushes in your bathroom, but according to our enquiries, you're single. There was also a sleeping bag on your sofa, and someone had been smoking a considerable amount of weed while playing video games. Sam's mum, when we first saw her, hoped that Sam was with a friend doing exactly that."

"Doesn't mean anything," Cal said, his voice dry, scraping his throat. He coughed to clear it. "That could have been anyone staying over."

His long, fine-boned hands were in his lap, and from the movement of his forearms he seemed to be twisting them.

"I didn't say I had proof, Cal. But I do know that Sam spent his last few days with you. And the fact that you haven't come forward and told us isn't making you look great. Now, you bust a gut searching for that boy on the hill. Way beyond the call of duty. The PolSA said they had to stand you down because you were determined to stay out until he was found. But from my perspective, perhaps that was all misdirection. Maybe you knew where Sam's body was and did your best to lead the search in the wrong direction, deflect our attention until we'd have very little chance of collecting forensic evidence."

"No!" Innes's head shot up and his deep brown eyes glowed gold with intensity. "I would have given anything to find him. I ..." He shook his head and buried it in his hands again.

Georgie waited before speaking, giving time for tension to

build. Or for him to finish what he had started to say. When he only sighed, she said, "Look, Cal, I can get a forensic team over to your house and turn the place over and I am one hundred per cent confident that they'll find that Sam spent time there recently. Why don't you save us all time and money and just tell us what happened? If Sam's death was an accident, then we can help you—"

"I didn't kill him!"

Georgie held out her hands in a gesture of helplessness and sat back again, giving him the floor. Cal Innes sighed and rubbed his hands over his head, pushing back the bandana. When he looked at Georgie his eyes were damp.

"Sam turned up at mine around two that night. Banging on the door. Wild. Off his face – almost hysterical. He said Davey had run off. He thought he might have killed him."

Though the red light on the recording equipment showed it was taking everything down, Corby's pen scratched on her notepad. Innes followed its progress as though hypnotised, then carried on.

"He told me about the Fight Club thing. That the others had started it but when it was his and Davey's turn, they got carried away. He said it was like they both got really dark. Like all the shit that had been going on with them the last couple of weeks kind of swelled up and they were really going at it. Like trying to hurt each other. And then Davey collapsed."

Innes was shaking and his eyes were no longer on Georgie. Their gaze had turned inward, taking him back to his cottage on that dark night, a few days before the snow fell.

"Sam thought he was dead. They all did. One of the lads did CPR until he was breathing again. And they got him in Jessie's car so Sam could drive him to hospital. Sam said that when he came round he was like a lunatic. Superhuman strong. Like he was on something. He got out of the car while it was still moving. Sam went after him – you know, parked up and ran. Said it was like a kind of out of body thing. Watching himself pelting along the road and then off over the hill towards Callow after Davey. All the time wondering what the hell he was doing but like he had no control. Like being in a movie." He looked wildly around and licked his lips, his breath rasping. "Can I have some water?"

Corby got up and fetched a bottle and cup from the bench by the wall. She filled the cup and handed it to the youth worker who drank as though he too had been running over the hill behind Sam and Davey.

"Sam saw him fall. Said it was like his body just stopped in mid-stride, like he'd had an electric shock or something. He was silhouetted against the sky. Like a shadow-puppet. Then he fell. Just keeled over the edge."

Corby stirred in her seat.

"He didn't think to call for help?" she asked. "Davey might have survived the fall."

Cal shook his head.

"He didn't fall that far. Got caught on some bracken. Sam climbed down. He said Davey was definitely dead this time." Silence sat heavily across the table. Then Innes spoke again. "Sam tipped him off the hillside so he wouldn't be seen from the path. Then he went back to the car and drove to mine. He called the others and told them Davey had run off. Told them not to look for him. And if they were questioned, to tell anyone that Davey had never been there. It was just him and the eight of them. He gave them the story of him going off in a strop because of a row with Jessie and told them to stick to it."

"He told you this?" Georgie asked.

"I heard him. He called them – like a group call. He said he was going to lie low for a bit and they mustn't tell anyone what had happened."

"Did he tell them Davey was dead?"

"I don't think so. But later he said to me that in a few days someone would find Davey's body and people would assume he'd been out doing his survivalist thing."

"Which is the line you fed me," Georgie said. "Did you think it was a good plan?"

Innes bit at the skin around his thumbnail, his brow creased in two.

"No. I told him he was crazy. What about his family? They were going to be worried. He and his mum were close, I couldn't believe he ..." He shook his head. "He told me that yeah, his mum would be worried but that he'd wait for things to die down and then let her know he was OK. In a way, he needed her worried or people wouldn't think he was missing. He was planning to go to London for a bit, he said. More likely Birmingham. He still had contacts from when he was doing a bit of dealing."

"It didn't occur to you to go to the police yourself?" Georgie tried to keep the judgement from her voice. "Concealing a death is a serious criminal offence. And you know how much manpower a misper enquiry takes. You work for Search and Rescue."

"He didn't give me any choice," Cal Innes said, at last.

The story came out in chunks, as though the youth worker was dredging it up from deep inside like undigested food. It was not a good idea, he said, if you worked with young offenders, for anyone to know you were gay. Particularly if you worked with vulnerable young men in a mentoring position. It was all too easy to be accused of grooming. He knew. A friend of his had lost his job and been subjected to police harassment when some piece of shit he was trying to help decided to spread rumours about him. Cal couldn't afford to lose his job. It was all he had. It was his life.

"My family are Jehovah's Witnesses," he said, looking

straight at Georgie, his eyes having taken on that intense amber hue again. "Do you know what happens to a gay Jehovah's Witness?"

Georgie could make a guess but shook her head.

"You're shunned. Disowned. Unless you submit to a cure. Conversion therapy. Homosexuality is an abomination. I, because I'm gay, am an abomination. I haven't seen or spoken to my family in ten years. They live seven and a half miles away. In Craven Arms."

Onnyford was only a mile from Craven Arms. Georgie drove through the small town every day, passing the Kingdom Hall of the Jehovah's Witnesses as she neared the A49.

"If I told anyone where Sam was or what had happened, he would tell the police I had sexually assaulted him. That I had groomed him when he was on the programme and had been abusing him ever since. He made it very clear he wasn't joking."

How had it been for Innes, having Sam under his roof? Getting on with his life, going to work, carrying on as normal, knowing that Sam had an axe suspended over his neck. Had it all got too much for him?

"I thought I could persuade him. If I let him stay, maybe I could make him see sense. And then on Saturday afternoon I went to the shop to get some milk. When I came back, he was gone. I looked in the barn where we'd hidden the car. That was gone too."

"He didn't leave you a note or text you? Give you an idea why he'd left?"

Cal shook his head.

"It was nearly dark. I wondered if he'd gone off to meet someone. Jessie maybe. Give her car back. Anyway, he didn't come home. And then Sunday morning when Mike Harley called about the car ..." He chewed at his lip. "I thought we were going to find his body in it. Thought maybe it'd got too much and he'd driven over the edge."

Georgie pressed her fingertips together like the child's game. *Here's the church, here's the steeple.* Innes drained the last of his water and pushed the cup around the table. He seemed to have run out of words.

"So why," Georgie said when she had watched the digits on the recording equipment scroll through a full minute and Cal had still said nothing, "after Sam disappeared didn't you come clean about the fact that he'd been staying with you? When you met us on the Burway on Sunday morning. We could have conducted a proper search using your house as the last known position."

"Because I didn't know he wouldn't turn up, did I? And he might still go through with his threat."

"And after his body was found?"

The plastic cup crumpled under pressure from his fingers and his eyes flared again at Georgie.

"Why d'you think? You were bound to think it was me. I was the last person to see him alive, wasn't I?"

Georgie touched the tip of her steepled fingers to her lips and watched him. He had what she would call an honest face. But she'd also been in the game long enough to know that appearances could be deceptive.

"Not if you didn't kill him, you weren't."

Shortly before the team's evening briefing Georgie received a call to say that Jessie Pritchard was waiting in reception. Descending the stairs from her wing of the building she saw the girl sitting neat and trim on the bold blue seating, not hard plastic like the waiting area in her last London station, but semi-circular sofas made of composite units, too low-backed for anyone to get really comfortable but giving at least an illusion of welcome. Flashes of red and yellow accented the white walls and the whole gave the impression of bright, modern efficiency. It set off to perfection Jessie's black coat and boots, the broad black band holding back her glossy hair.

"Jessie," Georgie said. "You're a long way from home. How did you get here?"

The girl stood up and smiled, her face pale.

"Borrowed my mum's car. I wondered when I can have mine back."

"Not until forensics have finished with it, I'm afraid. And even then we might need to hang onto it. Sadly, it's classed as evidence in a murder investigation. Would you like a cup of tea, or is that all you came for?"

It wasn't, of course. No one in their right mind would drive from Church Stretton to the far side of Shrewsbury in a borrowed car and winter weather when a phone call or email would have done the job just as well.

Jessie said yes to the cup of tea and Georgie took her to the children's interview room where she had talked to Andy Morgan. On the way she sent a message up to the incident room asking for Corby or one of the other officers to join them. "Just in case we need to take some notes," she said. "My memory's not always the best."

"I was hoping to talk to you," Georgie said, once she had fished the teabags out of blue Ikea mugs and added milk to Jessie's and oat milk to hers. "There's something been bothering me about Sam and Davey and I thought you might be able to help."

"Is that why your sergeant came to see my mum today?"

"Did she tell you about it?"

Jessie nodded. She unbuttoned her black coat and pushed it off her shoulders, revealing a pale pink mohair sweater with buttons at the high neck. While very pretty, Georgie thought it would probably make her itch.

"What did she say?" she asked.

"That you wanted to know about someone Davey's mum used to know."

"And is that why you came in?"

The girl's eyes swam with tears and she set her handbag on her knees, busied herself opening the clasp and searching for a tissue. As she pulled one from a plastic travel pack, there was a knock on the door and Ali Corby came in with a matching blue Ikea mug in her hand.

"Ooh good," she said, "I'd just made a cuppa but I didn't want to be rude if you two weren't having one. I brought biscuits." She put a packet of custard creams on the coffee table and sat in one of the squashy armchairs, leaving the sofa to Jessie. Georgie took the other. Folding the tissue, Jessie dabbed carefully beneath the line of her eyelashes so as not to smudge the wet mascara.

"I love your jumper," Corby said. "Gorgeous colour. Where's it from?"

Jessie mentioned a vintage shop in Ludlow and for a few minutes she and Corby discussed the pros and cons of Shrewsbury and Ludlow for clothes shopping. With every sentence, the girl's shoulders dropped a fraction until she helped herself to a biscuit. Georgie judged she was ready to continue with the conversation.

"So, Jessie, what did your mum tell you about this man Davey's mum knew?"

The shoulders went up a centimetre.

"Not much. But I already knew about him," she said, a faint blush staining her smooth cheeks. "Davey told me."

"Would this have been Colm Doherty?"

Jessie nodded and nibbled the corner of her custard cream. Perhaps she needed the comfort of sugar.

"And what had Davey told you?"

Georgie was fairly sure she already knew. With no evidence whatsoever to support her theory, nonetheless it had seeded itself in her mind with the similarities between Davey and Sam's stories, the photos of the two boys lounging in the caravan and those taken beside Colm Doherty's grave.

Jessie took a deep breath before she spoke and squared her shoulders as though bracing herself.

"Davey reckoned Doherty was his dad," Jessie said, her eyes dry now she had steeled herself to be brave. "He found an old diary of his mum's. In stuff my mum had boxed up for him. Some letters and a photo. The diary said his dad was a pilot.

And he worked as an instructor at the gliding club. He was Irish."

Paper crackled as Corby turned to a clean page in her notebook.

"His mum always said his dad was Irish and Davey thought that was why he wasn't around. That he'd gone back there. When other kids at school talked about their dads or we had to make Father's Day cards, Davey always said his dad was in Ireland. But when his mum died, he found out his dad was dead too. There was no name on his birth certificate so he couldn't find anything about his family. His mum had only said his dad's name was Colm – and there are a few of those in Ireland."

"When was this?" Georgie asked.

"When he found the diary? About six months ago. And then about two months ago, he was in Greenhills – you know, the cemetery – and he saw this grave for Colm Doherty. He'd died a year after Davey was born and there was a glider on the gravestone. So it all kind of made sense."

"What was he doing in the cemetery?" Corby asked.

Jessie shrugged.

"He just liked places like that. He said you could find stories on gravestones. He wanted to be a writer. He was writing a graphic novel. About a pilot who could fly between different worlds. It was good."

Her eyes brimmed again and she dabbed the tissue into each corner, soaking up the tears before they could make black rivulets on her cheeks.

"When did he find out about Sam?" Georgie said, hoping to God her hunch was correct. Although if it wasn't, then at least that would stop her haring off after a red herring. The worst that would happen was that she'd look a bit daft. And it was always better to know. "That Colm was Sam's dad too, I mean."

Jessie's head snapped up.

"How did you know? Did Sam's mum tell you?"

"Not yet," Georgie said. "My sergeant went to see her this afternoon."

"So how did you ...? No one knew, Sam said."

"There was a photo on Davey's phone. The two of them together on Davey's bed. Their heads next to each other. Something about their noses. And chins. I just remember thinking, they could be brothers." She remembered too the picture captioned 'My Brother In Arms'. And Sam, pissing on the grave while Davey captured it on film. Two lost boys.

Jessie's eyes seemed to be looking back into her memories.

"I always thought Davey looked like his mum. His blond hair and those big eyes." Her voice wobbled. "I never thought he and Sam looked alike at all."

"Maybe you knew them too well to see it," Georgie said. She waited but Jessie was lost in thought.

"Was that why Davey was arguing with Sam's mum? One of the neighbours told us," she added, when Jessie's eyes swung onto hers. "A full-blown row on the doorstep in the middle of the night."

"Chelle refused to believe Colm Doherty was Davey's dad too. He was her secret love, Sam said. Chelle had always told Sam his dad had been married to someone else and that was why she had to keep it a secret. But that he'd loved her and even left them some money when he died, even though Sam hadn't been born yet. He made a will and they were in it."

"And how did Sam and Davey find out? That they shared a dad."

"I was there," Jessie said. "We were at the Costa in Shrewsbury. We'd been to the cinema. *The Banshees of Inisherin*. There was a character in the film called Colm Doherty. And Sam said that was his dad's name. And Davey said his too. I remember Sam saying what are the chances? There being a character with the same name as either of their dads. Let alone both. It was a while – like a week – before they twigged it was the same man."

"How did they feel about it?" Corby said. "It must have been weird for them."

"They were pleased at first. They thought it was funny. And cool. They were brothers." She smiled sadly. "And then, a bit later, I thought that in a way it made them ... I don't know ... sort of jealous of each other. Like they'd both had this idea of what their dad was like and now they were going to have to share him."

Georgie looked up at the strip of window that ran around the top of the room, designed to let in light but retain privacy. It was getting dark, although whether that was because the sun had gone down or because snow clouds were piling in she wasn't sure.

"When they had their fight, up at Pole Cottage," she said, "someone heard them arguing about money. One of them said, 'I could just kill you now and then I get it all'. Was that about their dad?"

Jessie blinked.

"I don't know. Davey's mum reckoned Doherty's family was quite rich. Chelle told Sam she only got a bit and the rest of his money had gone back to his folks. Davey reckoned he and Sam had a claim on it. They were going to try to trace their grandparents in Ireland, or uncles and aunts if the grandparents had died."

Brothers in arms. United for a short while with a new-found kinship and a common goal. And now both were dead.

"Jessie, did anyone else in the group know about this? Seth or Lucas maybe?" According to Alfie, those two boys had been closer to Sam than any of the others, Davey and Jessie excepted.

The girl shook her head, pushing her Alice band a little further back from her forehead.

"I don't think so. No one's ever said anything. Seth didn't like Davey much so I don't think Sam would have told him. And Lucas and Sam didn't hang around that often anymore."

"And no one else took Sam or Davey on in the Fight Club game?"

"Seth wanted to. It was meant to be him and Sam after Seth and Lucas had a go but Seth said he was too pissed by then." She smiled. "And there's no way Lucas would have done. He only had a go with Seth to impress Alisha. He's been mad about her since school but she's never going to look at anyone local. She's got her eyes on London."

Sam had planned to go to London too, according to Cal Innes. Had that been a plan he'd made with Alisha? His stepdad might have said the only girl Sam cared about was Jessie but how often were men privy to their stepson's love lives and daydreams? Davey had been mad about Alisha too, according to Alfie. Had a fight that started as a game turned sour over their claims to an imaginary inheritance from their shared father? Or had it all been simpler, as it had first been presented? A fight over a girl. Georgie sighed. None of these musings took her any closer to who had killed Sam Gray.

ONE GOOD THING about the team's exhaustion levels was that everyone was one hundred per cent focussed on getting through the evening briefing efficiently so they could head home. A few flurries of snow had fallen since the morning but nothing too heavy, and by and large the main roads were clear. The gritters were out in force though, expecting another heavy frost overnight. Weather bulletins flashed statistics about the longest cold snap in early December since records began and, on the local news, Georgie heard the story of the Reverend Carr who'd lost his boots on the Mynd when he'd been stranded in a blizzard.

Chowdhury, who had visited Chelle Gray and Sarah Pritchard with PC Holton, kicked off the meeting. Their interviews had yielded little more, if even as much, as Jessie Pritchard's. Chelle had begun defensive. Why the bloody hell should she have told them about the doorstep row with Davey Whelan when he was talking bollocks? *He was a fantasist that boy, you couldn't believe a word he said. And he dragged my Sam into his stupid games.* Sarah Pritchard, while outwardly co-operative, had been unwilling either to besmirch her old friend's reputation or to unwittingly incriminate Davey. Neither could see how the boys' relationship to Colm Doherty could have had anything to do with their deaths, especially given that Doherty himself had been dead since Sam was a baby. Both Chelle Gray and Sadie Whelan had believed Doherty to be married, with a wife back in Ireland. Neither seemed to resent his being unwilling to settle down with them, especially as he had been generous with them while alive.

"He never pretended to be anything he wasn't," Chelle Gray had said. "I went into it with my eyes open and having Sam was the greatest blessing I could have asked for. Honestly. I never regretted it for a second."

When Chowdhury had finished his report, Georgie fed back her interviews with Cal Innes and Jessie Pritchard.

"Which leaves us with more rather than less in terms of lines of enquiry," she added. "We'll need to check Innes's account of his movements on Saturday, see if we can corroborate the time of his trip to the shops. In the evening he claims to have been out with Tom Edwards from Mountain Pursuits and a couple of other friends so we'll need to check that. Maybe you could do that tomorrow, Mike. And find out what kind of mood he was in. If anyone noticed anything odd about his demeanour."

The sergeant nodded and made a note.

"One other thing, boss," he said, just as Georgie was planning to draw the meeting to a close. "While you were in with Jessie Pritchard, Annemarie Glover came in." Georgie raised an eyebrow and he continued. "Seth Glover's mum."

Bob Carradine laughed darkly and, when several eyes turned on him, said, "You don't want to get into a fight with her. Her fella's all right. Owns the garage down at Newington. Quiet man. But Annemarie. Hellcat. Could start a fight in an empty room."

"Well, she was true to form here, then," Harley said. "Fuming that her son's being treated as a suspect and says it's having a massive impact on his mental health. Asking me what the hell we're doing and why we haven't got to the bottom of it yet. According to her, it's clear as the nose on her face that the two lads killed each other and we're just too stupid to have worked it out. I think she called the police collectively 'thick as mince'."

"Interesting," Georgie said.

"So how does she reckon Davey Whelan stabbed and buried Sam Gray when he'd already been dead for three days?" DC Hallam asked.

Harley grinned.

"We didn't get into the specifics. I just told her that new evidence was coming to light and we hoped to have an answer for her soon. In the meantime, her son's been a great help and we're taking the mental health of all these young people very seriously."

"OK, great, thanks Mike." Georgie sent a smile around the room which warmed as she took in their faces, eyes ringed with charcoal shadows and heavy with fatigue. "Now if there's nothing else, let's get off home. Bright and early tomorrow, eh?"

They left in dribs and drabs with hopes of a thaw. The snow, which, Georgie observed, always brought a feeling of excitement when it first appeared, had lost its magic and was now nothing more than a nuisance. She had always thought snow best enjoyed on a holiday, preferably in an Alpine resort with nothing to do but ski. UK infrastructure wasn't set up to deal with it and all it did was add a layer of complication to life and work. As she gathered her things, her phone buzzed and she saw Marianne's name flash on the screen with a short message telling her that she was going to Effie's for supper and asking Georgie to join her there. Joe had asked them to come, apparently.

Wondering if Niamh would be there too, and how Marianne would feel about it if she was, Georgie replied with a thumbs up. In all honesty she would have preferred to head home to a bottle of cider, tea in front of the fire and a hot bath, but maybe she could have all those things afterwards. With her own family hundreds of miles away on the Isle of Mull, Marianne's surrogate family of Effie and Joe were dear to her and she reckoned a bit of effort was merited. Besides Effie was a mine of information on the Stretton area and had lived there for the past fifty years. It wasn't beyond the bounds of belief that she might remember Colm Doherty. Her husband, if Georgie remembered rightly, had been a member of the gliding club.

It was only when she headed for the door that she realised the incident room wasn't empty. Mike Harley was waiting for her.

"I don't want to hold you up, boss, but can I have a quick word?"

"Of course." She sat on the edge of a desk, her bag over her shoulder. "Everything ok?" His face, always so easy to read, said not.

"It's just ... well, Annemarie Glover's not the only one losing sleep over her son's mental health."

"You're worried about Lucas?"

"Suse, my sister-in-law, is. And Terry – my brother. Say he's gone all withdrawn. Depressed. And it's not like him. He's always been an equable lad. Takes everything in his stride."

Georgie resisted the temptation to say, well, what do they expect? Two of his friends have turned up dead and he's been up to his neck in the cover-up. Instead she smiled as gently as her impatience to be finished with the day's work would allow.

"It's not surprising these lads are finding it hard to cope. What are they ... eighteen? Nineteen? It's a lot to deal with. Losing two of your friends in a week is bound to affect anyone."

Mike gave a half smile. Georgie suspected that he had given his all, reassuring his brother and sister-in-law that their son would be all right. Now, he needed to hear the same from her.

"I don't think Lucas liked Davey much," he said. "Thought he was a bit wild. But I suppose if someone your own age dies it makes you aware of your own mortality. And maybe not liking him is making him feel guilty. Sam was a good mate, though, especially when they were younger. Besties at primary school. It was only when Sam went off the rails they drifted a bit."

"Why don't you have a chat with him? Informally. He might open up to you in a way he can't to his parents." And give us some more information without meaning to. She still reckoned at least one of those kids hadn't told everything they knew.

Outside, darkness had settled over the car park, the orange glow of lamps casting pools of warmth onto the tarmac, blackly clear of snow where it had been gritted. Georgie watched Mike to his car and waved before getting into her Land Rover. Her mind drifted to what Jessie Pritchard had said about Lucas only playing the fight game to impress Alisha.

She hadn't given much thought to Alisha Johnson since she and Corby had gone to see her at work. Now, she had a fleeting image of the girl with her dangerous beauty, so self-possessed that even two CID officers turning up at her place of work didn't throw her from her usual cool. Too big for the local area, her sights set on the bright lights of London. What if Sam had somehow got in the way of her plans? Sam had left Cal Innes's remote house suddenly and without explanation. What if he'd had a call from Alisha and had gone to meet her? She might have been the only one with enough power to tempt him from his sanctuary. Jessie had said her requests to meet him had fallen on deaf ears.

Sam's phone hadn't turned up either in Jessie's car or on his body. And, although a request had been made to his service provider to furnish his phone records, nothing had come through so far. Before starting the engine, Georgie sent a message to DC Hallam, asking him to put pressure on them first thing. They needed to know who he had called and when. Or, perhaps, more importantly, who had called him. Something had tempted him away from Cal Innes's place. When they found that, Georgie reckoned, they would know what had happened to Sam.

24

Even here, there was no escape from Georgie's investigation. Marianne had hoped that, at least over dinner, they might talk of other things, but Effie loved to reminisce about her late husband and it turned out that the Irishman Georgie had asked after had been a good friend.

"Oh, he was a hoot," Effie said, bringing a dish of apple crumble to the table, waving away Marianne's offer of help. Aware that Marianne spent her days waiting on others, Effie insisted that at her house, she should be waited on. It made Marianne uncomfortable which, Effie always said, was all the more reason it should happen.

"A good twenty years younger than my George, of course," she went on, breathing a little hard and wincing as she sat, her hip giving her pain, "but they got on like a house on fire. He came to the manor for dinner several times; Sunday lunch, the odd party." She launched into a story of how Colm Doherty had arrived unannounced one evening, three sheets to the wind and a woman on each arm, insisting that they had invited him to dinner. He had mistaken the day, of course, but not only had he rustled up a meal for everyone from the contents of Effie's fridge, he had called on friends to swell their numbers, most of whom had brought champagne. It turned out later that had been a condition on which they had been invited, then they entertained everyone with an evening of songs around the piano.

"There was nothing he couldn't turn his hand to," Effie said. "And what a voice – could sing the birds right out of the trees. A horseman, too," she added, in Marianne's direction, perhaps sensing her reluctance to discuss Colm Doherty and hoping that revelation of an affinity with animals might soften her. "He organised a gymkhana on our land once, for the local kids. Turned into a sort of village fête, everyone turning out, stalls and a tombola, the works." She sighed. "And then it turned out he was ill. Cancer. Such a shock. 'Live fast, die young', he used to say. No one was surprised when his glider came down. How he would have wanted to go."

She served large spoonfuls into four bowls and pushed them across the table, pointing out a jug of thick cream and telling them to help themselves. Marianne couldn't abide cream and watched as Joe poured a stream onto his own dessert, winking at her when he caught the expression on her face. She smiled. At least she got to spend the evening with her son and, so far, there had been no mention of the skeleton in the closet that had rattled between them the past week or so. And no Niamh, who was out with college friends.

"So was this Doherty fellow ever married?" Georgie said, taking the jug when Joe had finished and helping herself.

"Not a bit of it," Effie said. "Not the settling down kind. Though he put it about that he was. Even wore a ring. His way of keeping the girls from getting too serious." She took a spoonful of crumble, chewing and swallowing before going on. "He loved women. In the same way that some men love wine or cars. But no staying power. It was all about the hunt, I think."

"Were there ever any rumours of ..." Georgie hesitated and

Marianne wondered what was coming, "complications, shall we say? With local women. Unexpected pregnancies, for example."

Effie's brow wrinkled.

"I do remember one, I think." She sipped her wine. "Colm was a Catholic. Or perhaps that was just an excuse. Whatever the reason, he didn't see contraception as his responsibility. As far as he was concerned, it was up to the women. And when this woman fell pregnant, well, there was no way he was going to marry her. He looked out for her, I think, provided for the child. I don't remember there being any trouble about it."

Marianne wondered what part Colm Doherty was playing in Georgie's investigation into the deaths of these two young lads.

"We're trying to trace his family," Georgie said, "but not having much luck so far. I don't suppose your George would have had an address in Ireland for him?"

As she dabbed cream from her lips, Effie's brow wrinkled again.

"I think George visited when he was in Ireland. Not long after Colm died. A condolence visit since he was there anyway," she said. "But I don't know about an address. Kildare, I think it was. His family were horse-people. Owned a stud over there, as far as I remember." She promised to look for her husband's old address book the following day and see what she could turn up. So far, she had shown a remarkable lack of curiosity for why Georgie might be interested in her husband's old friend and now asked, only to be met with a rueful smile.

"All I can tell you is that his name's cropped up and the more I can find out about him the better. You don't know if any of his relatives have ever come over here? Settled here, maybe."

Effie shook her head. "Not as far as I know. It's not that common a name, though. I'd have thought you could look them up on the electoral role or whatever."

That, Georgie said, had occurred to them. The local team was on it.

"You don't know who Shona Doherty might have been? Mother or sister?"

Effie had never heard of her. Georgie sighed and thanked her anyway. She and her team would just have to do some more digging.

"And how's the boy's mother?" Effie asked. "I saw some terrible stuff on the news. All the things people have been saying on those websites. And camping outside her house. No respect, if you ask me."

Desperate to be away from the topic, Marianne collected the empty bowls and took them to the sink, offering to make coffee.

"And I'm doing the washing up too," she said to Effie, "so don't go arguing with me. I saw your face when you sat down. Have you been to the doctor about that hip yet?"

"Appointment next week," Effie said, with something like triumph in her voice that Marianne had not been able to catch her out. "And I know what they'll say. Old age and I need a replacement."

"Sooner you get on the waiting list the better, then," Marianne said. She suggested that she and Georgie should go through to the living room where Effie could sit with her feet up and she and Joe would wash up while she made coffee.

"You don't mind helping me?" she asked as he cleared the table, taking a cloth from by the sink to wipe it.

"Course not. Gives us a break from Colm Doherty. What's that all about, anyway?"

Marianne shrugged. "No idea. You know she doesn't tell me details of cases." She turned on the hot tap, water streaming into the deep porcelain sink. "How are things at work? Any more true crime tourists?"

Joe sighed and shook his head, in despair rather than as a negative.

"Crazy," he said. "Ranger Dan and I put that Heras fencing round the whole enclosure today. And the pond. I'd locked the gate and taped off the shelter the day Niamh and I found the knife but they've been climbing in. Wanting to take selfies and that." He grinned. "Some dickhead got stuck driving up from Ratlinghope today. Thought they could get up in a Nissan Micra in the snow. Put a stop to anyone else coming up by car anyway and we've got that section of the Burway closed off. Plowden route's still OK but there's too much snow still for the rest of it."

Too much snow and no sign of a thaw. When it did come there would be floods; the Onny, Severn and Teme were already running at full capacity. Surrounded by snow, Marianne found it hard to imagine that it would not stay for the rest of winter. It suited the landscape. Would there be a white Christmas? For her animals' sake, she hoped not, though there was no doubt it was beautiful.

"Ma," Joe said as she put the last plate on the rack and he picked it up, tea towel in hand. His tone had changed, the skeleton rattling its chains. "I know you probably don't want to talk about it but I've been thinking."

She should ask about what, but the words wouldn't come. Instead she focussed on the movement of the brush in the water as she swirled it around the inside of a pan.

"I know if you could tell me, you would. And maybe you're trying to protect me. Or you think it would be bad for me to know what happened."

So far, at least, he was right. She rinsed the pan under the tap, took another from the draining board.

"So I just wanted to say that you don't have to. I mean, I don't need to know." He half laughed. "I mean, it's not like I'm planning to have kids soon or anything so the genetics don't matter."

Marianne tried to smile, feeling his eyes on her, but a lump was swelling in her throat, hard and uncomfortable. Whatever happened, she mustn't cry. He didn't need that. Her hands arrested in the water, her eyes fixed on the yellow rubber gloves. Dimly, she was aware of Joe hanging up his tea towel. He picked up the kettle and came closer, moving the tap across to the drainer sink so he could fill it without disturbing her washing up.

"I just wondered though, if it might be good for you to talk about what happened," he said, then. "To someone else if you don't want to talk to me. Like a therapist, or something. Or maybe you have already."

Marianne's tongue was stuck to the roof of her mouth, tamped down sobs choking her. Though she squeezed her eyelids tight shut, rebellious tears oozed beneath them and trickled wet on her cheeks. Metal bumped softly on wood as Joe put the kettle down.

"Ma," he said, and she felt his arms close around her, moving her gently away from the sink and pulling her against his chest. He was warm and solid, his heart beating a calming tattoo beneath her ear. "Come on," he said. "It's OK. We're in it together. You and me. No one else's business. Unless you want it to be."

She stayed in that warmth and comfort for a moment until the closeness became too much and pushed herself away on the pretext of needing a tissue. Then she wiped her eyes and blew her nose, focussing on her breath until it became slow and rhythmic. Joe watched her but didn't speak or come closer, knowing her well enough by now to understand that for her, physical contact could be overwhelming.

"I can't tell you ... who he was ... because I don't know," she said, at last. "I've been talking about it to Georgie. She thinks she might be able to find out whether there were any other ..." Her words stopped abruptly. In her confusion, she had almost lost sight of the fact that Joe was ignorant, not only of his father's identity, but the whole story. That he had no idea that there was more than one contender for his paternity. "From police records," she said. "But it seems I'd have to make a formal complaint, register it officially. And it was a long time ago."

She was telling him in the only way she knew how. Without explicitly saying, *your father was a rapist.*

"Twenty-six years," he said and she nodded, twisting the tissue between her hands. She breathed deeply and squared her shoulders, standing up a little straighter. The cloth Joe had used to clean the table lay by the sink and she picked it up, rinsed it under the hot tap to wipe down the draining board.

"Still worth doing," Joe said. He took mugs down from the cupboard. "Not for me. I don't give a shit who he was. But for you. If you want to. Justice or whatever."

How would he have felt if his father had been a man like Colm Doherty? She remembered Georgie's question about unexpected pregnancies. Had Doherty left behind children who, like Joe, didn't know who their father was? Doubtless many of the women who had been swept along by him had believed that he would be different for them. That they would be the one to change him, to make him want to settle down. Even if they had believed he had a wife back in Ireland, they would still have wanted to win him for themselves.

She thought of herself at fifteen, so sure that her surfer boy loved her as she had loved him. She had believed it not because of any outward sign that he gave but because it was what she had wanted to believe. Of course, what she had felt for him hadn't been love but a need to escape, infatuation fuelled by a diet of the trashy romance novels her parents had banned, where love was always the answer. Then she thought of Susanne Morris, director of the Geoscience Trust, an accomplished, respected scientist, beautiful and clever, who had spent twenty years sure that, one day, Dr Neil Traynor would realise, after all the hundreds of women with whom he'd dallied, that she was the true love of his life. Until he had died. Perhaps some women needed to love a man who demonstrated consistently that he would never be constant. Some inbuilt yearning for the unobtainable.

Joe was making coffee and the smell pierced her thoughts, reminding her as always of Georgie. What she felt for Georgie was love. And, in a different way, what she felt for Effie and Joe. Completely different from her feelings for the surfer who had let his mates have their way with her once he was done, and left her bruised and bleeding in the sand dunes.

"I know you lived in Devon then," Joe said, turning away from the coffee and leaning against the counter, still giving her plenty of space. "If you wanted to go to the police there, I could go with you. I know you probably wouldn't want to stay with ... with Mum and Dad. But we could find somewhere nearby for you and Georgie to stay."

She wondered for how long he had been thinking this. How long ago he had guessed how he had been conceived.

"Thank you," she said. "But I don't think it's your responsibility to babysit me."

He raised his eyebrows, a silent rebuke for her defensiveness.

"It wouldn't be," he said. "I'd be doing it because I wanted to. Because you'd do the same for me if I needed it. Because you're my ma."

His phone buzzed in the pocket of his jeans and he frowned as he tugged it free.

"Niamh," he said, swiping the screen. "She's out in Shrewsbury."

Marianne was almost grateful to the girl for interrupting a

moment so fraught with emotion that she might have imploded under the pressure.

Joe was still frowning as he read the text.

"Weird," he said. "She met some girl who was slagging off Georgie. Well, the police in general I think, but mentioned Georgie. Called her a policeman in a skirt. Says she knew Sam Gray and Davey Whelan and that the police have fu ..." he stopped himself, "messed everything up. Name's Alisha."

25

By Friday, Georgie felt the investigation was flagging. There was always an element of that, she supposed; the first few days a flurry of urgent activity, new lead after new lead, falling over themselves. But when all those leads led nowhere a mild gloom set in. Where do you go when you have followed everything up and there remains only a murky sense of nothingness?

Pitbull had descended on Shrewsbury for the morning briefing, bringing his peculiar brand of no-nonsense motivational speak, which roughly equated to 'pull your fingers out and get this sorted or we'll all be relegated to traffic by Christmas.'

When Georgie had first met the DCI, he had been a battered hulk of a man, thirty-eight days into his second AA journey, and a hefty chain-smoker. Now, still sober, he was down to about fifteen stone and most of that was muscle. He'd taken up veteran's rugby and half marathons and Georgie was relieved that he still vaped. Without one vice he'd have been unbearable. Fit and slimmed down though he was he still carried his old persona, clothes crumpled, tie stained with coffee and shirttails escaping from his waistband, though his buttons no longer strained over his belly.

"Get the thumbscrews on Innes," he said to Georgie as he was leaving. "And put some pressure on those kids. I don't care if that mum's been in bellyaching," he added, before Georgie could say anything. "They might be a bunch of snowflakes but it's odds on one of them knows more than they're telling. Kids lie, don't they? I know I did."

It was true, she supposed. She had spent much of her young life lying and had considered it the only way to keep herself safe. Telling the truth would have involved not only breaking her parents' hearts but exposing herself to ridicule and probable shunning, much as Cal Innes had described from his community. Inclusive as it was now, rural Mull might have struggled to accept her as Georgie rather than Gregory back in the early 2000s.

Pitbull jangled his car keys as he pulled open the door.

"Harley's lad's your best bet, I reckon. Lean on him a bit. He's not going to want to cause shit for his uncle. Get him to talk and that's your way in."

Georgie wasn't sure the Pitbull was right in that respect. While she agreed that one or other of the group knew more than they were letting on, it didn't follow that all of them did. Someone might be guarding a secret closely and no amount of leaning on Lucas Harley could get him to reveal something he didn't know.

"Problem, boss," DCI Corby said as Georgie went back to her desk. She raised an eyebrow and the constable went on. "Twitter. Or X, I suppose I should call it. Probably best if you come and look for yourself."

Corby had the app open at the Friends of Sam Gray account, for which she'd taken responsibility for daily monitoring. On the day the lad had been found, it had been decked with black mourning flags. This morning, it sported a new border of Union Jacks and England St George crosses.

"This post," Corby said, pointing at a photo which clearly showed Georgie. It had been taken outside Chelle Gray's house on their first visit. She was wearing her hi-vis police jacket, her face red and pinched with cold.

Whose idea, the post said, *was it to put a freak in charge of this? We've lost our golden boy and all we get is some trans *woman* who was kicked out by the Met because he couldn't make the grade. #TransWomenAreMen #IStandWithJKRowling #ProtectThe Children #BiologicalMale*

"Nice," Georgie said, noting the account that had posted it. *TruMum @EnglandfortheEnglish*. "But not unexpected. With all the social media interest since Sam went missing they were bound to get onto me. Far as I'm concerned, it's a distraction we don't need."

"Shall I get Hallam to investigate the account?"

"Keep an eye on it but I don't think it should be a priority. It's not like it'll get in the way of our investigation."

"Unless Sam's mum gets on the bandwagon," Corby said. "If she starts badmouthing you that could cause trouble."

"I don't know. Pitbull's already had to pull one DI off the case. He might dig his heels in if she tries it again. Besides, we're making good progress." Say it often enough and it might become true.

Georgie thought of the text that Niamh had sent Joe while they'd been at Effie's the night before. She had been in charge of the case for five days. Now, within less than twenty-four hours of each other, two more people were raising the gender angle. Coincidence? Mind you, she hardly thought Alisha Johnson would be on X as TruMum, if she was on X at all. From what she knew of it, which wasn't much, it wasn't the kind of platform young people bothered with.

However blasé a face she presented to Corby, the post lowered her already flat mood and she wished the work day was nearing its end, that she could drive home and take the dogs for a walk by the river with Marianne. Even without the dogs and the river, just being with Marianne would soothe her. As she sat back down at her desk, steeling herself to go through the transcripts of the youngsters' interviews again in case they'd missed something, her phone buzzed against her thigh.

A text from Marianne, the first part of which showed on her lock screen.

Hey love, was just thinking how tired you... Georgie felt her shoulders drop. Without realising, she had been anticipating something to do with Marianne's conversation with Joe the night before, her tentative intention to face up to her past. She swiped across the screen to read the rest of the message. *Hey love, was thinking how tired you looked this morning so wanted to send some love and hugs to get you through the day. Pip, Mags and I all looking forward to a walk with you later and it's FRIDAY!!! B's out so we can have the place to ourselves xx*

Warmth bubbled through her, beginning at her heart and stealing through every blood vessel. Marianne often still found it difficult to be physically communicative and, though Georgie never blamed her, she sometimes felt that her love for Marianne was greater than vice versa. Gradually, though, Marianne was losing her tight-held reserve, more able to trust that verbal affection would be gratefully received. Only an actual physical hug in place of the proffered text-based one could have warmed her more.

"Boss?" Chowdhury's voice broke in and she was aware of the smile that had spread across her face. "Just found an interesting voicemail. Left about two a.m. Think you should have a listen."

Georgie took the handset that he held out to her and pressed the pause button which flashed red and imperious. She heard first a scuffling noise, as though a hand was covering the receiver, then breathing, fast and laboured.

"It's about Cal Innes," a male voice said, low and muffled. "He left the Yew Tree at eight forty-five on Saturday night not ten-thirty like he said. Just thought you should know." The message ended as though the caller had dropped the receiver like a hot potato. Georgie pressed the button and listened again. And again. She looked up to find Chowdhury still next to her.

"OK, thanks, Haris. How are you getting on with tracking down the Dohertys of Kildare?" She half listened as he updated her, in a little more detail than had been shared with the DCI at the briefing, all the while gathering car keys and phone. "Great, well keep pushing on the sister. She's not Shona, is she?"

Chowdhury shook his head. "Maeve."

"Well, get the local Gardaí onto it, if needs be. We need to speak to one of the family today, if possible." She looked around for Corby who was just heading for the printer in the corner. "All. With me. We're off out for a bit."

GEORGIE DROVE fast towards Church Stretton, her mind spinning in several directions at once. Beside her, Corby sat placidly looking out at the snow-covered verges, made grubby by dirt and engine fumes. Another of her valuable attributes. Whatever curiosity lurked beneath her calm surface, she knew Georgie would share her thoughts when ready. Quizzing her would only irritate.

Every space in the small police station car park was full but there was a space on Sandford Avenue just opposite Mountain Pursuits. Georgie crammed the Land Rover into it, clearly annoying an elderly lady in the Peugeot behind who had also been indicating.

"Couldn't we have parked on the yellows, boss?" Corby said as they got out and the Peugeot juddered off towards the Pay and Display car park. "She probably only wanted the Post Office."

"No one's above the law, Corby," Georgie said, with a lightness she didn't feel.

An old-fashioned bell rang above the door of Mountain Pursuits as they pushed it open. The shop had a scent very familiar to Georgie after her years of climbing and mountain walking, though she couldn't quite pin it down. A touch of oil, leather and Gore-tex, if Gore-tex even had a smell. Damp too. Though the pavements were relatively clear of snow and ice, there were wet patches on the black rubber mat just inside the door and both officers stamped their feet to shake off any traces of slush.

It wasn't only the bell that was old-fashioned. Compared to the large outdoor and camping stores with which Georgie was familiar, Mountain Pursuits retained the feeling of a pre-superstore era, perhaps owing to its size. Every available area of wall was filled with shelves or hung with equipment, every inch of floor space occupied with cabinets, hanging rails and stacks of boxes. There really was no room to swing the proverbial cat, despite a noticeable lack of customers.

Georgie moved towards a counter, its glass front showing a display of Swiss Army knives and Leatherman tools. A door behind it opened and a man stepped out of what was presumably an office. He had dense, curly nut-brown hair and a ruddy face which became even ruddier when he took in a pair of police jackets. Georgie noted the blush with interest and congratulated herself on her voice recognition skills. If she hadn't listened to the original team's recording of the man's first interview, she'd never have identified the mystery caller.

"Tom Edwards?" she said, holding up her warrant card as Corby did the same. "DI Georgie Fraser and DC Alison Corby. I understand you left a message on our incident room voicemail last night."

The blush deepened to an angry crimson. Bluster would perhaps best have described how the man answered, words tripping over each other, until Georgie interrupted.

"Please, Mr Edwards, it's fine. We're very glad you got in touch. And everything we talk about today is absolutely confidential." Unless it later had to be used in court, she omitted to add. No point alarming the man. "Is there somewhere private we can have a quick chat?"

Tom Edwards looked over his shoulder towards a steep staircase that curved upwards from the corner of the shop. Beside it, a large arrow promised a huge selection of tents and camping accessories upstairs.

"In here?" he suggested, gesturing behind him to the office. "I'll call the lad down. He's new but it's quiet enough."

Georgie didn't make out the name that he called up the stairs, her attention caught by a pair of Pyrenees waterproof hiking boots. Her old pair, at least ten years old, had developed a leak but she'd been wary of buying replacements online. Now wasn't the time of course but good to know he stocked them.

"Boss," Corby said in a low voice as boots clattered down the stairs. Georgie looked up to see Seth Glover slope into the room, squaring his shoulders as though in readiness for combat. She had a mental image of the Fight Club on top of the Long Mynd, the swagger with which Glover would have confronted his opponents.

"It's all right, Seth," she said, with a smile. The last thing they needed was his mum shouting harassment. "We're not here for you. Just need a quick word with Mr Edwards."

"How long have you been working here?" Corby asked and the boy's mouth curled in something like a sneer.

"What's it to you?"

"Hey!" Edwards said. "You're still on trial and you'll be polite to customers whoever they are. I had to advertise the job when Sam went missing," he added. "I've been short-staffed for a while and we have quite a big online business, even when it's quiet in the shop. There'd still have been a job for Sam if he'd come back."

Seth Glover turned to the counter, muttering something about them not even being customers. Tom Edwards brought him up sharply.

"Everyone," he said, stressing the word, "in this town, everyone who comes into the shop is a potential customer."

"I really might be," Georgie said, tapping the boots. "Another day, though. Can't do my shopping on police time. Shall we?" she added, gesturing to the office.

It was part office, part store-room, the walls lined with cardboard boxes which surrounded an old wooden desk that groaned beneath stacks of papers and a boxy computer. In one corner was a photocopier and printer and against the far wall a table bearing rolls of bubble wrap, brown paper and parcel tape. Edwards took the desk chair, offering a plastic chair to Georgie, and Corby pushed aside some bubble wrap to perch on the edge of the table.

"So," Georgie said. "What made you decide to leave the message?"

Tom Edwards looked at them with something close to despair then shook his head and glanced towards the window which was opaque and reinforced with wire. Georgie waited, giving him time to get his words together.

"Look," he said, at last. "Cal Innes is just about my best friend in the world. I'd do anything for him. We've known each other since we were kids. So when he asked me to tell you lot he hadn't left the pub until ten-thirty I was OK with it. He told me Sam had turned up at his place then disappeared again and he'd gone out to look for him. I didn't get why he needed to lie about it but I trusted him. If he wanted me to lie for him, he had to have had a good reason."

"What changed your mind?"

"Nothing," Edwards said. "I mean, I didn't change my mind. I still trust him." He sighed, shaking his head. "But I'm worried about him. Something's not right."

"Like what?" Georgie asked.

The man shook his head again and rubbed his dense curls.

"I called because there's no way you can sort all this shit out if people don't tell you the truth. I couldn't sleep thinking about it, so I called the number on the local police Facebook page. I thought if it was anonymous ..." His voice tailed off.

When, after a minute or two he'd said nothing more, Georgie said, "Well, you did the right thing. And you're correct. If people don't tell us the truth it makes the job much harder and wastes a lot of time. Just one thing before we go." She hesitated, unsure how to phrase her next question. "How would you describe the relationship between Cal and Sam Gray? Were they friends or ...?" Like him, she let her voice hover.

Edwards stood up, frowning.

"Look, I don't know what you're suggesting, but Cal is never anything but professional with the kids he works with."

Georgie smiled, though she didn't yet stand and willed Corby to remain on her perch. Tom Edwards' reaction interested her.

"I'm not suggesting anything," she said. "Cal hadn't worked with Sam for a few years as I understand it, not professionally anyway. But Sam helped with Time Out and Innes must have seen him when he came in here. Did they get on?"

"Of course. Cal was like a mentor to him. He was proud of how Sam had turned things around."

Georgie let her eyes rest on the shop owner for a little longer but, though his face remained defensive, he said nothing more. Nothing about how Sam had felt about Cal.

"Ok, then," she said, getting to her feet. Behind her, Corby slid from the table. "Thanks again for calling, like I said. We appreciate it. And I'd prefer it if you didn't let Cal know about our chat. Or that you called us. We'll speak to him later today. You wouldn't know where he is, I suppose?"

Edwards shrugged.

"At work, I imagine. He does support work at the sixth-form college on a Friday, I think."

They went out of the cluttered office into the sudden chill of the shop which didn't seem much warmer than outside. Perhaps because a couple of customers had come in, bringing the cold air with them. Two middle-aged men were examining a rack of fleece jackets, checking the size labels and wondering whether to try a large or an extra-large. Seth was helping a woman try on a pair of walking shoes.

As Fraser and Corby made for the door, it opened with a clang of the bell. A tall man with a bandana around his hair closed it behind himself. Like they had earlier, he stamped his boots on the mat to shake off the slush before he looked up and saw them. As though he'd walked in on a game of musical statues, his body froze.

"Hello, Cal," Georgie said. "Fancy seeing you here."

Cal Innes followed them to the police station in Monkmoor in the blue pick-up that Georgie had first seen on the Burway when Joe had found the car. They had offered him a lift but he'd said he'd rather go under his own steam. Then he could go straight to work when they'd finished. Confident he wouldn't be detained, then, Corby had remarked to Georgie as they'd turned out of Church Stretton onto the A49.

Before they'd left, George had recommended he contact a solicitor.

"Or we can find you a duty one, if you'd prefer. But I think you should have someone with you."

Cal hadn't protested. On the contrary, he'd seemed almost relieved and said he'd bring his own.

The man who walked into reception with him a half hour after they'd left Church Stretton wore a red Search and Rescue jacket over his smart suit. A mixture of snow and sleet had begun to fall as they drove and droplets glistened in both men's hair. Fraser and Corby, who'd arrived about ten minutes ahead of them had had time to warm up and sort out an interview room.

"This is Alex Popescu," Cal said.

The man shook both their hands before hanging his jacket over the back of one of the interview room chairs.

"My office is in Church Stretton," he explained. "Opposite Tom's shop."

"Do you work out of the community hub as well?" Corby asked, sitting down facing him. "I'm sure I recognise you." As ever, she spread the air that they were all friends gathering for an informal chat. No question then about who would play good and who bad cop if it came down to it.

Alex Popescu explained that he and several others in his practice, which also had offices in Ludlow and Shrewsbury, volunteered a half day each week. "With legal aid having been cut for so many ..." There was no need for him to finish his sentence.

While Cal took the seat next to his solicitor, his skin a pale shade of beige and the half moons beneath his eyes almost purple, Corby busied herself with the recording equipment, naming those present and making sure Cal understood that he was there for a voluntary interview. As yet, there were no charges. As yet. The words hung in the air.

"So, Cal," Georgie said, "we know that you left the Yew Tree pub last Saturday night at 8.45. Although when previously asked, you said you were there until 10.30. Where did you go?"

Cal Innes looked at his solicitor who nodded, conveying solid reassurance in a single movement of his head. Georgie imagined he was a valuable presence on any Search and Rescue team.

"I went home first to see if Sam was back. Then out on the hill. Walked out from my place all the way to Pole Bank." His voice was husky and he cleared his throat. "I thought Sam might have gone back to the shelter. I'd heard him on the phone earlier. Not what he was saying but just that he was talking to someone. I thought he might have arranged to meet them. From the summit, I could see there were no lights. No fire. But I went down anyway to have a look. Just sat there for a bit, hoping he might turn up."

"And did he?"

Cal's brow furrowed.

"No." His voice cracked. "I told you, the last time I saw him was Saturday afternoon when I went out to get the milk. And when I got back he was gone. Don't you believe me?"

How strange it was, Georgie thought, that people could lie to you one moment and then be outraged when you questioned their veracity.

"It occurred to me that you might have agreed to help him dispose of the car," she said. "If he was going to head off to London he couldn't very well take it with him. Jessie would need it back. I thought it might have been your idea to dump it. After all, it was you who told me how many cars go over the edge because people forget to put the handbrake on."

"I didn't see him. I swear. If I did, I would've persuaded him to come home with me."

Perhaps he'd tried. Perhaps that was when things had gone wrong.

"Did you see anyone up there? No one up there stargazing or night walking? It was a Saturday night."

"No one. It was cold. Bitter. The wind was coming over from Wales and you could feel the snow on the way. That's why I was worried. I didn't know if he was out in it. I didn't reckon he'd have gone off anywhere far away with Jessie's car." Innes bit the skin around his thumbnail, frowning. He looked again at Alex Popescu, a sideways swipe of his eyes. The solicitor nodded almost imperceptibly.

"I did think I heard something," Cal Innes said. "I'd been sitting there a while and I thought I heard ... like a slipping noise. Or someone falling over. But I called out and no one answered."

"Did you have a look around?"

"There was no one there. I went all round the fence line."

"And then?"

Innes shrugged. "I went home. Waited up half the night. Fell asleep on the sofa in the end. Next thing I knew, Mike Harley was calling me saying you'd found a car gone off the Burway."

The youth worker raised a hand to push back a coil of hair that had escaped his bandana. Fraser noticed how it shook as he sent it back to his lap to join the other. Again his eyes swiped sideways towards Alex Popescu who gave him a long, slow look. The solicitor cleared his throat.

"DI Fraser, there's something that Cal hasn't told you because he feels it places him in a compromising position. I've explained that it would be better to let you have all the facts. It may have some bearing on Sam's mental state."

Cal Innes shook his lowered head, muttering and twisting his hands below the table. The solicitor placed a hand on his arm. "Come on, mate. Trust me."

Georgie sat back in her chair and waited, watching the digits on the recording equipment.

"It was the first night," Innes said. "Sam was upset. Really upset. About Davey. That he'd killed his brother. He thought something must have happened during the fight."

Interest sparked in Georgie's brain, setting off tiny chain reactions.

"He told you Davey was his brother?"

"He told me about the glider pilot. His dad. And how he and Davey had found out. How Davey and shown him his grave and what they'd done. It was like he got kind of hysterical. I mean, I know he was off his face and in shock but he kept saying how he and Davey were being punished. Because he'd pissed on the grave."

Innes's voice caught in his throat and he reached for the plastic cup in front of him, water slopping as his hand shook. He took a sip and lowered the cup to the table slowly, gathering himself.

"I put an arm around him. Hugged him, you know, just trying to calm him down. And he ..." The man put his hands over his face, scrunching his long climber's fingers into his forehead. "He kind of leaned into me. And it felt like he was relaxing, you know. A bit calmer." He shuddered, his breath catching. "And then he kissed me. You know, like proper kissed me."

Georgie stayed silent, biting back her questions. What did you do, Cal? Did you kiss him back? Did one thing lead to another? Is that how Sam was able to blackmail you?

Cal had, he said, kissed him back. But only for a second. Then reality had pushed its way back in, all the implications of what might follow raining down on him. And besides, he didn't see Sam like that. He thought of him almost like a younger brother. It had felt wrong. Horrible.

"And then he kind of lost it," Cal said. "When I said we shouldn't. Ranting about how he knew I'd fancied him for years. About how now I knew about him and what he'd done, I thought he wasn't good enough for me."

It wasn't what Georgie had been expecting. Beside her, Corby shifted and she received a silent message to take her foot off the pedal for a minute. Trusting both her DC and her own instincts she sat back.

"That must have been really upsetting," Corby said. "It's difficult dealing with an unwanted move on you at the best of times but when you know the other person's just witnessed the death of a friend." Her voice, always down-to-earth, offered friendship and a sympathetic ear. Cal nodded and rubbed a hand across his eyes. Next to him, the solicitor watched his client, presumably monitoring that he didn't break down entirely and give away anything that might incriminate him. "What did you do?" Corby asked.

A thin tear snaked its way down the man's cheek, diverting around a patch of dark stubble when it reached his chin. He didn't seem to notice it.

"I didn't know what to do. I just told him it was nothing about him not being good enough. I couldn't take advantage of someone in the state he was in. And then he said it was the only chance I'd ever get with him. Now or never. So I said never. And the look he gave me ..." His voice choked on a sob. "I knew he'd never ... I don't know. Forgive me. I knew we wouldn't be friends again."

Georgie's mind was spinning. Every day on this case brought revelations that dragged her in different directions. Not for the first time she wished she could have met Sam. There seemed to have been something unquantifiable about him. Everyone who had met him described a different person. To Jessie, he had been not just a boyfriend but a best friend. To Davey, a brother in arms. To Alfie and perhaps the other boys in that group he'd been a bit of a wild boy, something of a hero. To his mother he'd been a golden boy, who'd overcome his troubles and made good, better than if he'd never had those troubles in the first place. No one, in all their conversations and interviews, had questioned Sam's sexuality. And yet she believed Cal. Both that Sam had made his move and that Cal had rebuffed it. The man's distress was too raw not to be real. But why had Sam done it? Had he genuinely been attracted to Cal? Had he, somewhere along the line, questioned his sexuality? And what about the local rumours regarding him and Davey? Had there been something between them before they knew they were brothers? And, if so, how did that change the anger behind their fight up at Pole Cottage?

And what about Cal? She wondered if he realised that, if looked at in a certain light, this revelation actually strengthened the case against him.

Perhaps Sam's behaviour had been nothing more than a cry for comfort. Though, given the many facets of Sam's character, it might also have been miscalculated manipulation, a way to ensure that Cal would look after him. By the sound of it, Sam had used it to his advantage despite Cal turning him down.

"Was that when he threatened you?" Georgie asked.

Corby took a pack of tissues from her pocket and pushed them across the table. Cal Innes took one and wiped his eyes, then blew his nose, all the while keeping his face turned away. His shame spilled across the table, like the floodwaters that were sure to come with the promised thaw.

"Next morning," Cal said. "He told me to fuck off that night. To fuck off upstairs to my sad, gay-boy bed on my own, which was how I'd always be because I didn't know how to appreciate people. So I did. I'd already got a pillow and a sleeping bag for him to have on the sofa earlier. I left him downstairs with a load of weed and the fire burning. But I didn't sleep. A couple of hours maybe, half sleep, just before dawn. And then in the morning, he told me how it was going to be." His voice cracked again and he covered his face with both hands, elbows jammed into the table.

"DI Fraser?" Alex Popescu sat forward, a hand on his client's arm. "I think we could do with a short break. Just time to take a breath."

Fraser nodded and Corby offered tea. Leaving Innes with his solicitor and a duty PC in the interview room, Georgie took advantage of the time to check her phone for messages and found one from Joe, telling her she might want to check out the

Friends of Sam Gray X account. *Sure your team's on it, but just in case. Same shit as Niamh heard last night.* Swatting her annoyance away as she might a wasp on a picnic, she swore under her breath and returned to the interview room.

CORBY HAD ALREADY RETURNED with tea and biscuits and Innes was looking a little more himself, his eyes red and puffy but dry, shoulders hunched over his cup of tea. Georgie asked him how he was feeling and if he was ready to continue. The man nodded and in a cracked voice, thanked them for the break.

"Cal, you mentioned earlier that you'd heard Sam on the phone to someone. Not texting but talking. When was that?"

"Saturday. But I heard him Thursday morning too. Before I went to work."

"And did he call them or the other way around?"

Cal Innes's forehead creased and he rubbed the tips of his thumbs together.

"I think they called him. But I can't be sure. I was in the bathroom. I thought he was talking to me at first. When I came down, I saw him on the phone."

"Did he try to hide the call from you?"

Innes shook his head and a smile tinged with bitterness played around his mouth.

"He raised his voice. Told whoever it was that he was 'at the paedo's house'."

Corby took in a sharp, hissing breath.

"Jeez, that must have hurt."

Georgie blessed her silently. Cal favoured her with a tremulous smile.

"You could say that."

"You must have been very angry with him." Georgie's tone was light but, if Innes was fooled, his solicitor wasn't. He flashed his friend a look which, with his eyes on Corby, George suspected the youth worker had missed.

"I wasn't angry. I mean yeah, for a second. But I was more hurt. Couldn't believe he'd talk about me like that, even after … you know. I tried to keep an eye out for him, let him come back to help at Time Out. I thought he liked me. But when he said it … it didn't sound like it was the first time, you know? It sounded like whoever he was talking to would know exactly who he meant."

Georgie decided to take her bad cop hat off, although in all honesty she felt she'd been wearing it pretty lightly. It was never a role that suited her. She was better at subtle persuasion than bullying.

"What he said doesn't mean you were wrong. At that age we can be many things to many people. Especially if we're a bit insecure. We'll say anything to be accepted. Maybe he thought whoever he was talking to would take the piss so he got in there first. Called you a paedo to throw them off the scent. And he knew you were listening. Probably wanted to hurt you after what happened the night before. Salve his pride."

Innes nodded, his movement effortful and as unconvinced as it was unconvincing. Georgie presumed that everyone around the table had made the same connection as her. Contrary to Cal's previous assertion that no one had known Sam was at his house, someone clearly had. Had whoever it was turned up while Cal was out getting the milk and tempted Sam from his sanctuary? And who would have had that power?

"You've really no idea who he was talking to?" she asked. "Boy? Girl?"

"Could have been either."

"If you had to guess?"

Innes exhaled heavily.

"Girl, I suppose. He was a bit cocky."

"Jessie?" Corby asked and Innes shook his head.

"He was always normal with her. Same as he was in the shop or helping with Time Out. He was different when he was with a crowd of friends."

Interesting. Only three girls had been there on that Wednesday night and, after the way she and Bryn Morgan had been, Georgie thought it unlikely to have been Lily Morpeth on the other end of the phone.

"Do you know Alisha Johnson?" she asked. Her interest flickered as a wave of colour spread up Cal Innes's face to stain his cheeks.

"I know who she is."

"Did you meet her through Sam?"

Innes chewed at the skin around his thumbnail again.

"I used to run a climbing club at the sixth form college. She came along for a while."

"Wouldn't have put her down as an outdoor type," Corby said, with a smile.

"Don't think she was. Came along with some friends." His awkwardness was striking and his next words made things clearer. "I had to ask her to leave."

"Why was that?" Georgie asked.

"She started hanging around afterwards. Helped clear up and stuff, put the ropes away. To be honest, she flirted. Anyway, one day she made it very clear it was me she was interested in, not the climbing. Asked me where I hung out and then kept turning up as if by accident. In the end, I told her I was in a relationship. A few weeks later I was in the Boujee Lounge in Shrewsbury with a guy and there she was. She saw us dancing together. That was when the rumours started. About me being into young boys."

She likes to stir things up, Alfie Rickard had said. Or was it Lucas Harley?

"How old was the guy she saw you with?" Georgie said. "Just out of interest. I'm not implying anything," she added, as the solicitor sat forward.

Cal Innes laughed bitterly.

"About twenty-eight. But he looks young. Babyface. I stopped the climbing club at the end of that term. The last thing I needed was rumours spreading."

Georgie tapped her pen on the table and smiled briefly at the two men, her mind already setting off down a new path.

Maybe it was time to talk to Alisha Johnson again.

"THING IS, BOSS," Corby said, "we only have Cal's word that he got back from buying the milk to find Sam gone."

She and Chowdhury were in Georgie's office after the interview with Cal Innes. Georgie's mind was still moving too fast to be of any use in the incident room and she'd hoped a half hour talking over the interview with Corby might help crystallise her thoughts. Chowdhury had tracked them down on his return from Davey Whelan's caravan where he'd been to search for anything that might hold a clue to any contact with the Doherty family in Ireland, and to collect Davey's notebooks and folders of drawings. He sat on the edge of a desk, a box of papers and A4 red and black hardback notebooks beside him. Georgie remembered using the same brand at university and was surprised they still made them.

"We've checked with the shop," Chowdhury said. "So we know that bit's true but who's to say what happened when he got back? Maybe Sam wound him up again and this time he lost it."

"It's possible," Georgie said.

"It's not like anyone's ever up that way," Corby said. "And if he'd been hiding Jessie's car in his barn all that time, it would have been easy to hide a body for a few hours. He could have gone to the pub for a bit, then driven Sam's body up to the Pole Bank shelter in Jessie's car after he got home."

"Made sure he took the knife and blood-stained clothing with him," Chowdhury added. "Then he dumped Sam in the bog, buried the knife and jacket and pushed the car off the Burway."

Georgie held back from saying it was possible again. It was, but several questions sprang to mind. Why had Innes bothered taking the jacket and knife and burying them behind the shelter where the kids had had their fire? He could have buried them anywhere out on the Mynd, in the rough wilderness that surrounded his cottage, or burned them to destroy any traces of DNA. Why risk driving a dead body in a car halfway across the Mynd, when there were plenty of other places he could have disposed of it?

"Maybe it wasn't a coincidence he was the first on the scene with Mike when he called Search and Rescue," Corby said. "He could have tweaked the rota to make sure he got any calls that came in. He'd have known the car would be found."

"OK, well we need to find out who organises the rota and when his name would have been put on. Or ask Mike if he called Cal directly."

Corby nodded.

"But I want it kept quiet," Georgie said. "Tomorrow morning, we'll have a full forensics team at Mytton's Fold – Innes' house. They can take the place to pieces." Pitbull might question her use of resources but, while her instinct argued against it, there was enough evidence pointing at Cal Innes to demand that he should be thoroughly investigated. "You can go out with them, Haris."

"What are we looking for?" Chowdhury asked. "If he did kill him there, we know he disposed of the knife and the jacket. He's not going to have left anything else."

"We're looking for anything to suggest that Cal killed Sam in the first place. Look at the kitchen knives in his drawer. Are there any that match the one found with Sam's jacket? Same make, different size. Check in the barn where the car was kept. If the lad was stabbed there, there'll be traces of blood somewhere, no matter how careful he was."

"What about the car?" Corby asked. "There'd have been traces there, if he'd transported the body. Wouldn't the forensics lot have found them by now?"

Georgie looked at the clock on the wall. Beyond the window it was almost full dark, the orange lampposts of the car park standing out like fire beacons against an obsidian sky. As they crept closer to the winter solstice, she was finding it harder to judge the time, the nights drawing in so early.

"Unless they've gone for an early Friday knock-off, someone should still be at the lab so let's chase them."

"He could have wrapped him in a tarpaulin or something, couldn't he?" Chowdhury said. "Anyway, Sam was in that car so many times, his DNA would be all over it."

"Not blood, though," Corby said.

"Unless he was bleeding after the Fight Club. We know he drove the car afterwards. All Innes's lawyer would need to do was offer that as a reasonable explanation for Sam's blood being in the car." Georgie wasn't sure why she even put the point forward. A need to discipline her mind, perhaps. To engage her left brain and work on evidence and facts, rather than intuition. Pitbull had no time for hunches. "The car's worth checking but not our best bet. Innes's house and barn are where we need to find evidence. We'll need to check all his clothing too, and look for signs of recent burning at the property. I think I spotted a small incinerator to the left of the barn when Ali and I were up there the other day."

It was, of course, also possible that someone else had killed

Sam up at Mytton's Fold. Perhaps Cal had returned to the house to find Sam not missing but dead and whoever had killed him gone. He might still have disposed of the body in fear of being blamed for his murder. Someone else had known that he was there. Cal had heard him on the phone. Always assuming Cal was telling the truth, of course.

A knock on the door announced DC Hallam, clutching a sheaf of printed papers.

"I thought you might want these, boss. Sam Gray's phone records."

Georgie laughed.

"Perfect timing, DC Hallam! You must have been reading my mind. Or my fairy godmother summoned you. Any headlines?"

"It's only the record of calls. No transcripts available yet. But I've cross-referenced them with the rest of the numbers. You know, the kids up at the Mynd."

Georgie stretched out a hand for the papers, although the fastest route to finding out what she wanted to know would doubtless be to ask Hallam. He had an almost photographic memory and a knack for remembering sequences of numbers.

"Any phone calls on Thursday morning? Calls not text."

"7.43 am," Hallam said. "I noticed because all the rest of the traffic is text or Snapchat. Alisha Johnson."

Georgie's interest flickered. According to Cal, Alisha had accused him of being into younger men. No prizes for guessing who Sam had been talking to when he'd called Cal 'the paedo'.

"Did he call her?"

"She called him."

"Any other calls? Voice or video?"

Hallam shook his head.

"Plenty of unanswered ones from his mum and other family. But from his mates, only Saturday afternoon. Same number. And she called him again."

When Georgie was young, she'd enjoyed the game Tetris. Now, it seemed that irregular geometric shapes were gliding before her eyes waiting for her to slot them together without gaps.

"Ok, we'll get her in, either this afternoon or tomorrow morning. Voluntary interview but advise her to bring a solicitor," she said to Chowdhury.

"Not being funny, boss, but if we've got our eyes on Innes why are we following up the girl? Don't we want to get the house search done first?"

Doing her best to keep her voice free of irritation, and wondering if Chowdhury had absorbed from Pitbull the ability to pursue only one lead at a time, Georgie said that whilst they had to cover all eventualities it was perfectly possible that Cal was telling the truth. If that was the case, someone – and most likely one of those kids – had lured Sam away from his safe house. Given that Alisha knew where he was and had spoken to him on that Saturday, they had to follow it up.

"And we'll get Mike to do the search up at Mytton's Fold. I want you and Ali to interview Alisha."

Chowdhury frowned.

"Don't you want to do it?"

"A little birdie tells me Alisha Johnson has an issue with my gender. I don't want to give her anything to use as a distraction. I'll observe and buzz in if I need to. Any more news on Shona Doherty?" she added, as Hallam turned back towards the door.

"Not confirmed yet, boss. I was going to tell you at the meeting. I think she might be Colm Doherty's daughter."

"And?" Georgie said.

"I found her on LinkedIn from her emails. Last year, on Father's Day, she posted a note about how she'd never known her father. He'd died in a gliding accident in England."

"Any idea where she lives?"

"Not yet, boss. Still looking."

Corby rolled her eyes. "Every time we think we're getting somewhere, something else pops up. What if she followed her dad over here? She could have been living in Church Stretton under a different name and we'd never know."

Briefly, Georgie wondered if it might be worth asking Niamh if she knew any other young Irish women in the area. Shona Doherty would be around the same age.

About ten minutes later, following Corby and the others to the incident room in time for the evening briefing, Georgie considered what Cal had told them about Alisha. How determined and pushy she'd been in pursuing him. Perhaps she had been the same with Sam. After all, according to Alfie's report, she had offered herself as the prize in the fight club knowing that Davey adored her and that it would hurt him to see her with Sam. And with Jessie there too. What kind of friend offered herself to her best friend's boyfriend with no concern for her feelings? Perhaps she had had her eyes set on Sam all along. What if, in the end, he had turned her down?

27

The dogs heard Georgie's Land Rover before Marianne did. They shot off towards the gate just as headlights swept around the bend in the lane, barking their excitement. Bill, the younger of the two donkeys, though old enough to know better, charged after them bellowing his hee-haw, while Ted, older by several years chewed on his hay, jaws moving rhythmically. Marianne often thought Bill was a dog trapped in a donkey's body. Earlier, when she'd first come to the field to chisel piles of hard-frozen dung from the ground into the wheelbarrow, Bill, not much bigger than Maggie, had played with the dog, bouncing and chasing, Pip snapping at both their heels. Josephine the goat, a little more sedate now that she was nearing twelve, had eyed them irritably and helped herself to chunks of hay from the wheelbarrow as Marianne stuffed it into feeding crates around the field and shelter.

"Perfect timing," she called, standing the wheelbarrow on its end against the shelter wall and tidying her rake and scoop away.

The gate creaked loudly and Georgie rounded the corner of the hedge, both dogs leaping around her and Bill trotting alongside, his *hee-haws* shattering the peace of the evening. Occasionally Marianne wondered if her neighbours minded but she'd lived in Onnyford for a year now and no one had complained yet. On the contrary, most days she saw dog walkers and locals stop by the field gate to admire them. She'd even had to put a sign up asking people to please not feed them.

"I've just finished," she said, switching off her head torch so as not to dazzle Georgie who looked shattered.

"Swap," Georgie said as she neared her. Marianne wrapped her arms around her. "You run my investigation for a day and I'll cook for people and look after the menagerie." She dropped a kiss on Marianne's head and hugged tight. "Lordy, I'm glad I've got you to come home to."

"Is that me or the donkeys?" Marianne asked, laughing as Bill butted Georgie in the back, making her stumble. "It's your fault. If you didn't give them treats, they wouldn't mug you." Georgie's coat pockets were always full of pressed mint pellets which Bill and Ted loved. "Anyway, I'm not sure your team would appreciate me being in charge."

Georgie took Marianne's hand and they walked towards the gate.

"Probably not. And I'd probably poison all your customers and destroy your business in one fell swoop. But tomorrow, I could really do with some donkey time. And dogs," she added to Maggie and Pip who had raced ahead of them, Pip squeezing under the five-bar and waiting for them on the grass verge of the lane.

Marianne opened the gate, latching it carefully behind them once they were out on the lane and leaving a reluctant Bill on the right side of it.

"Tough day?"

"Not the best. Actually, I could really do with talking some of it over, if you've got the mental space. Without names or anything, you know."

"Sure," Marianne said. "You talk, I'll cook." In fact she'd brought the remains of a lentil and vegetable bake back from the Geoscience Trust and planned that they could have that with some cheese to finish, but it would take her no time to knock up a loaf of banana bread for Georgie and she looked like she needed some nurturing. Besides, Georgie needing to talk was a relief. At least they wouldn't have to discuss whether she planned to pursue the case against Joe's potential fathers.

She'd lit the log-burner before going over to the field and warmth enveloped them as they brushed snow from their coats in the porch. Marianne dried the dogs' paws and sent them into the living room to laze in front of the fire while she and Georgie went through to the kitchen.

"Joe said someone's been making trouble," Marianne said, pouring Georgie a cider and fetching an apple soda for herself. Last night, washing up Effie and Georgie's glasses after dinner, she had caught a waft of red wine and almost crumpled with longing. And now, following the cool stream of golden liquid from bottle to glass, it hit her again. A yearning for the crisp sharpness on her tongue, the pop and fizz of bubbles in her mouth, the warm tingle as alcohol crept along her veins. She shut the fridge door with more force than she intended and Georgie looked up from her phone in surprise. Marianne handed her the glass with a smile and went to the cupboard for a loaf tin and mixing bowl. "I don't mean that girl Niamh met in the club last night," she went on. "He said something about social media."

Georgie sighed and took a sip of her drink.

"Someone's gender-trolling me," she said. "Questioning why they'd put a freak – and a reject from the Met, no less – in charge of an important investigation."

"Jesus," Marianne said. Her parents had used the Lord's name only in praise and she'd used it in vain to annoy them. Despite not having seen them for more than twenty years, the habit had stuck. "Do you know who?"

"More than one, I should think. It doesn't really matter. As long as it doesn't become a distraction from the investigation. It's more than a week since Sam Gray went missing. I can't blame people for wanting results. Maybe poking at me is just their way of expressing their frustration."

"But you're doing everything you can."

"Of course we are. The team's working flat out. And I think we might even have made some progress this afternoon. But these days it's too easy to bang the drum that someone else could do better."

"Like the prime minister," Marianne said. Georgie frowned. "You know, this constant speculation that it's time for Keir Starmer to be replaced. And the last government – five prime ministers in as many years or whatever it was. What is it they say? A new broom sweeps clean."

"Problem is," Georgie said, "Pitbull already pulled Harkness off the case because Mrs Gray didn't like him. He's not going to take kindly to being pressured to take another DI off. But he might decide he needs to assume responsibility and just nudge me out the side door."

Marianne wondered if that would be such a bad thing. The case seemed to be eating away at her. At the same time, she knew how much Georgie needed to solve the puzzle. That she couldn't rest until it was resolved. Her innate need for justice and resolution – and perhaps a hidden belief that she was the only one who could find it – often made her her own worst enemy.

"The thing that gets me," Georgie said, "is that there's all this fuss about Sam Gray. What about the other lad? Davey Whelan.

No one's kicking off about him. Why is one life worth more than another?"

"No family," Marianne said, without sentiment. The boy had been a loner, as far as she'd heard. Like her. When she had been sentenced for murder, rejected by her family and without powerful friends, there had been no one to fight on her behalf. No one to organise campaigns or rally the media. Or the press, as it had been referred to back then. At least Davey Whelan had Georgie to fight for his memory. She would give as much importance to Davey as to Sam, despite the Friends of Sam Gray group's demands for answers. Georgie was programmed to fight for the underdog. Perhaps the reason she had championed Marianne, when Pitbull had had her down as a suspect.

"So, what's bothering you?" she asked as she laid tins of plain flour and soft brown sugar on the counter, fetched spices and the pot of baking powder from the drawer. "Just the social media thing?"

Georgie shook her head.

"That's just noise. No ..." She took another sip of her drink. "We interviewed a suspect today. Credible motive, opportunity, means ..."

"That's good, isn't it?"

"It should be."

"So? What's the problem?" Marianne weighed out the dry ingredients and mixed them in one bowl. Four overripe bananas, saved from the tearoom, lay next to the larger mixing bowl and she peeled them, ready for mashing. Georgie was looking at her nails, inspecting them for chips, her fingers curled in towards her palm. At last she looked up, catching Marianne's eye as she reached for the potato masher.

"I believe him. I believe his version of events."

Marianne smiled.

"Maybe I should take over your job for the day. I rarely believe anyone."

"Like Miss Marple," Georgie said, her own mouth curling at Marianne's quizzical look. "I think Miss Marple said that was what gave her the edge as an investigator. She was never inclined to believe anyone."

"Whereas you want to believe the best of everyone, which means you're bound to be disappointed most of the time."

"Aye, maybe." The *aye* was a clue to Georgie's frame of mind too. The more off kilter she was, the more Scottish crept into her speech. "I don't necessarily want to believe the best of everyone. But I know Pitbull thinks I rely too much on instinct. And right now, my instinct's the only thing not pointing towards this person."

"It hasn't let you down so far," Marianne said. "Maybe you're right."

28

"Isn't it Saturday?" Liz, the café manager said, coming upon Joe as he climbed onto the quad bike in the yard behind the Chalet Pavilion.

"Just some finishing up from yesterday," he said, a politer response than he'd given Effie when she'd asked the same question. He'd had it in mind to visit the possible site of the peregrine's nest, at a safe distance of course, but with the clouds lowering and a thaw setting in he wasn't likely to see much. Why not finish off clearing the heather from the Shooting Box ditch?

"Well, I wouldn't be long if I were you," Liz said. "Weather's coming in." As she often told him, she'd lived on the side of the Mynd all her fifty years and knew the signs.

"You'll be telling me Devil's in his chair next."

Joe started the engine and raised a gloved hand as he drove through the tall green gates, taking care to stop and check before turning out onto the newly re-surfaced tarmac roadway. Accustomed to water-filled potholes, he couldn't get used to its sleek, black surface, nothing to impede the chunky tyres of the quad bike as he headed it down towards the car park. Where the shale track turned off up the hill towards the Burway, flanked by steep snowy banks, he paused, letting the engine idle as two women in their late sixties, if not early seventies, descended the path, crossing onto the road.

Neat and trim in their outdoor gear, with short-cropped silver hair and walking poles, they reminded him of Effie. It was a reminder he didn't need and brought with it a wave of guilt.

"But you're never going up on the hill today?" she'd said as he pulled his Ranger jacket on by the front door. "Can't you give yourself the weekend off? You were up there all last Sunday, too."

Niamh had said the same, and though he'd not heard from Marianne he'd imagined her voice too, chiding him for overdoing it, for going off on his own, even if it was a habit he'd somehow absorbed from her.

"Jesus, can't everyone just get off my case?" he'd muttered, and a flash of hurt had crossed his landlady's face, followed by annoyance. And she'd been right to be annoyed. He hadn't even had the manners to apologise before tugging open the heavy Victorian front door and stomping out into the porch. As he'd laced his boots, he'd been aware of the silence behind him. No cheery *bye, then,* or asking if he'd be in for his tea. Which was lucky because he didn't know what he'd have said.

Officially he was a lodger, with his own self-contained flat, but usually they ate together if he was in in the evening and he took his turn to cook. It was an arrangement that worked well for him. For both of them, he thought. Company and help for her if she wanted it and for him, as well as a very nice room in a beautiful house close to his work, it afforded a connection with his mother while allowing them space as they learned to know each other properly. Maybe he'd send Effie a message when he got to the top of the hill. Apologise for his rudeness.

As he turned the quad bike up the steep track towards the Burway, Niamh's parting hurled insult from their row the night before speared his brain again. *God, you're just like your bloody mother!* And he'd had nothing to say in return because it was true. But how was it possible that he and Marianne could be similar? They'd never lived together, apart from the few weeks he'd stayed with her before moving into Effie's, after the murder at the Geoscience Trust. Marianne hadn't brought him up, and the people who had were warm and open, not retreating into themselves and running off into desolate hill country when emotion threatened to overwhelm them. Emotion never had overwhelmed them. They had talked things through sensibly. No, this craving of his for solitude and wilderness was all Marianne.

The promised thaw had begun overnight, though here, on the hill, snow still lay thick on the heather that flanked the track. Below in the town, only traces of white frosting remained on the tiled rooftops, and all around was the steady drip of moisture from the branches of trees. In several places, thin streams crossed the shale track and the quad bike's wheels sent up satisfying clouds of spray. There were no walkers in his path so he opened the throttle, let the bike surge upwards until a clutch of straggly looking sheep scrambled up to his left, alarmed by his noisy progress. Their panic brought him back to himself and, by the time he reached the Burway and turned right towards Cow Ridge, his heart rate had slowed. A thin layer of shame settled over him and he reminded himself consciously of the joys of his job, of the luck he had in being able to live a life that suited him. Of all the good things that had come his way since he'd stepped out on the road to find his mother, hoicking his courage along with him, in blind faith that he was following the right path.

His phone buzzed against his chest. Niamh, he reckoned. She must have messaged about six times since he'd been up. Once he reached the Devil's Mouth cross-dyke, he pulled off the road onto the snow-packed turf above Devil's Mouth Hollow.

Weird to think that it was just under a week since he'd seen the car jammed between the rocks, halfway down the gutter. Those six days seemed to have expanded into a timeless span of blizzards and frozen whiteness, as though Church Stretton and its environs had been trapped in Narnia. Two lads, not much younger than him were dead and he'd held the body of one of them between his hands, manoeuvred it up the steep sides of Callow Hollow in a blizzard. The other had been found frozen in a shallow pool, hands outstretched beneath the glassy surface as though the boy was begging to be freed from his icy grave. In his head he saw it as clearly as if he'd discovered it himself, not just heard the scene described by Georgie.

Last night, he'd turned his anger and confusion on Niamh, blaming her for setting in motion the wheels that had so distressed Marianne and churned through his head, bringing to the surface the knowledge of where he'd come from. Of how he had come to be. How could his mother even bear to be around him? How could he ever be anything but a reminder of shame and regret, no matter how she seemed to love him?

Niamh had suggested a dinner date as an antidote to a stressful week. She had cooked for him in her shared house, still limping a little as she pottered around the kitchen, and afterwards they'd retreated to her room with the rest of the bottle of wine he'd brought. They'd been in bed when the shame had swooped down on him. He'd pulled himself roughly away from her and sat naked on the edge of the mattress, shaking and consumed with horror at the scenes that played in his head. Something he'd overheard between Marianne and Georgie that night he'd first brought it up with her, when they'd thought he was still upstairs. *But how can I ever know which one of them was his father? It could have been any of them.* How many had there been? What had they done to her?

Shaking his head to clear it of what he longed to forget, he took out the phone and pulled one glove off with his teeth. He'd been right. Niamh.

-Please call me. I'm worried about you x

He saw again the shock on her heart-shaped face as he'd spewed forth his garbled half-formed fears and accusations. The confusion that had sparked out of her as anger until she'd shouted at him to go. More shame at the things he'd said. He loved her. Or thought he did, anyway. He'd never felt that way about anyone else, the lift that seeing her or hearing her voice gave him. The peace he felt when they lay side by side, drifting off to sleep. The joy on opening his eyes and seeing her head on the pillow next to his, still wrapped in slumber.

Wearily he swiped at the phone to open it and typed a reply.

-im sorry for how i behaved. He couldn't say he hadn't meant anything he'd said, because he had. *- just need some time alone – gone up to shooting box.*

He sent the message, then read it again. Not enough. Not nearly enough.

- i love you – im sorry – explain later x

Then he put the phone back in his jacket and turned the bike north along the Portway.

THE SHOOTING BOX was a bronze age barrow, the only known disc barrow in Shropshire and the largest on the Mynd, with a mound about nineteen metres across and two and a half high. A ring ditch encircled it, surrounded by a heather-covered bank about four and a half metres wide. Nothing compared to a hill fort of course, but still an impressive structure. It took its name from a nineteenth century grouse shooting hut which had been removed in the early nineties, leaving behind a depression in the otherwise intact monument. Before the snow, Joe and Ranger Dan had noticed that the heather had begun to encroach on the ditch and, with everywhere too wet for burning, had begun to clear it by hand with the help of the Friday volunteer group. Joe had been up there with them again the day before, in reduced numbers thanks to the snow, but the work had kept them warm and by the end of their three-hour shift, shorter than usual owing to the temperatures, the trailer had been stuffed to the gunwales with twisting stems of heather.

There had been no need for him to come back today. Or rather no official need. His own need however, was great. To be alone, with the likelihood of seeing not a soul, surrounded by nothing but earth and rocks and birds and sky. And the odd sheep. True, walkers passed by the disc barrow which was just off the ancient Portway track but, with the weather closing in, he might have the place to himself. As he turned from the tarmaced road onto the rough surface of the Portway, gunmetal clouds skimmed the top of Pole Bank to his left. Instinctively, he looked across to the Devil's Chair, where he had first met Marianne, only to find it and the Stiperstones range rendered invisible by a thick charcoal curtain. Rain? It looked more like snow, though there had been none forecast. Fog, later, but he'd be down off the hill before it reached the Mynd. And then where would he go?

He had no energy for mending fences, though both Niamh and Effie deserved amends. He wanted Marianne's cottage, with the dogs and, across the lane, the donkeys and Josephine the goat. If Georgie was there, he didn't mind. He just wanted to sit with his mother and be.

As he neared the Shooting Box, it was clear he'd misjudged the weather. The scent of fog hung heavy in the air, even stifling the quad bike's diesel, and now it rolled silently over him, wrapping him in soft, creeping folds. Droplets jewelled his jacket sleeves and his gloves where they gripped the handlebars, and moisture clung to his face, cold and clammy.

As if from far away he heard Effie's voice, the sing-song tone she adopted when telling her local legends. *If you look across and can't see the Devil's Chair, it means he's sitting in it. Time to get off the hill, get inside and close the shutters.* He'd left it a bit late for that.

Where the Portway met the disc barrow's ring, he stopped the bike and killed the engine. Its dying sounds echoed in the fog, receding until all that was left was silence and, somewhere to his left, the calling of sheep. He stepped off the bike, his legs stiff with cold and turned through three hundred and sixty degrees. Visibility was, he reckoned, less than five metres, if that. He could see his hand in front of his face all right, could make out where the heather from the ring bank dwindled into the snow-covered turf of the ditch, but no further. Taking a few steps in the other direction, the ground began to rise beneath his feet and he knew he must be heading for the centre of the mound. But where on the barrow was he?

In the fog it was easy to lose all sense of orientation. Not that he was worried about the bike. All he need do was stick to the ditch and he'd find it. But, even with the Portway to follow, he'd be lucky to find his way off the hill without a few wrong turns. Once fog came in, shrouding any landmarks, everywhere on the heather-strewn plateau of the Mynd looked the same. With snow on the ground it would be unnavigable and he'd need the GPS on his phone to be sure of his direction. The last thing he wanted was to take the wrong way along the Portway and find himself heading north towards All Stretton and Woolstaston.

He stopped dead. From somewhere to his right came an eerie sound, low and moaning. Not a sheep. Nor one of Effie's Wild Hunt or Will-o-the-wisps. Joe listened, his ears at full stretch. A voice. Human, he was sure. Human and in pain.

"Hello?" he called. Nothing. If anything, the silence intensified. Then the sound came again. No words, only a low groan. Quickening his pace, Joe climbed the mound until the ground began to drop away again, then felt with his feet, wary of falling into the depression left by the old grouse hut. He might be nowhere near it, on the other side of the barrow even. The groan came again from somewhere nearby. Joe pulled out his phone and switched on the torch but rather than casting light it sucked and swirled the fog into whiteness and he turned it off.

"Hello?" he called again. As another groan pierced the fog, something clutched at his leg and he went down, falling hard across a bulky lump that gave an agonised yell. Joe scrambled away but whatever it was clung to him, pulling him back until he kicked out to free himself. He rolled onto his hands and knees, crawling back to the prone figure because now he recognised it as human. A man, or a boy even, younger than him and clad in waterproof clothing, a dark beanie covering his head, lay curled like a foetus.

"Hey!" Joe said, kneeling close. The boy's eyes were closed. "Can you hear me? What's your name?" He shook him by the shoulder and patted the padded arm, kept talking, kept asking his name. *Shit, shit, shit.* He had his phone. If he could get the casualty to the bike, he could call for an ambulance to meet them at the Burway. A fall maybe – he could have been there for hours.

"It's all right, mate, we'll get you out of here. We'll sort you out. Come on." Grunting with exertion, he slid an arm under the unresponsive figure and heaved him into a sitting position then recoiled, almost dropping him back to the ground. On the grubby snow where he had lain was a knife, its blade patterned with red. A dark stain spread across the young man's unzipped jacket. Beneath the hands clutched tight to his belly, blood oozed between clenched fingers, red and sticky.

Shit, holy shit. What the...?

"All right, mate. Hang on. We'll get you sorted. I've got stuff on the bike. By the ditch." His first aid kit was in his bag. Joe pulled off his scarf and folded it into a thick pad, prising away the rigid hands and pressing it firmly against the wound. "There, hold that there. Firm pressure, OK? Stay with me, you hear?"

Should he drag him? Or try to get the quad bike nearer? The boy was almost the same size as him and to sling him across his back might cause catastrophic bleeding. He needed a stretcher and a team. There was no way he'd do it alone.

Still talking, he pulled out his phone and pressed the Search and Rescue emergency number. Kneeling up, he strained his eyes towards where he thought he'd left the bike. How far was it? Could he carry him?

When it was answered, he didn't wait to hear who was on call. "It's Joe Ingles. I'm at the Shooting Box on the Long Mynd. I've got a casualty. Looks like a knife wound."

Movement caught the corner of his eye. A flash of dark. Before he could turn, someone stamped hard on his leg. White hot pain seared and he pitched forward, the phone springing from his hand. From somewhere near him came a scuffling noise, movement of snow and fog. His vision swam and focused again. A hard, black alien object protruded from his thigh, planted deep through his snowboard pants into his flesh.

As he reached for the handle of the knife, thick, dark liquid began to bubble around its base and he pressed his glove to it. *Don't pull it out. Don't pull it out. Press down. Firm pressure.* He tried to push himself upright but his arms wouldn't obey and he hunched on his knees, one elbow and his forehead tight to the freezing ground. He turned his head towards the young man who lay next to him. Barely more than a boy. Eyes open, teeth bared in a rictus grin. Words so quiet they were little more than a hiss reached him across the furrowed snow.

"No one's coming for us, mate ... we're gonna die here ... you and me."

29

Alisha Johnson's interview had yielded little. Georgie had watched from behind blacked-out glass, one eye on the text reports that trickled in from Mike Harley, updating her on the progress of the search at Mytton's Fold. Which so far had yielded nothing. Plenty of evidence that Sam Gray had stayed at the house, but none to suggest it had been the scene of his death. The incinerator had contained only garden waste, and there had been no traces of blood in the barn or anywhere else. The knives in the kitchen knife block and drawer were a mixture of French Sabatier and Japanese Miyabi, suggesting Cal Innes liked to cook. The knife that had killed Sam Gray had been identified as part of Dunelm Mill's own brand homeware collection.

Rarely had she seen a suspect so self-possessed as Alisha. Rather than cowed or intimidated by having been brought in to the station for a formal interview, she seemed galvanised by anger, outraged that anyone could consider her anything other than blameless.

"So I called him. So what? After what happened Wednesday

night, him disappearing off with Davey and then saying as we all had to keep quiet, you think I'm not going to check in with him? Just sit home like a good girl because he says so?"

"Yours was the only call, Alisha," Chowdhury had said. "What made you pick up the phone? He'd said on the group chat for you all to leave him be in case your phone was checked. Only use the group chat."

"And I had to do what Sam Gray said, did I? Who made him the boss of me?"

Had she known where Sam was staying, Chowdhury had asked. A question met with an eye roll and a sneer. Of course she had. Sam had told her, probably hoping she'd drop round. He'd been the one wanting to move things on with her, talking about going to London and leaving this shit-hole behind.

"What about Jessie?" Corby had asked. "I thought they were back together."

"He still cared about her. I didn't want to hurt her neither. But Jessie's never going to leave here, is she? Stuck in the family business. Sam had ambition. Wanted to go places. He wanted us to go together."

When Chowdhury had asked about her movements on the Saturday afternoon that Sam had disappeared from Mytton's Fold she'd crossed her arms and said she'd been shopping in Shrewsbury. Asked for a list of shops and the rough times she'd been there, she'd announced she'd had enough.

"This is meant to be voluntary, right? Well, it's not voluntary anymore. I'm done."

Her solicitor had backed her, pointing out that they had nowhere near enough evidence to hold her on any charge. Telephoning the deceased on the probable but still unconfirmed day of his death was hardly grounds for arrest.

Seeing a missed opportunity, Fraser, who'd been trying not

to interfere, had buzzed through to Chowdhury's earpiece, telling him to ask her if she'd told anyone else where Sam had been staying. Had anyone else in the group known?

"No comment. And any other question you ask, no comment. I told you. I'm done."

They'd had little choice but to let her go. Georgie had had to admit there'd been something magnificent about her. But it had been magnificence she could have done without.

Now she sat in her office, feet on the desk, staring out at the dreary sky. The snow had lost all its magic. Shrewsbury's pavements were dirty-grey, the gutters clogged with slush, and cars sent up showers of filthy spray. On the surrounding hills shimmers of whiteness still showed, but the town itself was cloaked in gloom. The air was dull, misty and though it was barely lunchtime, you could have mistaken it for twilight. She wondered if Marianne had finished work yet. Saturdays were busy at the tearoom but often she finished after the lunchtime rush, leaving her staff to run the afternoon and clear up.

Usually they went for a walk in the hills with the dogs, shaking off the stresses of the week, most of which were Georgie's. Until the question of Joe's father had reared its head, anyway. She realised now that, since that evening at Effie's and Marianne's conversation with Joe, she hadn't mentioned it. Or perhaps Georgie had been too preoccupied with her case to hear. Joe had said he didn't need to know and Georgie had sensed Marianne's relief. But underneath it, had there been anticlimax? Had Marianne come to the conclusion that it was time those who had assaulted her, whose actions had changed the course of her entire life, paid for their crime?

Thoughts of the bastard who'd inadvertently fathered Joe brought her mind around to Colm Doherty and the two sons he'd left behind. Had there been others? It seemed an unlikely coincidence that the man, with his penchant for women and reluctance to use contraception, had left two children in one small town and none anywhere else. Besides the daughter, of course. And where was she now? They'd had no luck so far in tracing her in Ireland. Had she come to England? To Shropshire? It wasn't beyond the bounds of possibility. But if she had, why was there no trace of her on council tax records or the electoral register? Georgie's phone rang on the desk and, with a sinking feeling, she saw Pitbull's name.

"Morning, sir," she said automatically.

"It's bloody afternoon, Fraser, and I've been waiting for your call. Update now, please."

She filled him in on the search so far – still unfinished, though Harley reckoned they'd be done in another half hour – and the interview with Alisha Johnson.

"And that's all I get for shelling out on overtime? That's you, Chowdhury, Corby, Harley and a full bloody search team. And sod all to show for it."

She couldn't disagree with him, though she had to put up some sort of fight.

"With respect, sir, ruling things out is progress of a sort. And I don't have Innes down as our man. Or Doherty's family. Whatever we do, I keep coming back to that group of kids. One of them has more to tell us, I'm sure of it."

"And in the meantime, we've got trouble coming at us from all directions. I presume you've seen all the shit on Twitter or X or whatever the bollocks it's called."

She had, although she hadn't looked that morning, regarding it as a distraction that they didn't need.

"And the *Shropshire Chronicle* has run an article on you being the only trans police officer in any force's CID. Which isn't true incidentally. There's one up in Merseyside too. But they manage to make it look as though I've demonstrated poor judgement in putting you on a sensitive case."

Would it be impolitic to tell Pitbull that she really couldn't give a shite? All that mattered was getting the job done. And it was his job to fend off flak from the press.

"We've got a complaint to add to that, now," the DCI said. "An official one. Came in ten minutes ago. That Johnson girl's solicitor."

"A complaint?" Georgie said, taking her feet off the desk and sitting up. A dull ache had started behind her eyes halfway through the morning and wasn't getting any better.

"You've had two suspects in for interview, one yesterday, one today. What do they have in common?"

Georgie frowned. Cal Innes and Alisha Johnson? Nothing, apart from that they both knew Sam Gray. That both had had contact with him in the days immediately before his death.

"Come on, Fraser, you're not blind. Or shall I get the solicitor to spell it out for you?" His voice broke into a pause, followed by a long exhalation. She imagined billows of pure nicotine vapour streaming from between his lips. No fruity scents for Pitbull.

"It's all over bloody social media. Of all the possible suspects, the only ones you've pulled in are black. Or turn it around. There are two black witnesses or persons of interest and you've labelled both of them suspects."

"With respect, sir, I haven't labelled anyone anything. I've followed up every lead that's come our way, even going back to an Irish connection from twenty years ago. Skin colour has nothing to do with it."

"There's one black kid in that group and she's the one you pulled in for a formal interview. What did you think people were going to make of that?"

Georgie's temper was rising, long days and poor nights catching up with her.

"What did you want me to do, sir? Arrest a token white kid?"

The door burst open without a knock and Corby surged in.

Georgie hadn't known she was still there, had thought she and Chowdhury had left once Alisha Johnson was off the premises. Pitbull was still ranting on – *well, maybe that wouldn't have been such a bad idea* – but Fraser's attention was firmly on Corby. Her face said she brought news that Georgie couldn't afford to miss. She nodded at Corby to go ahead, holding the phone away from her ear.

"It's Joe Ingles, boss. Up on the Long Mynd. Another of those lads has been stabbed."

Time slowed. Pitbull's voice still registered somewhere to her left but her mind turned only on Corby's words. *Another of those lads has been stabbed.* Corby hadn't finished talking.

"They don't know who yet. Search and Rescue called it in ..."

"Are you listening to me, Fraser?"

Georgie started as Pitbull's voice reached new decibel levels and put the phone back to her ear.

"Hang on, sir. Something's just come in."

"S and R said Joe called," Corby was saying. "He found the lad but now they've lost all contact. They think something might have happened to him. Joe."

Pitbull was still going.

"I don't care what's come in. We've got a press conference at three o'clock and at the moment, I've got nothing to deflect the mob's accusations of you being a freak and a racist."

At another time, Georgie might have considered making a formal complaint herself about Pitbull's language. Now her brain barely registered it. Another stabbing. And Joe had dropped out of contact. If there was fog in Shrewsbury it would be worse in the hills. Another young lad had been stabbed. Who was to say the killer hadn't still been there? What if Joe...? Marianne's face drifted between her and Corby, who was still talking. It seemed Georgie must have asked a question because Corby was trying to explain the order of events.

Pitbull growled again in her ear. The sound snapped her out of her trance.

"With the greatest respect, sir, we've got bigger fish to fry. There's been another stabbing. And Joe Ingles is missing on the Long Mynd."

30

Marianne was restless. She had left work once the lunchtime rush was over, hoping that Georgie might be home already, if not on her way. But, when she turned the key and opened the door, the only ones to greet her were the dogs, tails waving and full of joy. It never mattered how long she was gone, twenty minutes or five hours, their greeting was the same.

Checking her phone she found it switched off, as it often was, and turned it on to find a message from Georgie saying that she'd have to stay at the station until a search was complete but that she hoped to be home by three at the latest. Beneath the notification of Georgie's message was one from Niamh. Marianne frowned. She and Niamh were hardly in regular contact. In fact, they had only swapped numbers when Niamh had messaged to thank Marianne for a birthday present.

-Hi Marianne could you call me when you get this? I'm a bit worried about Joe x

Scrolling down through her notifications Marianne saw two missed calls, also from Niamh.

Knowing that if she stopped to think she would find a reason for not calling the girl, she pressed her number. The phone might go to voicemail. If Niamh hadn't answered within six rings she reckoned she could legitimately ring off, without anyone being able to say she hadn't tried to call back. Niamh answered on the second ring.

"Marianne, thanks so much for getting back to me."

"My phone was off," Marianne said. "I was at work. Is everything ok?"

"Not really. Well, maybe. I was worried because I hadn't been able to get hold of Joe all day. We had a bit of a row last night – my fault – and I wanted to check he was OK, but he just wasn't answering. He'd said he was going to do some more of the conservation work ..."

Marianne let the girl's words wash over her. Joe sometimes joked that Niamh would never use just one word if there was a chance to use fifty.

"... and I knew the weather was coming in. No more snow, but fog and all the tracks are so wet ..."

"Do you want me to try calling him?" Marianne interrupted. It wouldn't be like Joe to sulk and if the two of them had argued she hardly wanted to get involved, but the girl sounded worried.

"No, it's OK. He got back to me in the end. Said he was going up to the Shooting Box and that he'd call later."

"So?" Marianne said, not impatiently but aware that she could perhaps be showing more sympathy.

"It's just, well ... now, I can't get hold of him again. And the fog's come down. I'm over at Effie's. I'd been at work in the Pavilion café so I thought I'd drop in, in case he was back. I keep calling but he's not answering. The phone keeps going to voicemail."

"Could he be out of signal?"

"I don't think so. Not if he's at the Shooting Box. We were up there yesterday with the volunteer group and the signal was fine.

Just with the tracks how they are – now that some of the snow's melted. I'm worried maybe he's had an accident on the quadbike."

It was odd, Marianne thought, that she had such absolute faith in her son. Accidents happened of course but it never occurred to her to worry about him in that context. When he was in Devon, he had forever been out surfing and sailing. Having grown up by the sea, she knew its power all too well but Joe was practical and competent, not given to panic or recklessness. The same applied now that he had moved inland and was often up in the hills on his own. She had to admit, though, that it would be unusual for him not to answer repeated calls. And anyone could have an accident in treacherous conditions.

"Look," she said. "Why don't I try calling him too? And I'll come and meet you at Effie's. If one of us hasn't got hold of him by the time I get to you, we can maybe drive up the Burway and look for him. If Georgie's finished work, she can take us up in the Land Rover."

Loading the dogs into the back of her old Subaru Impreza Wagon, Marianne reflected that, given that she had four-wheel drive, there was no need to wait for Georgie and the Land Rover. Only she hated the Burway and the thought of driving up it in fog, with snowmelt running down its surface, made her feel sick.

As she turned onto the A49 towards Church Stretton, pushing through dense banks of fog which lifted and drifted, then settled again, she left a message for Georgie asking her to call and pressed Joe's number. No answer. Ten minutes later, passing Acton Scott's Heritage farm and the Marshbrook junction she tried again. Still no answer. Despite her habit of not worrying, low-level anxiety ticked away in her stomach. It wasn't until she turned into Sandford Avenue from the main road that her phone rang. Georgie.

She swiped right, switching the phone onto speaker in its holder.

"Have you heard from Joe?" Georgie's voice cut in before she could say hello. Its urgency made her stomach drop.

"What's happened?"

With the thaw, Church Stretton's snow-free pavements were busy and Marianne braked suddenly, swerving to avoid a man who had stepped off the kerb in front of the post office without looking. The jolt of adrenaline that surged through her had little to do with the near-miss.

"Georgie. What's happened?"

"He found a casualty up on the Mynd. Another young lad's been stabbed, we think. He called Search and Rescue but now his phone's dead. No one's been able to establish contact."

Georgie was using her work voice. Her work personality. Ice sluiced down Marianne's spine. Joe would never go up on the hill without his phone being fully charged. Not in this sort of weather. In the little town it was more like low cloud or mist but as she headed up towards Effie's the fog grew thicker, stained yellow by the street lights which had come on well before their usual time.

"I'm on my way to Effie's," she said. "To meet Niamh. We were going to drive up the Burway to meet him if he hasn't called by the time I get there."

"Don't," Georgie said. "Stay at Effie's."

"But what if—?"

"Search and Rescue are sending a team up. Corby and I are on our way. You know you hate the Burway. Stay where you're safe. I'll keep you posted, I promise."

Marianne pressed her foot to the accelerator as the car growled its way up the foot of the Burway and onto Effie's steep drive.

"I've got the dogs with me. They could help find him."

"Sweetheart, Search and Rescue will find him. I promise. Look I've got to go. We're heading up from Woolstaston and the mist's like soup."

Don't you sweetheart me. Anger flooded Marianne's veins, making her arms and legs tingle. *That's my son, out there. My son, not answering his phone. My son with a boy who's been stabbed, and who's to say he didn't run into whoever did the stabbing?*

"Fine," she said, turning off the engine, her car sprawled across Effie's drive. No point parking carefully. She wouldn't be there long.

"Marianne, honey ..."

"Just keep me posted." She ended the call.

Leaving the dogs in the car, she ran to the door and hammered on it with its heavy brass knocker. Niamh opened it so fast that Marianne almost fell through into the hall. Behind the girl, Effie stood with a thermos flask in her hands.

"Georgie just called," Marianne said, and told her story in as few words as possible. Niamh's mouth fell open, shock and fear scrawled across her face.

"We'll drive up the Burway," Marianne said. "You can direct me to the Shooting Box. The dogs'll find him."

Niamh grabbed her jacket, a red National Trust one like Joe's, from the pegs behind the door. Marianne turned towards the car and only then noticed that Effie too was pulling on a long waterproof coat.

"You stay here," she said. "We'll need someone here for when we bring him back."

"Nonsense." Effie followed Niamh through the front door and pulled it shut behind her, the thermos flask still in one hand. "You hate driving up that road. We can take my car."

. . .

HALFWAY UP THE BURWAY, Marianne's stomach was churning with nausea. Anxiety for her son or fear of the sheer mountain road? The fog almost helped. At least she couldn't see the two hundred foot drop where the road fell away to her right down Devil's Mouth Hollow. She kept the car tight to the wall of rock on her left, praying that they wouldn't meet anyone coming the other way. At least, if they did, the passing spaces were all on her side. It would be them that would have to face the side of the road with its unfenced drop. Every so often saliva flooded her mouth and her heart missed a beat, thumping hard against her ribs. Perhaps she should have let Effie drive. The thought of sitting helpless in the passenger seat had been unbearable. As had been the time it would have taken transferring the dogs between cars.

"Nearly there, love," Effie said from the passenger seat. "Two more bends and you'll be at Cow Ridge." And there the road crested onto the plateau, broad stretches of turf on both sides, and no more risk of a car plunging off the edge into the valley below.

"I've got my GPS on," Niamh said. "We need to keep going until we get to the Portway. I can track Joe's phone too." Some app the two of them used, Find My Friends or something. "It's not dead. It's showing over to the north-west, about where the Shooting Box must be, I think."

But if his phone wasn't dead, why wasn't he answering?

In the boot the dogs shifted restlessly, picking up on the energy that bounced off the shell of the car. Pip had been whining since they began their ascent of the Burway. As they reached the plateau and the road flattened, Marianne's shoulders dropped a millimetre and she exhaled, her knuckles white on the steering wheel.

"That's it, my girl," Effie said. "You've been holding your breath since the bottom. Worst is over now. Just keep going."

"I'm not going back down that way," Marianne said, her voice catching. "When we find him, Georgie can take him down and I'll go back via Ratlinghope or Plowden."

"Cross that bridge when we come to it," said Effie, her tone easing Marianne's heart rate.

"Slow down a bit." Niamh was leaning over the back of Effie's seat, phone in hand, craning to see through the windscreen. "We'll be coming up to the Portway soon. We don't want to miss it. Jayz, you can barely see five metres."

Marianne's phone buzzed suddenly, making them all jump. Joe's name filled the screen.

Marianne swiped across it, almost knocking the phone from its holder.

"Joe? Are you OK?" She could have cried with relief.

"Ma?" His voice was faint, as though the phone was a long way from his mouth. "Ma? I couldn't ... lost my ..." Silence.

"Joe?" Niamh called from the back. "Joe? Where are you? Here!" she shouted to Marianne. "Turn right here."

From the speaker of Marianne's phone came only a faint hissing. Sweat beaded in her armpits, goosebumps prickling on her arms. Behind her, Niamh began to cry, calling Joe's name again as the phone maintained its stubborn silence.

"Slowly, love," Effie said. "We don't want to go off the track. Keep going slowly. Niamh, you keep an eye on that GPS. Tell us when to stop. Come on, love. He'll be all right. You've heard his voice, he's still with us."

"Joe!" Marianne thumped her hands on the steering wheel, calling out loud in her frustration and fear. A faint groan issued from the phone then, even fainter, so quiet she might have imagined it. "*Ma?*"

"We're on our way, Joe. Just hang on, OK? We're nearly there. Georgie, Search and Rescue, we're all coming. Just hang on."

31

Time lost all meaning. Wrapped in thick, eerie fog, his body pressed against the cold ground, Joe slipped between fear and grim determination to hold on.

At first when he'd seen the handle of the knife standing proud out of his thigh, shock had robbed him of rational thought. And those words, hissed by the boy who lay on the ground beside him; 'we're gonna die here, you and me'. They echoed in his head and came back to him now when cold and pain threatened to overwhelm him. Through half-closed eyes he saw his mother's face; that look she had when she was bracing herself to face the world. It must have taken unimaginable strength to rebuild her life after the terrible things that had happened to her. He was not going to die.

Beside him, the unknown boy gave a low moan. Since Joe had pressed the pad to his belly he'd seemed unconscious. Periodically, half-crouching, forehead resting in the snow while he harnessed his strength, Joe had spoken to him, tried to keep him going. Responsibility for another gave him an added reason to hang on.

As the initial shock receded, his rational brain took over.

Despite the pressure, blood continued to bubble between his fingers, seeping through his snowboard pants into the snow on either side of his leg. Too far to the bike for his first aid kit. One-handed, he burrowed beneath his jacket and fleece and pulled his belt free of his trousers. Not leather, thank goodness. Some sort of webbed fabric. Leather would slip. Snaking it under his thigh, he threaded it through the ring buckle with a shaking hand. He used his teeth to pull it tight, holding it in place above the wound, before making a loop and tying it. A slim torch from his bag served as a windlass, pushed though the loop and wound tight until the bleeding subsided.

For a while afterwards he lay still, recouping his strength. If the boy beside him was not to die, and he along with him, he must find the bike. He must find his phone. The barrow rose behind him and he reckoned he had come over it in a fairly straight line. If he retraced his steps, surely he must come to the quad bike. And he needed to move soon, before the pain became any worse. It felt as though a dull, heavy vice was trying to snap his femur. A sharp, biting pain seared where the belt edges dug into his flesh.

Summoning effort, he took off his jacket and laid it over the boy.

"I won't be long. I'm going to get something to help you." There was no response. Surely it couldn't have been the boy who stabbed him. He'd seemed to have no strength left. And why would he? But Joe had seen no one else. Only that quick flash of movement in the fog.

There was no question of him standing. Even crawling seemed impossible. Using his elbows and his one good knee, Joe dragged himself on his belly, his injured leg trailing behind him, useless. He tried not to notice the slick of red that followed him through the snow, or the excruciating pain that burned through his left leg every time he accidentally flexed a muscle or forgot to hold it completely still. The blade of the knife must have passed right through his quadriceps, or perhaps between the femur and his IT band. Thinking of the muscles, visualising the anatomy helped somehow.

Low to the ground, the visibility was better than when he'd been standing. He crested the rise of the barrow, felt the slope begin to descend. At least he would be able to follow his blood trail on the way back. As he slid head first down towards the ditch, something black loomed into his vision. A thick, chunky tyre, clogged with snow and mud. Even up here the thaw was starting. Behind the bike, two thick black tracks showed between dirty white edges like crushed Liquorice Allsorts.

Summoning the strength he was sure would soon be lost, Joe hauled himself up the side of the quad, balancing on his right knee, keeping the left leg out to his side. Pins and needles stabbed at his calf like electric shocks and every so often the part of his leg below the knee jerked and spasmed. He breathed deeply, forcing himself to concentrate on his task. The first aid kit was in his bag, strapped to the carrier, and he tugged it free from beneath the webbing. The tools he had brought to clear the heather were there too; shears, secateurs and a spade. He could think of no use for them and anyway wouldn't have the strength to take them with him.

The weight of the bag brought to mind the flask of coffee he'd packed at the last minute and, feeling a stab of guilt for the boy who lay semi-conscious on the other side of the barrow, freezing and bleeding to death, he eased it free from the bag. His hands shook so hard he struggled to unscrew the lid, his gloves slipping on the smooth metal. At last he managed it and held its mouth to his lips. Scalding liquid spilled over his chin but some found his tongue and he gulped it down, heat stealing down his oesophagus. There was chocolate in the bag too and he found it with his free hand. He put the flask back and broke off a few chunks of sweetness, stuffing them in his mouth before closing up the bag again. He had a long way to crawl back to his prone companion. And he needed to find his phone.

The trail of blood was easy to follow. Somehow, though, the distance had grown, further than on the way over. Each pull of his elbows and forearms required more strength. He kept himself going with the promise of more coffee. More chocolate once he reached the other side. His leg dragged like a dead weight. When the slope began to descend again, he lay flat on his belly and let himself slide down into the hollow where the boy was.

"Hey! Can you hear me? We need to get you warm."

No reply. He hadn't really expected one.

Pushing himself into a sitting position he dragged the bag onto his lap, his injured leg sticking out almost at right angles to his body. The buzzing pins and needles had faded into a heavy, cold deadness and when he tried to move his toes it felt as though his foot was made of wood. He pulled a foil survival blanket free of the bag and used his teeth to open the plastic wrapper. The boy lay curled on his side, hands still holding the pad of Joe's scarf pressed against his belly. Joe took his jacket back, aware that without it he might freeze to death himself, and tucked the silver blanket around the boy, lifting him to push it beneath to insulate him from the snowy ground. The lad must have been lying in the freezing wet, bleeding for a good hour. If the stab wound didn't finish him, hypothermia might.

Once he'd struggled back into his jacket, he followed the same procedure with a webbing bandage. Tearing it free with his teeth, he rolled the boy from side to side as he wound it around his torso, securing the padded scarf tightly in place.

For what could have been five minutes or fifteen he rested. Until, forcing away the sleep that threatened to overcome him, he pushed himself upright again and drank more coffee. He let the chunks of chocolate dissolve slowly in his mouth, reviving slightly as sugar seeped into his bloodstream. Then he began the hunt for his phone. On his hands and knees, he probed through pockets of snow until his gloved fingers closed on something smooth and hard. Joe thanked the God he didn't believe in for the chunky waterproof case that all the Search and Rescue volunteers used for their phones.

His tasks complete – the phone in his hand, the boy beneath his foil blanket – all strength suddenly left him. His arms gave way, weak and trembling, and the hollow ache in his leg seemed all-consuming. For he knew not how long he lay semi-conscious in the snow, overwhelmed by nausea and dizziness.

Far distant, he heard his mother's voice. Thought for a second that she was leaning over him. Smelled the scent of her hair when she'd just washed it. He dragged the hand that held the phone nearer to his face. Though it swam in front of his eyes, something brought the screen to life. Thank God for facial recognition. How strange that it worked, even in such extreme circumstances. Using voice controls he told it to call Marianne.

She answered straightaway as though the phone was in her hand.

"Joe? Are you OK?"

Scared. Urgent.

He spoke, though he didn't know what he said.

He heard her voice and Niamh's too. Heard her promise that she was on her way. That Georgie was coming. His friends at Search and Rescue.

He reached out and found the boy's shoulder.

"They're coming. Search and Rescue. My ma. She's coming."

Then he laid his head on his bag and let sleep steal over him.

The next he knew, something cold and wet was pushing at his face. Hot breath and wet fur. A deep bark, loud to his ears. A large dog paw scraping at the snow by his face. Maggie. He recognised her smell. Pip, smaller and furry, wriggled against him, squeaking. Then Marianne's voice. Niamh crying. Gulping down words. Strong firm hands on his shoulder, then his face. His mother told him he would be all right. That they were there.

"Can you hear, Joe? That's Georgie. And your friends from Search and Rescue. You're going to be OK. Hold on, my darling." His mother's hand gripped his. "Niamh's here. Niamh, talk to him." And he'd heard the spill of his girlfriend's words, garbled and choked with sobs, and tried to smile.

He wasn't unconscious. He could hear. The grumble of an engine. Tyres crunching over snow. Another engine. Men's voices calling to each other. Georgie's Scottish lilt shouting orders. He was almost preternaturally aware of everything but something cocooned him tightly and he was unable to speak or respond in any way. All he needed to do was open his eyes or move his lips but every muscle seemed frozen.

The hollow was suddenly full of movement. Large boots. Snow crunching all around him. The metallic creak of a stretcher. He recognised Cal Innes's voice and Andy Morgan's. The medic called Liz. They were talking to someone called Lucas. Someone said something about the air ambulance.

Georgie's voice. His mother's again and a gulp of Niamh's tears. A hand on his shoulder and Georgie spoke close to his ear.

"Well, look at the state of you, Joe Ingles. We'd better get you off this hill, I reckon." A gloved hand stroked over his head. "Now, you take a deep breath and hold tight to your ma's hand. We need to get you on this stretcher and it's going to hurt like hell."

Then, beating the wind, came the whirling thud and thwack of rotor blades. A fine spray of cold powder dusted his face and he felt himself swept upwards in a spiral of freezing air.

32

Niamh's intense distress was, Georgie found, easier to cope with than Marianne's shutdown. Besides murmuring to Joe as she held his hand, kneeling in the snowy hollow while the Search and Rescue team and later the paramedics did their stuff, she hadn't said a word.

Niamh, quite naturally, had sobbed, terrified by the sight of her boyfriend on the ground, a knife embedded in his thigh and the snow around him soaked in blood, however well he had managed to stem the flow. Effie had wrapped the girl in strong, sinewy arms and held her tight, dispensing firm, no-nonsense assurances that Joe would be all right, that they had reached him in time, Corby echoing her like a Greek chorus. And all the while Marianne had knelt as though carved from alabaster.

Lucas Harley was in a bad way. If he survived there was no doubt that it would be down to Joe. Hypothermia may well have set in without the foil blanket and he was not safe from it yet. Without the pad that Joe had clamped to the wound, the boy would undoubtedly have bled to death.

The air ambulance crew were sure of it. Full of praise for the way Joe had taken care of Lucas and himself. Whether either Joe or Marianne heard their praise was debatable.

And for Joe there was no air ambulance. It was equipped for only one casualty and, though the doctor on board had seen to Joe before the helicopter took off, he was then strapped to a stretcher and carried to the Burway where an ambulance waited. Carried, Georgie realised, by the same team with whom he'd retrieved the body of Davey Whelan, Joe's place taken by Malcolm Tucker. There was something poignant in that. Cal Innes avoided Georgie's eye and for that she didn't blame him. It said much, and validated her belief in him, that he was there, despite having had his house and barn torn asunder by the police that morning.

Georgie, brought up a Catholic, though fairly laxly, gave thanks to God that Joe, unlike Davey, had survived. So far. Despite Effie's assurances to Niamh, there was no guarantee he would make it. As, she suspected, Marianne knew. There had been a horrifying amount of blood in the snowy hollow. As though gladiators and lions had ripped at each other in the barrow's half-amphitheatre. How much was Lucas's and how much Joe's had been impossible to tell.

Marianne had had to let go of Joe's hand while the team carried him to the Burway. He had made one sound, a brief staccato yell as they had lifted him on to the stretcher, but for the rest remained unconscious. Or unresponsive. The strength with which his fingers had found and gripped his mother's when they first arrived suggested some consciousness.

By the time they reached the Burway, the fog had begun to lift. They passed Marianne's car crouched by the side of the Portway and a little further on, Georgie's Land Rover next to Cal Innes's pick-up which had brought the rest of the Search and Rescue Team. As the paramedics lifted Joe and his stretcher into the ambulance, the realisation dawned that now they would have to make their way down off the hill.

Marianne, still silent, a smudge of her son's blood on her cheek, watched the ambulance team close the doors as, around her, arrangements were made and thanks given to the Search and Rescue Team. Effie insisted she would drive Marianne's car back down and Niamh begged them all to hurry. She wanted to get to the hospital at the same time as Joe.

As they turned to walk back towards the cars, the rear door of the ambulance flew open.

"Joe's mum?" The paramedic's voice wove through the mist, no longer thick enough to be called fog. "Have we got Joe's mum there?"

Marianne turned like an automaton.

"He's asking for you. Come and ride in with him?"

When Georgie had first met Marianne, her blue-grey eyes had been hidden behind shutters which had lifted over time until Georgie barely remembered them. Now they were back and the eyes that sought hers gave nothing away. Georgie took her hand.

"Come on. You go in the ambulance with Joe. I'll drive your car and Corby can bring the Land Rover. That way Effie can look after Niamh while I drive. No arguments," she added to the others as first Niamh, then Effie had protested. "We'll drop the dogs at Effie's when we go past."

THE LAST TIME Georgie had been to the Royal Shrewsbury Hospital's Accident and Emergency department with Marianne was after a midnight near-death experience at the Devil's Chair. Then their friendship had been only nascent. Marianne, newly transitioned from suspect to key witness in that murder enquiry, had offered her a lift home from the hospital. It was that night, too, that Georgie had hinted to her that Joe, also a suspect in the murder enquiry, was her son. Unprofessional, perhaps, but then she'd always sailed a little close to the wind where humanity was concerned. And Joe, that night, had just saved her life.

As they turned into the hospital car park from the Mytton Oak Road, they passed the Emergency Department. Stark and red against the brick building, the air ambulance crouched like a giant dragonfly on the helipad. Georgie wondered how long it had taken to spirit Lucas here. Had he survived the trip? Between the helicopter and the department's doors stood two ambulances. Presumably one had transported Joe down the steep winding Burway and made good time. At any rate there was no activity around them now. Georgie had floored it in Marianne's Subaru, but stopping at Effie's to drop the dogs off had cost them five minutes and there had been no sign of either the ambulance or Corby in the police Land Rover on the A49.

She saw Marianne as soon as they passed through the doors into A&E. Still carved from alabaster she stared straight ahead, seeing nothing. Beside her stood Ali Corby, who did turn her head as they entered and raised a hand. Casting a glance down at Marianne, she came across to Georgie. Niamh and Effie went over to where Marianne sat.

"Mike Harley's on his way," Corby said. "He's bringing Lucas's parents."

"What have the doctors said?" Georgie asked, one eye on Marianne. It was like being split down the middle, her brain functioning on two levels. On the one hand, she was desperately worried for Marianne and for Joe. The ramifications for their lives if Joe didn't pull through didn't bear thinking about. Better then, not to think about it but to trust the medical team.

The other train of thought was far simpler. She needed to question Joe as soon as he was fit. Had he seen who had stabbed him and, by assumption, had also stabbed Lucas Harley?

"No news yet," Corby said. "I got here just after they'd taken Joe through. The doctor was talking to Marianne but all he said was that it would be some time before they had any news. Joe needs surgery but until they've assessed him, they can't be sure exactly what."

Georgie nodded. Niamh and Effie were seated one either side of Marianne, and Effie had taken her hand. As she watched, Marianne turned her head slightly towards Effie and spoke one or two words, but her face and eyes were blank. She had withdrawn into her shell like a mollusc. Briefly Georgie cursed her job which meant that, instead of supporting the woman she loved, she must maintain some semblance of professionalism. Perhaps it was better for Marianne. She had the look about her that Georgie had seen during the Devil's Chair case, wrapping her coat around her as though its fabric might prevent her from shattering all over the floor.

"What about Lucas? Did he make it?"

"Still unresponsive when the air ambulance got him here. They took him straight into surgery. The doctor from the air team said he might be lucky. It looked like the knife had missed the aorta otherwise he'd be dead already. Whoever stabbed him missed his mark."

Phrases kept ricocheting through Georgie's mind. Snatches of interviews and statements, the first briefing in the incident room when Corby had talked the team through the youngsters who'd been up at the shelter that night. She saw again the photos displayed on the Smartboard. There had been ten of them at that party. Now, two were dead and another halfway there; one it seemed by accident, and two stabbed. From what she'd seen of the knife in Joe's leg, it matched the one that had been used to kill Sam Gray. Had anyone noticed that their kitchen was missing two knives? If nothing else came to light, she would have to ask the parents of all those involved to go through their cutlery drawers.

But something else was tugging at a loose thread in her brain. Since she'd first seen that blood-soaked hollow where the old grouse-shooting box had been, a scenario had suggested itself to her but floated ghost-like and insubstantial, just out of reach. If she pulled hard enough at the thread, maybe she could drag it towards her.

"Oh lord, there's Mike," Corby said and Georgie turned to see the tall glass doors slide apart, admitting her sergeant. He was accompanied by a man so similar as to be unmistakably his brother and a woman of around Georgie's height, her hair scraped back in a ponytail, a coat thrown roughly over the kind of clothes you'd wear for decorating. Harley's brother was wearing paint-splashed overalls. News of their son's accident had interrupted a run-of-the-mill Saturday. Both looked shaken and grey-faced and the woman's cheeks were streaked with tears.

Georgie went to meet them.

"Boss, this is my brother Terry and Suse, my sister-in-law. This is my DI, Georgie Fraser." He turned somewhat helplessly, his own face drawn and Georgie held out her hand, shook both Terry and Suse's firmly.

"Pleased to meet you," she said, "and sorry it's in such terrible circumstances. We don't have any concrete news of Lucas yet. But he made it here and that's a good start. He was taken straight into surgery and for the moment no news is good news."

One of the triage staff came out from her glass-partitioned office and Georgie flagged her down, asking if there was a room where they might wait, explaining who they were. Without three hi-vis police jackets in the waiting area she doubted her request would have been met, but as it was, the receptionist showed them through to a small room with plastic chairs arranged around a low table.

"We'll get some teas," she said, pushing her debit card towards Corby. Thank goodness for contactless. No need to be ransacking pockets for loose change. Almost as an afterthought, she asked Corby to let Marianne know where she was.

"Please," she said to Lucas's parents. "Have a seat." She waited a few seconds to allow them time to settle but putting off the moment wouldn't make it any easier. "I'm really sorry but I need to ask you some questions. We're trying to establish why Lucas was up on the Mynd today and who knew he might have been there."

"It's OK," Suse said, taking a tissue from her pocket and scrubbing at her face. "Mike said you'd want to talk to us. And while we're waiting, we might as well ..." She reached for her husband's hand and he grasped hers with both of his, their knees pressed together as they sat side by side on the hard plastic chairs.

Her sergeant sat one chair removed from them, offering solid support but giving space for their intense grief.

"How's Joe?" Mike Harley asked. "Ali said if it hadn't been for him ..." He left the sentence unfinished. Georgie told him that as yet, they didn't know. They were keeping everything crossed. She strung the conversation out until Corby returned, bringing a small tray with five plastic cups of weak-looking milky tea and several sachets of sugar.

"So," Georgie said. "First of all, do you have any idea what time Lucas left this afternoon. Was he at home in the morning?"

"He usually works Saturdays but he'd called in sick," Terry said, his voice so similar to his brother's that Georgie almost did a double take.

"He's not been right this past week," Lucas's mum said. "Not since you found Sam up by that shelter."

"They'd known each other since nursery," the dad said. "It really threw him. The other lad, Davey, well, they weren't really pals. But Sam – that knocked him for six."

Beside Georgie, Corby had surreptitiously opened her notebook and taken out a pen.

"Do you think Lucas had any idea who killed Sam? Might that be why he was so troubled?" She remembered Jessie saying that Lucas had been head over heels for Alisha. Had Lucas's thoughts run along the same lines as hers? If he adored her and yet suspected her of Sam's death, might that have explained his low mood?

Both the boy's parents shook their heads.

"He didn't want to talk about it. Just shut himself in his room," Terry said. "I mean, Mike'll tell you, we're a close family. Just the four of us and we all talk about everything."

"Lucas's sister is quite a bit younger," Suse said. "Another thing he and Sam had in common. She's the same year as Sam's little brother at school. But they've always been close, Lucas and Rose."

"Even she couldn't bring him out of himself," said Terry. "He wouldn't talk to any of us."

"So, do you know what time he left today? Did anyone call him before he went out?"

"We'd gone to B&Q," Terry said. "In Shrewsbury. We're doing up the spare room. When we got back he was out."

"Was Rose there?"

Both parents shook their head. Rose had been at a trampolining class at the Sports Centre. Where Bryn Morgan worked. They would, Georgie realised, for the third time need to find out where every one of those youngsters had been that afternoon. Again that loose thread in her brain caught, making her wish she was alone with peace and quiet to think. Not crammed into a hospital visitors' room with the parents of a boy who teetered between life and death. And, just the other side of a door, the love of her life waiting to hear if her long-lost son, newly brought home to her, would live or die. If Joe had left Lucas to his fate, hadn't dragged himself over the snowy barrow to fetch the first aid kit and survival blanket, or had used them for himself rather than Lucas, his chances would have been much better. Marianne had given up any belief in God when she was a teenager. If they lost Joe, Georgie might have to turn her back too.

"So, no idea if anyone called him?" she said.

Suse shook her head, breathing in with a rattling sob.

"I went up to his room when I got back. Thinking he'd be in bed, you know. But he was gone. His bed was neatly made, the room like he usually leaves it. He likes things tidy."

"Did you notice anything else? Anything unusual."

Another shake of the head and she gripped her husband's hand more tightly.

"There were some photos on the desk," she said then, as though the thought had only just occurred to her. "A school trip they went on. GCSE year. To Yorkshire. Geography, I think it was. Camping. Up near Hebden Bridge."

The thread tightened, pulling a few thoughts free.

"Can you remember who was in the photos?"

Suse looked up, a spark of curiosity in her washed-out face. How could photos of a school trip be relevant? If she'd asked, Georgie wouldn't have known how to answer her. She was just suddenly sure that they were.

"Sam," Suse said. "And Lucas, of course. There were a couple with that pretty girl, Alisha. And Jessie. Most of them were just Sam and Lucas. They were still really close then. It was after that summer, when Lucas went to college and Sam got his job that they drifted."

"So not when Sam went off the rails?"

This time Terry answered.

"No. Lucas stood by him, even when Sam was tricky. And he was a right pain for a few years. They just grew apart when he went to sixth form. It happens."

A knock at the door interrupted them. A nurse in blue scrubs stuck her head around it.

"One of the doctors has just come through. I thought you'd want to know."

"Do you know which patient?" Georgie asked.

"Joe Ingles." There was a slight uplift at the end of the name, making it a question. Perhaps the nurse was trying to assess to which trio of shell-shocked relatives the boy belonged.

"Any news on Lucas Harley?"

The nurse shook her head, then smiled. "No news is good news."

Georgie thanked her, her chest suddenly tight, sweat breaking out on her palms. Did that mean the news of Joe was bad?

"I'll be back in a moment," she said to the Harleys. "I just need to be with Marianne for this. Find out how Joe is."

She barely heard their good wishes as the door swung shut behind her.

33

It was midnight before Joe was through surgery. While he was not quite out of the woods, all the signs were good.

"The knife pierced the vastus lateralis – one of the larger quadriceps," the doctor had explained when Georgie had left her interview with the Harleys, "and nicked a branch of the profunda femoris artery. He was lucky. It's deep so bleeding was slower and there was no arterial spray. The lad did well not to pull it out. If he had, he wouldn't have made it. But there's also some damage to the bone caused by his moving with the knife still in place."

Marianne's fingers had convulsed in Georgie's. Beyond that there had been no sign that she had even heard, although her eyes remained fixed on the doctor. Beside her, Niamh had given a strangled sob and Effie had uttered a low, "Oh, thank God."

"What now?" Georgie said.

"He's gone into theatre and we're optimistic he'll make a full recovery. He might well have sustained greater damage from the tourniquet than from the injury itself – though it's a cleft stick situation." The doctor was matter-of-fact, though not offhand.

She had introduced herself as Dr Pereira and looked Spanish but her English was unaccented. If anything there was a hint of Manchester beneath the cool tones. "Without it, he'd almost certainly have bled out before the ambulance got there. With it, he's at risk of having sustained nerve damage. Cutting off the circulation causes the nerves in the lower leg to misfire. He's going to have a painful recuperation and it may not be complete but we'll cross that bridge when we come to it. For now, he's in good hands."

She had advised them not to wait but one look at Marianne's set face had told Georgie she was fighting a losing battle. They had joined the Harleys in the small family room where the hours had ticked by. Around eleven, had come the news that Lucas was out of theatre and had been transferred to Intensive Care. All the surgeons and his family could do was wait and see. The Harleys had taken their vigil to the ICU, leaving the visitors' room to Marianne, Georgie, Niamh and Effie. One hour later Dr Pereira reappeared, accompanied by an older woman in scrubs, tall and thin with tired eyes.

"You can breathe again," she said, looking at Marianne. For the past few hours, Georgie, Effie and Niamh had maintained desultory conversation, interspersed with long bouts of silence, and all the while Marianne had held tight to Georgie's hand, frozen. "He's in the recovery room and should be on the ward in about half an hour. Mum can go and sit with him then, if you want to stay. But he won't be with it for a while, so if you want to pop home and come back early morning that's fine too."

"I'll stay."

There had been no question of anything else. At Georgie and Marianne's insistence, and acknowledging that there was nowhere for them to sleep and that someone needed to go back to Church Stretton for the dogs, Niamh and Effie left. When a nurse appeared to take them up to Joe's ward, Georgie stayed just long enough to see him safe, if pale and motionless, then left Marianne to spend the night at his bedside.

Having never had anyone to lean on in times of trauma, Marianne preferred to be alone and Georgie comforted herself that her office in Monkmoor was at most twenty minutes' drive away. Besides, the loose thread that had begun to tug in the snowy hollow, and gathered speed when she spoke to the Harleys, was now demanding to be unravelled. She needed time and space to let the details of the case percolate. She knew now who had stabbed Lucas but still was not sure why.

Drifting in and out of restless sleep on the sofa in one of the interview rooms, a week's worth of conversations, scenes, photographs and soundbites kaleidoscoped through her head. Then, at around six, after a phone call from Marianne to say that Joe had just woken after four hours' deep sleep, she went back to her desk and re-read every statement given by the group that had partied up at the Pole Cottage shelter ten days earlier.

Either lack of sleep was playing tricks with her brain or all the original statements, those taken before she was put in charge, were almost word for word identical as Corby had said in the first team briefing. All except one detail in one statement. Georgie went back, found the corresponding sentence on each typed sheet and read them again. In seven out of eight, Sam Gray had argued with Jessie Pritchard before storming off in her car. In one – Lucas Harley's – Sam had argued with Alisha Johnson. How had they all missed this the first time around? Was it relevant? And how did it fit with the theory that kept worming into her mind?

At last, when it was far enough past seven o'clock to decently call someone, she rang Jessie Pritchard.

"It's OK, I've been up a while," Jessie said, when Georgie

apologised for disturbing her. "I'm seeing Sam's mum later. Helping her go through his things."

"It's quite soon for that, isn't it?"

She could almost hear Jessie's shrug down the phone.

"I think she just wants to spend time looking at them, really. Feel close to him. I don't mind helping. And there are some of my things in his room still."

Dawn light was just grazing the sky beyond the window. Almost the longest night. Almost Christmas. And today, a bereaved mother and girlfriend would sort through their deceased loved one's possessions. It made the questions she needed to ask now seem very trivial.

"I heard about Lucas," Jessie said. "How is he?"

"He's in intensive care," Georgie said. "They're doing everything they can. We have to hope it's enough. Listen, I'm sorry to disturb you with something that might seem unimportant but I wanted to ask you about a camping trip you went on in your last year at Church Stretton School. Geography, I think it was."

Jessie paused.

"Yorkshire," she said, with a hint of question in her voice. "Something Bridge."

"Hebden Bridge," Georgie said. "Lucas's mum told me he'd been looking at some photos from then. You and Alisha were in a couple of them. I wondered if anyone else from your group had gone. Anyone else who was at the party last Wednesday, I mean."

"Just the four of us. None of the others did geography."

"Would you tell me about the trip? Anything you remember, even if it seems silly or irrelevant. Just your memories."

Jessie didn't have that many, she said. They'd done some orienteering and caving which Alisha had hated. It had been wet some of the time but the camping had still been fun. They'd been allowed to go to the cinema one evening but she couldn't remember what they'd seen. She'd shared a tent with Alisha and Sam with Lucas. There had been twenty in the group but they'd spent most of the time hanging out just the four of them.

Georgie had been on the odd geography field trip herself. As far as she remembered there'd been quite a bit of boys and girls sneaking into each other's tents. Had any of that happened in Hebden Bridge?

"Only Alisha," Jessie said. "With some guy who wasn't even from our school, just someone from the campsite. I don't think she got up to anything, just having a drink and hanging out. She said I was boring because I didn't want to but I didn't think it was worth getting kicked out of school for."

"How about Sam and Lucas?"

There was another pause.

"I sort of hoped Sam might come in with me. We weren't really seeing each other yet but we'd had a kiss or two at parties. You know."

"But he didn't?"

"He just kept saying it wasn't worth getting caught. It was just after he'd finished his community service so it made sense."

"And Sam and Lucas were good friends?"

"The best," Jessie said. "They were even after they fell out, really. Lucas just didn't like some of the people Sam hung out with. Like Davey. His uncle being a police sergeant probably didn't help."

Georgie asked a few more questions but Jessie had little more to tell her. There was a bleakness in her voice that was hard to hear in one so young. Nineteen and already coping with the loss of her first love. There would come a time when Sam would be a distant memory but at that age, life seemed to stretch for eternity, Georgie remembered. On this damp, cold Sunday morning, Jessie must feel that she would miss him forever.

.   .   .

AT EIGHT O'CLOCK on a Sunday morning, the roads were quiet and it took Georgie only thirteen minutes to drive from Monkmoor to Shrewsbury Royal Hospital. The thaw had set in with rain overnight, which according to the local radio had fallen as snow on the hills. The SOCOs had had little time before dark had fallen to inspect the Shooting Box hollow, although Bob Carradine, who'd been on call from the local team, had said they'd carried on working until after eight pm with arc lights. This morning, presumably, they would continue, unless they felt they'd gleaned everything there was to be found. In an hour or so, she'd need to update the Pitbull and find out if the social media furore had escalated as a result of the attack on Lucas. But first, she needed to see Marianne. And Joe. When she had called the medical team, they had said they would make a decision as to whether or not she could question him officially when they had done their rounds at nine am.

Corby rang, her voice still fuzzy with sleep, just as Georgie was parking the Land Rover, fat drops thudding on its roof and splattering the windscreen, halfway to sleet.

"I'm so sorry, boss, I've only just woken up. Do you need me to come in?"

Georgie laughed and told her to stay put.

"I'll call you after I've spoken to Joe and we'll see where we are then. You could all do with a few hours off, I reckon. And for the moment, no one's going anywhere."

Joe had been given a side-room off a ward, presumably to allow him privacy when pesky police officers came to question him. When she poked her head around the door, Marianne held a finger to her lips and got up soundlessly from her chair. Joe lay on his back, sleeping soundly, an oxygen tube in each nostril and a drip draining into his right arm. On the locker beside the bed stood a tray with a carton of orange juice and a yoghurt pot. The blue curtains were half drawn, showing a lowering sky.

"How is he?" she asked, as Marianne pushed her gently outside the door.

"I don't want to wake him. He had a lot of pain earlier and it took them quite a long time to get it under control. His nerves waking up, they said. He's only just gone back to sleep."

Georgie wrapped her arms around her and pulled Marianne close, feeling the resistance in her ribcage, the iron bands with which she'd bound herself to keep from dissolving.

"And how are you? Did you sleep?" she asked as Marianne levered herself gently away. In the early days of their relationship Georgie would have found it hurtful. Even now, she had to consciously remind herself that there was no rejection. For most of her life Marianne had kept herself safe by eschewing human connection, especially physical contact. It was a hard habit to break and one to which she reverted at times of crisis.

"I dozed a bit," Marianne said. "You?"

"On and off."

Joe, Marianne said, had managed a bit of breakfast before falling back to sleep, which gave Georgie the perfect opportunity to say that she was taking Marianne to the canteen for some of the same. And, as if the universe was on her side – and about time too, given the way the investigation had been going – Effie and Niamh arrived, wiping out Marianne's protestations that she didn't want Joe to be alone if he woke.

"We'll be back well in time for the doctors' rounds, I promise."

And they were. While Georgie had downed coffee and a granola yoghurt, Marianne had played half-heartedly with a piece of toast, only forcing it down when Georgie pointed out that she would be no use to Joe if she fainted from low blood sugar. In the canteen they saw Mike Harley fetching provisions for his brother and sister-in-law, his eyes red-rimmed from lack of sleep. Lucas's surgery had been successful but there were concerns about how much blood he'd lost and whether his brain had suffered from lack of oxygen. And hypothermia. The stab wound to his stomach might have missed his aorta, but it had pierced his spleen which had had to be removed, increasing the risk of infection.

"They're telling us to go home," Harley said. "He's in an induced coma and they won't be bringing him out of it for at least twenty-four hours. If he makes it that long," he added quietly. "Terry and I are just working on Suse. She doesn't want to not be here if ... well, you know."

Georgie nodded and offered to look in at the ICU when she'd finished talking to Joe. Mike thanked her but said that wouldn't make much difference to Lucas's mum.

"Home for a few hours' kip and she can come back later," he said. "Our mum's with Rose but they must both be worried sick, too. Good for us all to be together for a bit."

"All the best to Joe," he added, when Georgie and Marianne said they should go. "Thank him for us."

Unsurprisingly, the surgical team were reluctant to allow four visitors in the room when they came to examine Joe. Marianne was allowed to stay, and only when Joe asked if Georgie could stay too, did they relent. Niamh and Effie slunk away like dogs booted out into the rain.

"It'll be quicker," Joe said, his voice slurring a little from morphine. "Otherwise the DI will only stop you outside the door to get an update."

The surgeon with the tired eyes, who they had seen the night before, laughed.

"Well, if your sense of humour's anything to go by, you're heading in the right direction," she said.

As the team quizzed Joe about how he was feeling and

explained the process of his nerves healing, Georgie watched Marianne, whose eyes never left her son. There was a serenity now about her. Last night, she had been frozen. This morning, she was still.

"Ten minutes," Dr Pereira said to Georgie as the medical team left. "And I'll be sending a nurse in to make sure you stick to it. He needs rest."

"Better get cracking, then," Georgie said once the door had closed behind them. "You sure you're feeling up to this?"

Joe nodded, a slow up and down that seemed the most he could manage.

"Not sure how much good I'll be though. I didn't see much."

"Tell me what happened when you found Lucas."

His account came in fits and starts. The disorientation brought on by the fog. Hearing groaning when he came to the Shooting Box. Falling into the hollow. Falling over Lucas. The blood and the knife on the ground. His panic, keeping it at bay to remember his Search and Rescue training. Calling the team. Then the sudden, searing impact on his leg.

"It felt like someone stamped on me, at first," he said. "And I kind of fell forward. It was only when I saw the handle sticking out of my leg that I ..." His voice tailed off.

"Did you see anyone? I know it was foggy but they must have been pretty close."

Joe shook his head.

"I heard something. Behind me. When I was on the phone. And movement out of the corner of my eye. But like I said, I fell forward. I was kneeling and just remember my forehead hitting the ground. The snow, you know."

Georgie nodded. In Corby's absence, she had her phone on record so as not to have to take notes.

"And you didn't see anyone running away? Or hear footsteps?" There should have been sound, surely. The fog might have prevented him seeing someone, but often fog seemed to amplify sound. In Georgie's mind, there was only one explanation.

"Was Lucas conscious at this point?"

"He spoke to me. I fell next to him and he opened his eyes."

"What did he say, Joe? Try to remember the exact words."

His silver-grey eyes, their luminescence duller than usual, found hers.

"I'm not likely to forget."

A FEW HOURS LATER, once Georgie had at last persuaded Marianne to come home, leaving Joe in the hands of the medics for a few hours, she called Pitbull.

"About bloody time," he said, and then at least had the decency to ask how Joe was. When she'd told him, there was an awkward pause until Pitbull, sounding perhaps even more forthright than usual, said, "Look, I'm sorry Fraser, and I don't want you to take this as me not having faith in you but I need to run this case myself. The nation's police forces are getting enough shit in the press without us giving them any more ammunition and this social media stuff is getting out of control."

Georgie's stomach prickled with what might have been annoyance but could also have been triumph. Thank goodness he hadn't made his decision the day before when she wouldn't have had enough to even scramble for a toehold.

"That's a shame, sir," she said, keeping her voice even, "because I don't think there'll be much for you to do. You see, I know who stabbed Sam Gray and Lucas Harley."

There was a long pause before the Pitbull said, "You're kidding."

"Did you ever know me to kid about anything serious, sir?"

"Go on, then," Pitbull said. "Tell me." Though he didn't articulate it, there was a clear subtext of *it had better be bloody good*.

Keeping to the chronology as accurately as her sleep deprived brain would allow, Georgie outlined her theory, referring back to small details that had seemed irrelevant at the time they had been shared, and admitting to distractions that had led her off down several blind alleys.

Pitbull listened without interrupting. Only when she'd finished did he bark, "Evidence?"

"Nothing conclusive, but several lines to follow up. The knives were from the same set and it'll be fairly easy to check who's missing them. The SOCOs have found Lucas's phone at the Shooting Box so it won't be long before we have access to that. And in a few days I should be able to talk to Lucas himself. In the meantime, with this different point of view we can check DNA samples on the items we found buried at the shelter. There's lots to keep us busy. While we have evidence, I wouldn't say that we had proof. But there's enough for you to keep the social media lot quiet, surely."

Pitbull inhaled deeply and she imagined clouds of vapour billowing out of his mouth and nose before he spoke again.

"What do you reckon, then?" he said. "A press conference this afternoon?"

Confident that she couldn't be seen in the privacy of Marianne's cottage – it would always be Marianne's cottage no matter how long she lived there – she rolled her eyes. What she really wanted now was to curl up for a few hours with Marianne and sleep. But she had to concede the press conference was necessary. Pitbull wouldn't want her, with her toxic social media presence, to appear, but she would have to write a statement for him.

Even after working with him for almost two years, it turned out he could still surprise her.

"I want you to front it, Fraser. And I'll have your back. All that shit they've been saying about you, they can eat their sodding words. But we'll have to word our statement carefully until we have absolute proof. Plenty of *we've apprehended a suspect and are awaiting on forensic confirmation* or what have you. The family aren't going to be happy."

"That's an understatement, sir."

The family were going to be broken-hearted.

34

Two days later, Lucas Harley was released from the ICU and transferred to a ward, with the promise that Georgie and her team could interview him the following morning. Those two days had been spent chasing every loose end until everything had been neatly tied. Lucas's parents had given their consent to his fingerprint being used to unlock his phone and there Georgie had found more evidence to support her theory. And Sam's phone had at last come to light, carefully hidden away where no one would have thought to look. Even so, without Lucas's testimony the case was tenuous. And with all the media attention, they needed it iron-clad.

Joe was doing well. His medical team had promised to have him home in time for Christmas and for now, frenzied negotiations were going on between Marianne and Effie, with Niamh as second, as to where 'home' would be. Effie's house was bigger and they had all spent Christmas there the year before. Niamh planned to abandon her family in Ireland and stay until New Year. But Joe would need a fair amount of care for at least the first week. His bedsit at Effie's was on the top floor which wasn't ideal, and while Niamh had promised to nurse him, Georgie didn't like her chances. Marianne, having almost lost her son twice, wasn't going to let him out of her sight until she was sure he'd made a full recovery.

Ultimately, though, it would be Joe's decision. Georgie had promised Marianne who was back at work that day, that she would drop in on him when she had interviewed Lucas. But on no account would she mention arrangements for Christmas.

"Are any of the Harleys going to be there?" Corby asked, as she squeezed the Land Rover into a space meant for a smaller car.

"I hope not," Georgie said. "He's less likely to talk freely in front of family. But ultimately it's down to him. If he wants one of them with him, I don't plan on saying no."

The car park was clear of snow apart from a few grubby patches that lurked on grass verges, and a cold wind scoured the tarmac, the sky heavy with clouds. That morning, the weather forecast had promised more snow on high ground and there were hopes of a white Christmas. Georgie pulled her beanie down over her ears and shoved her hands in her pockets. As if on cue her mobile rang, forcing her to expose at least one hand to the elements again.

"Chowdhury?" she said, putting the phone on speaker so Corby could hear.

"Wanted to catch you before you went in, boss. Had a call from Ireland."

"Did you indeed, sergeant? Well, perfect timing, we've just got here. Go ahead."

"Call was from a Shona Doherty, boss. Colm Doherty's estranged daughter."

Well, well, well, thought Georgie.

"The Gardaí tracked her down, at last. She lives somewhere on the west coast but she'd been off on a business trip in the US for a couple of weeks. Only just got back."

"And has she ever been to Church Stretton?"

"Only been to England a couple of times and that was Liverpool. Some family connection on her mum's side. It turns out Sam and Davey did manage to get hold of her, though. Exchanged emails. She was hoping to meet them in the New Year."

Another tug of sadness dragged at Georgie as she ended the call. Maybe it was the age of the protagonists in this case that made her so melancholy. Just on the cusp of adulthood, so much promise ahead of them. She hoped those who'd survived would make the most of life from now on, use this tragedy as a springboard and never look back. For one of them, that might be harder than for the others.

LIKE JOE, Lucas had been given a side room. Both officers used the hand sanitiser by the double doors of the surgical ward and Corby remarked how accustomed everyone had become to slathering their hands with alcohol gel since the pandemic.

"I was wondering if they might give us PPE," Georgie said. "If Lucas' surgery has put him at greater risk of infection."

The nurse on duty at the station in the centre of the ward didn't hand out any white plastic overalls, but did ask them not to touch Lucas and to keep their distance from his bed. "It's not the wound," she explained. "Just that with the splenectomy, his white blood cell count will be well down. And it's still early days. Mind you he's about fifty percent antibiotics at the moment."

As they approached the side room she checked, almost as an afterthought, that neither of them had recently had contact with anyone suffering from an infectious disease, and gave them each a face mask. Beata had sneezed once or twice the night before but Georgie reckoned that was more down to her donkey allergy than to a cold. Nevertheless she put the mask on.

When they entered the room, Lucas was lying with his face towards the window, dark hair stark against the white pillow. He neither moved nor acknowledged them but his mother jumped to her feet from the padded, high-backed chair next to his bed.

"I won't stay," she said, picking up her jacket and a newspaper. "Lucas said he'd rather talk to you on his own. But if you need me ..." She raised her voice a little to reach her son, "I'll be in the canteen. And then Dad's coming later, he's bringing Rose after school. Last day of term so she'll be dead excited."

Was it Georgie's imagination or was Suse talking too fast? Perhaps it was exhaustion. Or simple relief that her son had survived when it had seemed impossible that he should. Perhaps any parent felt anxious and resented having to leave when their son was about to be questioned by the police.

"How are you doing, Lucas?" Georgie said, taking a seat where Suse had been and leaving the other chair to Corby and her notebook. Slowly, the young man turned his head. Young man. He was barely more than a boy. All these kids. One misguided party up on the Long Mynd and all their lives had changed forever.

"You don't have to wear those, you know," he said. His voice was hoarse, presumably from being intubated for days. "I don't care if you take them off."

"Better safe than sorry," Georgie said, with a smile. What a stupid phrase. Lucas was, she imagined, both safe and sorry.

"I'd rather be able to see your face," the boy said. He sounded almost angry. Bitter. Georgie didn't blame him.

"And you're sure you're happy to talk to us without anyone else present? If you don't want your parents, you could ask for a chaperone. Or a solicitor."

He looked at her for a long moment. Years of practice at keeping her face blank earned its keep.

"On my own. Might as well get it over with."

"Ok. I'm going to be recording this." Georgie smiled and held up her phone. "And DC Corby will be taking notes. Is that OK?" The boy nodded, a single jerk of his head. "Can I start by asking you why you went up to the Shooting Box on Saturday? Did you arrange to meet someone? Or was it just on a whim?"

"I was heading for Pole Cottage. But there were people there so I turned round and went the other way. The Shooting Box was just there."

"And were you planning to meet someone? Your phone showed you had a call from Alisha Johnson just after one pm."

Lucas turned his head back towards the window. It gave a view of a flat, grey rooftop covered in ducts and pipes. Pigeons perched as though holding a conference, every so often swapping places like a game of musical chairs.

"Yeah, I said I'd meet her. But not till later. I wanted to be on my own."

"Were you intending she should find you?" Georgie asked. Across the small room from her Corby frowned, her pen hovering over her notebook.

"Would have served her right," Lucas said. "I didn't mean it to be that Joe, anyway."

"Why would it have served her right?"

If Lucas had been sitting, he would have shrugged. Lying propped on pillows it was just a twitch of his shoulders

"Way she played us. Me and Sam. And Davey."

Georgie let the silence hover for a while. Lucas must want to talk, to explain. Now that his plan had ended in a way he hadn't expected. Sam Gray's murder should have remained unsolved. And Lucas should have died with no explanation, perhaps hoping to save his family the shame that they would no doubt feel. Or that he had imagined they would feel if the truth came out. His parents might feel pain, grief and unimaginable sorrow but she doubted they would be ashamed. He was not a psychopath, a thug or a brutal murderer. He had just made a terrible mistake after years of his own shame and confusion. When he showed no sign of saying more, she asked:

"So why did you do it, Lucas? What did Sam do or say?" What straw had finally broken the camel's back?

Even more slowly than he had turned it away, he turned his face back towards her. His eyes were dark and bottomless. The eyes of an old man, not a nineteen-year-old.

"You reckon I'm going to blame Sam? It was my fault. All of it. That was why I had to die like he did. Same way, same place. On my own in the snow." His voice cracked and he closed his eyes. "But those people were at the shelter. And then that stupid bastard Joe came along." He breathed in with a shudder, his hands clenched on the sheets.

"But Sam didn't die on his own did he, Lucas? You stayed with him. Someone else went looking for him that night and stopped at the shelter for a bit. They heard you."

There was a long pause. When Lucas spoke again his tone was bleak but steady. Resigned. From her childhood, Georgie remembered the principle of the confessional. That confessing one's sins brought relief. Perhaps Lucas was relieved that she had guessed what had happened and wanted only his confirmation. And, when he felt able to give it, an explanation.

"That youth worker. Just sat there. I thought he'd never go. Seemed like I lay in the heather for hours."

"Was that when you buried the knife and the jacket? After he'd gone?"

Lucas nodded. Despite the recording on her phone, a formal statement would have to be taken once he was charged. Pitbull might throw the book at her for not sticking to the rules but she didn't think Lucas would change his story. It had been eating him up for two weeks. He had been prepared to end his own life, to be his own retribution. Now that had been denied by Joe, he would demand retribution from her.

"Lucas, I have to caution you before we go any further. You do not have to say anything. But it may harm your defence if you do not mention when questioned something which you later rely on in court. Anything you do say may be given in evidence."

The boy let out a sigh that carried with it a cresting wave of pain.

"Yeah," he said. "Whatever. And I don't want a solicitor."

"Do you want to tell us what happened? Or would you rather I asked questions?"

For a while, it seemed the silence was answer enough and Georgie would have to ask her questions. Until Lucas asked his own.

"How did you work it out? That it was me, I mean."

"I didn't until Joe found you. Even then, I thought maybe you'd been covering for Alisha." Lucas shook his head as though her name hurt his ears. "And then your mum told me about the photos you'd been looking at from the trip to Hebden Bridge." Georgie smiled. "I don't know if you know but Hebden Bridge has a reputation for being LGBTQ+ friendly."

"You'd do all right there, then," the boy said, the corner of his mouth twitching.

"Aye, I would," Georgie said. "But I do fine here, too. Anyway, maybe that sparked something in my mind because I started thinking about things a bit differently. About whether Sam was a bit confused about his sexuality. I know everyone thought he was keen on Alisha but maybe that was just cover. I know he loved Jessie, so why did he break things off with her?" She recalled the last interview with Cal Innes. "And something else that came up in our investigation made me wonder."

Lucas rubbed his eyes, the cannula in his hand tugging at the tube of his drip with the movement.

"It only happened once," he said. 'On that camping trip. I'm not gay. I've never … apart from then."

"Do you think Sam thought he was gay?"

It was odd to hear so bleak a laugh in someone so young.

"Most of the time, Sam just wanted to be adored. Loved, whatever. I don't think he cared much what gender anyone was."

"And did you love him?"

The deep brown eyes, so like her sergeant's, met hers with an honesty that almost made her flinch.

"He was my mate. From when we were, like, four. But then, after that thing in the tent, he kept wanting to … and I didn't. So we kind of fell out. Only hung out if there was a group of us." He took a deep breath. "And then all that flirting with Alisha, not just that night up at Pole. All the time. Like, rubbing my nose in it. He knew how I felt about her."

"Did you arrange to meet him that Saturday? The day he died. We didn't find any calls on his phone from you. Apart from the group chats."

"Alisha told me where he was. I went up to Mytton's Fold to see him. I wanted to know what had happened with Davey. The truth, I mean. Jessie wanted her car back. He couldn't go on hiding forever."

It wasn't yet the time to ask him why he'd taken a kitchen knife with him. Perhaps Lucas heard her thoughts.

"I took a fucking picnic with me. There was this cheese he really liked. I thought if I got him away from Mytton's Fold and we went back to Pole, maybe had some beers, I could talk him round. My uncle's a policeman for fuck's sake, and we'd all been lying to the police for him."

'So you persuaded him to go up on the hill in Jessie's car with you?"

Lucas nodded.

"And it was working. I thought he was starting to see my

point. But then it was like he got nasty. Kept talking about Alisha and how he was going to London with her ... about how she'd never be interested in me. Not after he'd told her about Hebden Bridge." A slow tear trickled down his cheek towards his ear. Lucas let it fall. "He thought it was funny. All that shame I'd been carrying around with me for years. I couldn't think about it without feeling sick. And he just thought it was funny. He laughed at me."

Georgie waited to see if he would continue. Then she said, "Was that when you stabbed him?"

The boy nodded again.

"I didn't even know I had the knife in my hand. I just hit him. Like punched him hard in the gut. And then there was all this blood. Everywhere. Like gushing out of him ... and I ..." He broke into sobs, choking on his words.

Georgie had noticed the line on the heart monitor behind his bed begin to resemble a mountain range and sure enough, the door swung open and a nurse came in.

"Hey, there, what's all this?" She crossed to the bed, making soothing noises, pressing a button on the machine and laying a hand on Lucas's forehead. He continued to sob, flat on his back and helpless. The nurse turned to Georgie.

"I think that's enough, don't you? Mum's outside. When you leave you can send her in."

Lucas's voice burst out, rasping through his tears. He didn't want his mum. He didn't want anyone. He wanted to be alone. Why couldn't they all have just let him die?

35

Joe came home on the winter solstice.

Georgie often teased Marianne about being a pagan but, like Midsummer, it was a celebration that felt important to her. The turning of the year, the changing of the light, seemed to bear much more relevance than a festival that celebrated the birth of an undoubtedly inspirational man which sadly had led, like most religions, to so much strife. She had a partner in crime in Beata, whose mother had once been known locally as a white witch. In part to remember her mother, Beata liked to celebrate the moon and the solstices and together, she and Marianne had planned a small party whose main function, along with celebrating the passing of the year, was to welcome Joe home.

Together they built a bonfire in the garden, well away from the menagerie field, and made a midwinter punch, with both alcohol-free and full-spirit options.

Georgie had collected him from the hospital after work and, when she heard the Land Rover's wheels crunch on the gravel drive, Marianne's heart skipped several beats. Had they made the right choice, her and Joe, bringing him here for Christmas and his first week out of hospital? She and Georgie were heading up to Mull to see the New Year in with Georgie's family and Joe would then go back to Effie's. All she asked was a week to make sure he was firmly back in the land of the living and then she would let him fly free again.

"Careful on those crutches," she said, meeting him by the gate and opening it as wide as possible. "It's dead slippy on the path now we've had a frost again." She had shut the dogs inside, worried that they might send Joe flying, and shadowed him towards the front door, carrying his bag while Georgie put the Land Rover at the far side of the lane.

He teased her now for being fussy but the hug he gave her, crutches pressed against her back, told her he was glad to be home. Of course, the cottage had never been his home but he'd said, when he decided to spend Christmas there, that home now was where she was.

Just for a second, she'd wondered if he'd abandoned the idea of trying to identify his father. Georgie had told her something of the two lads whose deaths she'd been investigating and their quest to find their father's family. Perhaps it was something peculiar to boys, a need to know who your father had been. Part of her couldn't understand it. Who cared who had provided their genetic material? She hadn't seen her parents since she was fifteen and had no plans to remedy that. But perhaps that was different. Perhaps, if she hadn't known them, she would want to, as Sam and Davey had wanted to know their father even if only by proxy. Georgie didn't believe for a second that they were really after a share of his will. Neither boy had known their father. What they wanted was connection. As Joe, aged twenty-three, had decided to come and find her.

"Are you going to be able to be outside with this bonfire?" Georgie asked, carrying a folding wheelchair in through the front door. "Or is that what this is for?"

"I'll make it for a bit, I reckon," Joe said.

"And we'll be able to see the fire from inside," Beata said, appearing from the bottom of the stairs and giving Joe a clumsy hug around his crutches, "so you can go inside if your leg starts to hurt."

"It would make a change if it stopped hurting. Maybe the cold will freeze it a bit."

As the doctors had predicted, despite his wound healing well, he was in constant pain from the damage the tourniquet had done to his nerves. A small price to pay, he'd said, for being alive.

"What time are people coming?" Beata asked, following Joe into the living room where Marianne had lit the fire an hour earlier. No need for anyone to chase the penguins out. She'd wanted it warm for when her son came home.

"Not for an hour or so," Marianne said, "so you've got time for a rest if you want to lie down."

"Sofa's fine," Joe said. "I can't face the stairs yet. Are you going to let the dogs in?"

"Once you're sitting down. Wait!" she called to Georgie, whose voice had just drifted through from the utility room. Too late, though. Paws scrabbled and slid on the quarry-tiled floor of the hall and the dogs burst into the living room then skidded to a halt as Marianne whistled to them.

"Sit!" she said, holding up a finger. "Not until he's sitting down."

For some reason, when Beata had helped him install himself, with his legs up and his crutches out of the way, Marianne found herself moved to tears by the greeting the dogs gave him. Sometimes, she felt that the dogs were her familiars, expressing the feelings that she couldn't. Joe might have found it a little overwhelming if she'd flung herself on him, yelping with joy, her metaphorical tail wagging.

. . .

EFFIE AND NIAMH were the first to arrive, followed not long afterwards by Ali Corby. With the exception of Niamh, it was a reunion of those who had gathered at Marianne's old cottage over by the Stiperstones, when Georgie had explained the identity of the killer at the Devil's Chair. Marianne hoped it might be the last such gathering. Georgie had come to Shropshire to head up the Rural Crime unit. Eighteen months in, she had had three high-profile murder cases.

"Is Joe the only man?" Niamh asked, sitting on the floor next to the sofa to be as near to Joe as possible. Marianne wondered if their relationship had recovered from the row they'd had the night before he'd gone to the Shooting Box. They'd hardly had time to work things out with him stuck in the hospital. But then, they were young. For all she knew, they'd been communicating online day and night.

"I invited Frank," Marianne said to Joe, suddenly remembering. "He was asking after you today and I didn't think you'd mind."

Frank Markham was the groundsman at the Shropshire Geoscience Trust and Joe had briefly worked with him when he'd first come to Shropshire. Both practical and taciturn, the two had hit it off and met every month or so for a drink. Given that Joe's adoptive dad was all the way down in Devon, Marianne was pleased that he had some sort of father figure here. The only company she'd been able to offer him was female.

When Frank arrived they went outside to light the fire. Georgie did the honours while Beata recited a Polish poem to celebrate the turning of the year and Marianne handed round cups of hot punch. Joe sat in his wheelchair, his leg resting on an extender plate and for a while the talk was all of Christmas and the weather, as people watched the flames send sparks shooting high into the star-strewn sky. It would be cold again tonight.

With the certainty that always proceeded unpleasantness, Marianne knew that the time would come for Georgie to answer the questions that still hung over the disappearance and death of Sam Gray. The media furore had died down, and Pitbull had even managed to twist an apology from the editor of the *Shropshire Chronicle* for their abuse of Georgie. A full retraction and a grovelling apology. Georgie had accepted the apology gracefully but drawn the line at a double-page spread detailing her triumphs since joining the West Mercia force. The social media trolls had been suspiciously quiet too, their guns spiked by the 'freak' not only solving the case but proving their half-baked theories entirely inaccurate into the bargain.

Frank Markham asked the first question. It had been meant as a private question to Joe, just after they had all gone inside where they could see the fire from the French windows.

"Why did he stab you, though? That was hardly going to help him."

Joe shrugged and looked across at Georgie.

"He didn't want Joe to call for help," she said, adding, "I don't think he meant to kill him. I don't think he meant to kill anyone."

"Just happened, did it?" Marianne said, unable to keep the bite from her voice. She had once stabbed someone. With a pair of dressmaking scissors. She had meant to kill. Or if not to kill, to maim as viciously as the man had maimed her. Her legal team had presented a defence of temporary insanity and self-defence. She had been sentenced to fifteen years for murder.

Marianne stole a glance at Beata. Her mother too had stabbed a man, but only because she had thought he was already dead. And to save her daughter. According to Georgie, very few murders were the fiendishly clever puzzles set by psychopaths in TV dramas. Most were messy, clumsy and poorly planned, if planned at all.

"How is the boy's family?" Effie asked

"Devastated," Ali Corby said. "As you'd expect. He was always their golden boy. I went round to see his mum the other day. His uncle's on our team, you see, and she's been struggling. Mind you so has he. Mike, I mean. He's applied for a couple of months compassionate leave."

Marianne knew that Georgie had done everything to support Mike Harley's application. She had derived no pleasure from charging her sergeant's nephew with murder.

"With a good lawyer, Lucas might get off with manslaughter," Georgie said. "For Sam, I mean."

"He took a knife with him," Beata, who had heard the story from Alfie, said. Alfie's parents were friends with the Harleys. No matter what steps the Pitbull had taken to keep gossip locked down, it had leaked out like water through a sieve.

"But there was a reasonable explanation for that," Corby said. "And the knife he used to stab Joe, he'd taken to use on himself."

"You're all making excuses for him!" Beata said. "It's sad, of course it is, but the fact remains he stabbed two people and one of them died. The only reason Joe's still here is because he had Search and Rescue's number on his phone and he knows his first aid." No one had given her mother the benefit of the doubt. Marianne was hardly surprised Beata was reluctant to afford it to Lucas.

"What about the Irish connection?" Effie asked into an awkward silence and Niamh looked alarmed. "An Irish fellow Georgie was asking me about the other week. Something to do with the case."

"Something and nothing," Georgie said. "Sam Gray and Davey Whelan found out that they had the same biological father. We were just following up a few leads but it didn't come to anything. Did you know, though," she added to Effie, "that Colm Doherty had a daughter in Ireland?"

"Well, I never. And he never said a thing."

Colm Doherty, Marianne reflected, seemed to have made a habit of fathering children and abandoning their mothers. She wished that Effie hadn't liked him so much. Marianne had always considered her discerning.

"But she's been in touch with us and said she might visit Church Stretton," Georgie said. "See the gliding club and what have you. I've told her to look you up."

"Oh, that will be lovely!" Effie said.

Suddenly overwhelmed by the warmth and the press of people in her living room, Marianne excused herself with a promise of making tea. While the kettle boiled she slipped out through the back door and stood on the terrace, face turned up to the stars. The night was clear, a spiralling column of smoke drifting up from the bonfire and Orion stood stark above her, his sword bright.

The door latch clicked behind her and she wasn't surprised to hear Georgie's voice.

"Come out for some peace?"

Warm arms closed around her and Marianne leaned back against Georgie, her head resting against her shoulder.

"It just feels so sad," she said. "All that young life wasted. And I still don't understand how it all happened."

Georgie sighed, her breath drifting past Marianne's ear, lightly scented with punch.

"Sam Gray was a very confused boy," she said. "Confused about a lot of things. His sexuality. His feelings for his newfound brother. For his mentor, Cal Innes. For his girlfriend. I think she knew something of how he was feeling." Jessie's quiet mourning had spoken volumes. "And quite by accident, he killed his friend and brother. Or at least had a fight with him that resulted in his death. Then he pushed another friend too far. Neither of them was what you'd call a murderer."

Marianne laughed without amusement.

"Funny. Murderer sounds like a role, doesn't? Some people just end up killing people. They never set out to be murderers."

Georgie put her hands on her shoulders and gently turned her towards the French windows. In the shadow of the terrace they were concealed from those inside and yet had a perfect view into the room.

Joe sat on one end of the sofa, leg propped on a padded stool with Niamh curled at his side. Beside them was Effie, laughing at something Beata had said from where she sat cross-legged in front of the fire, both dogs sprawled beside her. Frank Markham had one armchair and Ali Corby the other. Marianne had decorated the room with swathes of ivy and yew, bound with bright ribbons, and a tree with white lights and handmade baubles glittered in the corner. It looked every inch the perfect Christmas scene.

"Look," Georgie said. "This is what we have. This is what you've built. Look at all the love in that room."

Marianne looked. It was true. All that love. Enough to siphon some off and send it to Sam Gray's family; to all those who mourned Davey Whelan; to Lucas Harley and his family; to their friends who would need a long time before they could put that fateful party behind them. In the far distance, the brooding hulk of the Long Mynd was just visible hunched against the dark sky. Above it was a scatter of stars. The turning of the year. A new beginning.

AUTHOR NOTE

As I write this, the Long Mynd is firmly embracing spring, the heather coming into bloom and the streams tinkling down lush valleys. Skylarks and meadow pipits swoop overhead, lambs totter after their woolly mothers, and the herds of wild ponies are enjoying a burst of sunshine.

In winter, however, it can be a very different landscape; bleak and malevolent. Earlier this year, the roads from Ratlinghope to the Mynd and the Stiperstones were impassable and we had to turn back when cars in front were being pulled out of drifts by a tractor. In snow or fog, it is easy to lose your way and you can wander for miles before you find a path.

The story of Parson Carr – or the Reverend Edmund Donald Carr – referenced by both Georgie and Marianne is absolutely true, although his boots are no longer on display at either the Carding Mill or Shrewsbury museum. The full story of his miraculous twenty-seven hour ordeal on the Mynd in a blizzard can be read on my website in the explore folklore section or in his own book, A Night in the Snow: Or A Struggle for Life which is still available on Amazon.

All the locations in the book are real and you can visit them yourself, although don't be tempted to climb down Callow Hollow as it really is very steep. I believe it is now accessible via Minton but in twenty years or more, I have never seen a human there. The campsite at the foot of Ashes Hollow, Small Batch, is where I used to stay with my children before I moved to Shropshire, and makes a perfect base if you want to visit the area; there is also an excellent pub, The Ragleth Inn, just along the lane. Packetstone Hill (so named because it was where parcels were left on the old packhorse route over the hill) and the Gliding Club can be found at the south end of the Mynd, and the shelter where the young people partied is on the site of the old Pole Cottage, just south of the summit at Pole Bank. The Shooting Box, where Joe and Lucas so nearly met tragedy, is further north along the ridge beside the Portway, an ancient track which is believed to date back to the Bronze Age. At any rate, most of the scheduled monuments (of which there are, I believe, twenty-six) are to be found close to it.

If you find yourself driving between Shrewsbury and Ludlow ever, make a point of dropping into Church Stretton. There is plenty of parking from which you can explore the Long Mynd to the west or Caer Caradoc, Hope Bowdler Hill and the Lawley to the east. There is also a wide selection of excellent places to eat or have a coffee, a regular market, quirky shops, and a summer arts festival. You will also find a friendly, local independent bookshop, Burway Books, which kindly stocks my books in its well-curated collection.

Of all the locations featured in my books, the Long Mynd is the one closest to my heart because it was my introduction to Shropshire when I was a child. *Mystery at Witchend*, the first Malcolm Saville Lone Pine adventure, is set there and its setting captured me in a way that is hard to describe. I knew it was a place that I longed to see, and when I did, about thirty years later, it did not disappoint. Now, I see it each morning from my bedroom window; apart from on a foggy, bleak day when the hill tells me I would be well-advised to stay at home.

AFTERWORD

Thank you for reading Lies Beneath the Mynd. If you have enjoyed this book, I would be delighted if you would leave a review on Amazon, Goodreads or wherever you like to read book reviews.

If you would like to keep up-to-date with the Shropshire Mysteries please visit:https://saskiavanderzee.com/ and sign up to my author newsletter. You will also find background on Georgie's other cases, audiobook links, Shropshire folklore, Marianne's recipes and a free short story. More coming soon!

ACKNOWLEDGMENTS

I am, as ever, very grateful to those who kindly gave their time and knowledge to bring this book into being.

My thanks go to: Alex Bodza of West Mercia Search and Rescue, and Patrick Edwards, National Trust Area Ranger for the Long Mynd, both of whom were incredibly generous with their time and information; Christian Owens of Genderspace UK for insight into a trans police officer's experience; and my brother, David, who happily answers my questions on police procedure at random times. Please remember, though, that this story is fiction. Any inaccuracies are one hundred percent my responsibility.

As ever, my editor Liz Ward and cover designer Tim Byrne have done a great job. I'm also grateful to Sophie Hannah and the Dream Author programme for mentoring, and to my MA writing group for monthly support and inspiration.

Lastly, I would be nothing without my family: my brothers and sisters-in-law, nephews and niece; my uncle and aunt, still holding the fort for their generation; my children, Molly and Jake, and my children-in-law, Joel and Mia; and Paula, who makes every day an adventure.

West Mercia Search and Rescue is an essential service and entirely charitably funded so if you are ever looking to donate to a good cause, you can find them on Facebook or at https://westmerciasar.org.uk.

ALSO BY SASKIA VAN DER ZEE

Death at the Devil's Chair

Death by Relic